NEVERNESS

David Neilson

Cover art by David Neilson
Rear cover inset 'Pyjama Scuffle' by Binky

Note for Librarians: A cataloguing record for this book is available from Library and Archives
Canada at www.collectionscanada.ca/amicus/index-e.html
ISBN 1-4251-1007-x

PUBLISHING

Offices in Canada, USA, Ireland and UK

Book sales for North America and international:
Trafford Publishing, 6E–2333 Government St.,
Victoria, BC V8T 4P4 CANADA
phone 250 383 6864 (toll-free 1 888 232 4444)
fax 250 383 6804; email to orders@trafford.com
Book sales in Europe:
Trafford Publishing (UK) Limited, 9 Park End Street, 2nd Floor
Oxford, UK OX1 1HH UNITED KINGDOM
phone +44 (0)1865 722 113 (local rate 0845 230 9601)
facsimile +44 (0)1865 722 868; info.uk@trafford.com
Order online at:
trafford.com/06-2766

10 9 8 7 6 5 4 3 2 1

STANDSTILL revisited…

After the others had gone to bed, he and Mike had migrated up to the observatory and were now sitting amongst the debris of empty bottles and overflowing ashtrays. It was early morning and had just started to get light.

'Urrgghh, I'm knackered…might turn in for a few hours,' said Mike, with a long yawn.

'Looks like another fine day, pity we're going to miss most of it,' he said, peering out of the window.

'Oh shit, I've just remembered something.'

'Yeah?'

'We've got to get all the equipment back to the attic in case…'

'Jesus, what the hell is that?'

'What, what is it?' said Mike, jumping up. 'Shit, where have they all come from?'

'This is scary, what the hell's going on?'

'Oh my God, it's worked! I forgot to tell you, I set the beam to suspend the stratosphere before we came up here last night. I wanted to see if I could trap some more meteors. But why are there so many? There are thousands and thousands of them!'

'They don't look like meteors though,' he said, gazing through his binoculars. 'They look all smooth. Must have been melted like that on entry.'

'None of this makes any sense…the beam's only been going overnight.'

'I'll take a closer look with the telescope.'

He gawped in disbelief at the close-up view of thousands of shiny spaceships as they hung motionless on the edge of the atmosphere. Immediately they called everyone to an emergency early morning meeting and Mike explained the truth about last night.

'What a load of cobblers, suspended the stratosphere indeed! Ha haha! You got us all out of bed at the crack of dawn for this crap?'

'William, have you seen outside yet?'

'You want me to check the weather?'

'Here, use the telescope.'

Shock travelled around the group as they took it in turns to have a look. William was left speechless for once.

'We're in deep shit here, and I can't think of a way out at the moment,' said Mike.

'Why deep shit? We've got them trapped, haven't we?' said Anna.

'Yes, but if the power plant or SAR generator fail, we're finished!'

'Zey could be friendly,' offered Gina.

'I don't think so. The sheer quantity screams invasion,' he pointed out, with everyone nodding in agreement.

'Ze aliens zey come. I say before. Now zey get us,' said Serge.

'Oh my God, we're done for!' cried William.

'Well, we're safe for the time being. I've got some confidence that the kit will be okay for a week or so,' said Mike, trying to be positive.

'A week, why only a week?'

'Well, the beam tube must be on its last legs by now, it's been going for two years, remember?'

'Oh dear God, it could fail at any second. You've got to think of something quick, otherwise it's certain death for all of us.'

'Shut up William. How long does it take to change the tube?' asked Carmen.

'About an hour.'

'An hour? It's going to take them less than a millisecond to get down here!'

'How many spare tubes do you have?' continued Carmen, ignoring William's hysteria.

'None, I make them myself.'

'How long does it take you to make one then?' she persisted.

'About a month.'

'A month?' screamed William. 'We're all dead! Well, it's been nice. Oh my God, what are we going to do? Wait a tic… I've got an idea! Why don't we blow them out of the sky? Go and get some surface to air missiles and…'

'Won't work. The missile will never reach the target, it'll get frozen itself.'

'Oh no! Oh no, we're all dead I tell you…'

'Don't panic William, Victor and I will take care of it. With everyone's help, I'm sure that we can get a standby kit set up by the middle of next month. Of course it'll mean we'll need everybody's full co-operation.'

'Oh dear God, I've got to live on a knife-edge for a whole month,' sobbed William. 'I'll go mad.'

'You're mad already, so no change there,' quipped Carmen.

'Yeah, we'll have to send down for food and drink and things like that,' said Mike.

'And there'll be a lot of errands to run,' he chipped in, obviously very pleased with the instant new committee, which consisted of, well just him and Mike really.

Carmen took Stefan and Serge over to Kibble Science Park to collect a mini dome, which would protect the SAR generator from potential bad weather. Mike drew up lists of materials and sent everyone else off in small groups to track the items down.

'Hey, this can be our headquarters, hold our meetings with them in here,' suggested Mike.

'Yeah, let them do the hard graft for a change,' he said, stubbing out his joint. 'You know, I got really fed up having to check the swimming pool chemicals *every day. I've never even had time to use it myself.'*

'You'll like this then, I've got a drawer full of spare tubes in the lab.'

'Hey, that's brilliant! So, while they're running around like idiots, we can have some time off!'

'No, it doesn't get us off the hook, we still have to get the standby kit made. I'm really worried that the tube will fail. There must be something we can do...'

'Hang on, I know how we can get out of this!'

'Go on,' said Mike.

'Er...nah, it's gone. I hate it when that happens. Wait, it'll come back...'

Chapter 1

'Ah, I thought I might catch you two hiding in here! Right, I've searched the grounds and I can't see it anywhere...come on Muffton, own up, where have you hidden it?'

He looked up from his notes to see William standing over them wearing an artist's smock and beret, threatening Mike with a paintbrush.

'Leave it out William, we've been up all night.'

'I wasn't talking to you Ogroid.'

'Hidden what, anyway?' asked Mike.

'My caravan.'

'Oh, that.'

'Yes, that. Come on, where is it?'

'It's gone.'

'Gone? Gone where?'

'I don't know exactly. The *Neverness* maybe?'

'Well I want it back, do you hear? If you don't return it, there'll be trouble. Thinking about it, you're overdue dental treatment, aren't you?'

'I'm not letting you do my teeth again. Victor's got some dentistry equipment in his room, I'm going to him in future.'

'You'll regret this Muffton, when you're rolling around in agony with toothache. Oh yes, Anna's told me to tell you that you're dumped...and I've a good mind to throw you out on your heels!'

'What is wrong with you? Have you forgotten that we're in the middle of a crisis?'

'It's my caravan that's bugging me, if you really want to know. You've hidden it and I want it back, the joke's gone on long enough. And as for you Ogroid, I don't remember giving you permission to set up a dental practice in my house.'

'Oh, give it a rest. Anyway, why are you dressed in that stupid outfit?'

'Stupid outfit? Ha! You're so uncultured that you don't even recognise an artist's smock when you see one. Painting is something that I'd always promised myself I'd do at some time in my life and I'm therefore doing it while I've still got the chance. I could have been the new Rembrandt or Cézanne. Damn it, I was so looking forward to doing a painting of my caravan, now I'll never have the opportunity, thanks to you morons.'

William took three attempts to break the paintbrush over his knee, then threw the pieces across the observatory and stormed down the stairs.

'He's really lost it,' said Mike.

'Ignore him, it's delayed shock.'

'Did he say Anna's dumped me? Why would she do that?'

'A knee-jerk reaction most probably. She must have thought you were going to ask her to marry you.'

'What?'

'Well, it did sound a bit strange, didn't it? *Listen everybody, I'd like to make a special announcement…*'

'Hmm, I didn't think of it like that. Oh well, never mind, I wasn't that keen on her anyway.'

'Come on, we'd better make a start. Let's go to the workshop and get some materials together.'

He found it difficult not to keep staring up at the sky. It reminded him of a bedroom he'd once occupied at the orphanage. He'd acquired a nice collection of model aeroplanes as the result of a bet and had fixed them above his bed with fishing line. He remembered that he'd spent weeks painting them in great detail, even down to the pilots' helmets and flying suits.

'Mike, I wonder what sort of creatures are sitting inside those things? They could be really big and…'

'I'd rather not think about that.'

Coming out of the workshop a little later, they noticed that William had set up his easel on the edge of the lake. They sneaked across the grass and hid behind a tree to get a better look. Oblivious of their presence, William hummed loudly to himself while making extravagant strokes with his brush.

'Whaaa!'

'Ahhhhh! Oh, you idiot Ogroid, now look what you've made me do! This spaceship looks more like a dodgem car. It's ruined and I'll have to start again.'

'Oh, I am sorry.'

'This was a masterpiece, now it's trash! It's all your fault and just for that I'm not inviting you to my exhibition.'

'Oh, having an exhibition, are you?'

'Yes. I'm holding it at the *Maxwell Grunting-Smythe Gallery*. It's the most revered venue outside of London.'

'How many have you done then?'

'None, thanks to you. Now clear off, the master has to work.'

It was midday when Carmen arrived back with the mini dome. Their immediate priority was to protect the *SAR* generator from the elements; even a light shower could short the electrics, then they'd be in real trouble.

'How long will it take to erect, Carmen?' asked Mike.

'No more than a couple of hours.'

'That's good. The sky looks clear at the moment, well apart from the spaceships... Oh, and try not to interrupt the beam with the panel edges, it can't penetrate solids.'

'No problem.'

'Keep William away from it too. If that beam gets broken, even for a split second, it'll set the spaceships free.'

'Won't they just get suspended again when the beam kicks back in?'

'It really depends on how fast they were travelling when they got trapped. Once free, they could easily swoop below the frozen layer of atmosphere and then there'll be no stopping them.'

'Oh right. Actually, I haven't even seen William. Where is he?'

'The last we saw of him, he was painting over by the lake,' he chipped in.

'William painting? What, the barn?'

'No, pictures. He's having an exhibition.'

'Really? That should be interesting,' she said, raising her eyebrows.

By late afternoon everyone had assembled on the lawn to admire the new dome.

'It's too small, we'll never all fit in there,' complained William.

'It's not for us idiot, it's to protect the equipment from the weather,' said Carmen, shaking her head.

'Oh dear, they're going to get free, I just know it. I'd better go and get father's shotgun.'

'Shotgun? This isn't a clay pigeon shoot,' he ridiculed. 'Why don't you go and hide in the cellar?'

'Can't, too much to do. How am I going to achieve everything in time? Let's see, sail around the world single-handed...umm, fly around the world single-handed for that matter. Ooo, I must produce an heir to keep the Smargle line going...umm Danii...?'

'Well, Victor and I are going up to the lab to make a start on the back-up kit,' said Mike.

'Is there anything I can do to help?' offered Danii, deliberately ignoring William.

'Actually, there is. I'm getting a bit peckish. How about three pieces of cheese on toast, only the upper side toasted though.'

'Oh, me too, but I'd like baked beans on top,' he added.

'Yeah, I'd like beans too.'

Well satisfied with their snack they went upstairs, stopping off at Mike's room for the lab keys. Anna had left a pile of clothes and bags by the door, which Mike just kicked inside, before going on to the attic.

They'd been working for about an hour and the framework assembly was progressing well.

'At least all this commotion has spared me from being crucified about

9

the magic show,' he said.

'Oh, I thought it was the best act. I didn't know you were concealing a streak of comic genius all these years.'

'Ha, ha. Gina was a bit unkind though, the way she forced me off the stage like that.'

'I think she was worried about overrunning.'

'Overrunning? We'd only just started. I was the first act...'

'Mike, quick!' shouted Carmen, hammering urgently on the door. 'Something's wrong with the equipment!'

'I'm on my way Carmen! ... Shit, this is it Victor!'

Outside things were critical. A dense plume of green smoke billowed from the dome, gently drifting towards the house and shrouding everything in an eerie haze.

'Oh God, the coils must be melting!'

'Quick Mike, do something!'

'What?'

'I don't know...get some more coils? Wait, it's just come back to me!'

'What has?'

'How we can get out of this. Increase the power to the beam and make them disappear, just like you did with the caravan!'

'Oh, I don't know about that. The tube's so old, a surge like that could blow it.'

'Can't you increase the power gradually?'

'Yeah, but it's a hell of a risk.'

They were interrupted by two shotgun blasts. He looked over to see William striding onto the lawn in a poncho, reloading from the cartridge belt that was draped diagonally across his chest. The beret still perched on his head and the artist's smock hanging out from underneath like a valance, rather took away from the tough gunslinger image. William squinted as the smoke from his chewed cigar drifted into his eye. Another shot rang off, breaking an upstairs window.

'What are we going to do?' asked Mike.

'I'll get a bottle of carbon dioxide from the workshop. At least that should stop it igniting.'

By the time he'd returned, the situation had worsened. He lifted the heavy cylinder from the wheelbarrow and dragged it inside. It was difficult to see anything at all and they struggled to remove the screws from the casing. After a lot of frustration, the panel fell to the ground.

'Increase the power Mike!' he said, spraying the gas into the case.

'Oh, I don't know.'

'Just do it, it's our only hope!'

The whirring sound rose in pitch with every turn of the dial and the kit began to shake around in its framework.

'Quick Victor, hold it steady, the beam could become misaligned!'

'What's going on?' shouted William, coming into the dome.

'Over here quick, we need your help!'

'Do either of you have a lighter? My cigar's gone out.'

'For fuck's sake William, just get over here, will you?'

'Okay, but I'm not putting my hand in your pocket, so you can forget that for a start.'

'Can I 'elp?' asked Xenia, calling from the doorway.

'Yes, hold the door open to get rid of these fumes…and keep an eye on those spaceships.'

'It's getting out of kilter,' said William. 'I knew it would turn out to be rubbish.'

'We need something to weigh it down!' he shouted, holding on for dear life.

'I've got some croquet hoops in one of the outbuildings, you could fix it down with those. I'll do you a favour and fetch them.'

'Croquet hoops? You're going for croquet hoops? Why don't you make some cucumber sandwiches while you're at it? Get back here, otherwise we'll all be dead!'

They gripped on to the equipment as it thrashed around like a badly loaded washing machine. The smoke had turned black and was pouring out through the open door.

'Turn it to maximum, time's running out!'

'Maximum? It'll blow!'

'Fuckety fuck,' complained William, 'my poncho's on fire!'

'Fuck your poncho!'

'Ooo, you can be so nasty Ogroid.'

'Come on Mike, there's no time left, just do it!'

Mike twisted the knob and the searing screech began to hurt his ears.

'Somezing is 'appening!' shouted Xenia. 'Ze spaceships, zey 'ave got a green light all around zem, just like wiz ze caravan!'

'Excellent! Come on, we can do it!' he shouted.

'It is working! Zey are shimmering…zey are shimmering very brightly and…ooo la la, zey 'ave gone! You 'ave done it, zey 'ave gone!'

'Right, let's get out of here,' said Mike. 'After three, let go and make for the door. One…two…three…'

As they burst outside there was a round of applause. The sky was now empty and everyone looked greatly relieved.

'Brilliant Mike, we're saved!' he said.

'Yes, they've buggered off,' said William. 'Must have scared them with my shotgun. You owe me a new poncho though. Look at this hole, it's burnt right through.'

'What? You think you scared them off? You're mental.'

11

'Yes, Victor's right William, you're mental,' agreed Carmen. 'You know full well it was all Mike's doing. His equipment saved us.'

'Well, I suppose he helped a bit.'

'Helped a bit? You should be grateful to have such a genius for a friend.'

'I know! Actually, I was only saying to Anna this morning that she should give him another chance.'

'Liar, you said he was an idiot and you were glad I was dumping him.'

'No, no, sis, I think you must have misunderstood... Anyway Muffton, I've decided that you can stay in my house, I won't hear any more of this nonsense about you moving out. So then, celebrations are in order I think. Let's go and open some champers!'

'I'd better cut the power first,' said Mike, 'just to be sure it's...'

There was a loud screech and muffled *pop* from inside the dome. He looked over his shoulder to see flames leaping from the casing. Within seconds it had developed into an almighty blaze and all they could do was stand back and watch.

In the sitting room, William pulled the cork from the last bottle in the case and topped up everyone's glass.

'No more for me thanks, I'm shattered,' he said, puffing out his cheeks. 'Champagne always goes to my head. I'm going to fall asleep any minute.'

'What about you Mike? Come on, have a glass with your old friend.'

'Okay, just a drop, then I'm turning in as well.'

'God, what a stressful day. Let's celebrate with a party next weekend, when we've had time to recover,' suggested Carmen.

'I agree. At the moment it all seems like a bad dream,' said Danii.

He'd slept for nearly twenty-four hours and woke hungry and thirsty. It was almost six in the evening when he ventured downstairs. After two mugs of coffee, he decided to get some exercise and took the dogs for a walk around the lake. Yesterday's events seemed unreal. He wondered if he'd imagined it all, but then saw the burnt out dome and blackened equipment on the lawn. By the time he got back inside, Xenia and the sisters had laid the table in the dining hall and were serving supper.

'So, my *SAR* kit was pretty useful in the end, wasn't it?' said Mike.

'Well, yesterday I was prepared to give you some credit, but now that I've slept on it, I'm not convinced,' said William.

'What are you talking about, they went, didn't they?'

'There, you just said it yourself, didn't you Muffton? They went! I think they decided there was nothing here for them and left of their own accord.'

'For God's sake William, we all saw Mike's beam making them glow,' said Carmen.

'A mass hallucination, that's what it was. Things like that do happen you know. Or perhaps Ogroid spiked our drinks? Actually, I wouldn't be at all surprised if those two were hoaxing us. That stupid kit could just be a projector. Yes, they shone pictures of spaceships into the sky to fool us!'

'Get a grip, it happened!'

'Oh dear, the spaceships were real, weren't they?' William suddenly conceded. 'I knew, I knew they were real. It's just that when anything nasty happened when I was little, Nanny Muttlecroft always made it better.'

'How?' he asked.

'Well, basically through denial.'

'Did this sort of thing occur often then?'

'Umm, not really, no.'

'Can you give us an example?' asked Carmen.

'Umm…ooo, like the day I was walking home from school and the wind blew my cap into a muddy puddle.'

'Sounds traumatic.'

'Oh, that wasn't the end of it I can assure you. As I bent down to pick it up, a big shaggy dog mounted me. Nobody could get it off. They all just stood there laughing while it shovelled me around the pavement. Totally ruined my new mackintosh.'

'Right…' said Danii, with some consideration. 'So, how did this Nanny Muttlecroft make it all better?'

'Well, we pretended it was just a nightmare I had while sleeping on the sheepskin rug in the nursery. Hmm, never been able to abide those things since. Still, I did get over it…eventually. Now then, where was I? Oh yes, okay Muffton, I accept that you made the spaceships disappear. There, how's that?'

'Well, it's a start I suppose,' said Mike.

'Yes, but something's still bothering me about what you said after the party.'

'What's that?'

'You said the whole planet had accidentally been suspended for two years, didn't you?'

'Yes.'

'Well, I've got a problem with that. If you did suspend the whole planet, then your automatic timer would have been suspended as well, wouldn't it? So, if the timer was suspended, it wouldn't move and we'd therefore still be suspended now. See, you can't fool me with your lies.'

'I made a special bit of kit to stop that happening. It's called the *SDD*.'

'What's that stand for, Stupid Dimwit Device?'

'*Suspension Defeating Device*. It defeats the effects of the beam. I'm pretty certain I can use it to enter another parallel.'

13

'Pah! What good would that be?'

'Well, we might be able to recover things that have disappeared. Your caravan for instance. It's all part of my *PooP* theory.'

'Oh yes, poop! Well, that's going to work, isn't it?'

'It's short for *Places of other Parallels.*'

'Anyway, even if it did work and you got into this other parallel, you'd probably end up setting the spaceships free, then we'd all be killed. I think you should leave well alone. We don't need you meddling about.'

'So, is zat where all ze spaceships 'ave gone, into anozer parallel?' asked Gina.

'Yes, I think so. I've called it the *Neverness.*'

'Oui, I am correct. I 'ave said before, you remember it?' said Nikki excitedly. 'I 'ave said about ze parallel universes, non?'

'So, is zis where everyone 'az disappeared to?' asked Nadesche.

'Possibly. I think it's something to do with the alien invasion.'

'How could it be that?' scoffed William. 'Everyone went missing a year before they invaded, idiot!'

'No, I think Mike's right. That massive meteor shower Gina and I saw on *Gypsy Girl* could have been alien spacecraft entering the atmosphere!' he argued. 'The aliens might have taken everyone to use as slaves. They could have been returning to do a mopping-up mission.'

'Oh really, you do talk nonsense Victor. Taken everybody for slaves, indeed! What about all the animals then? Can you imagine how difficult it would be to turn a sheep into a slave? Ha!'

'Non. Not for slave, for food. I say before,' grunted Serge.

'Ooo, I wouldn't mind being a slave,' said Stefan. 'We had such fun at a party in London one weekend…'

'Oh yes!' interjected Marco. 'Brill, wasn't it? My neck was sore for a week!'

'Your neck?' he queried.

'Yes. I was Stefan's sex slave, but my collar was a bit tight. It chaffed my skin terribly. I had to use some special oil to soothe it. Sazoa, do you remember that?'

'No, I wasn't there. I was convalescing after getting my boobs done.'

'Oh, so you were. Ooo Stefan, remember Rupert with the enormous…'

'That's quite enough about that that!' said William curtly.

'Do you zink zat we are safe from zem now?' asked Nikki.

'Well, you girls haven't got anything to worry about…'

'Non Victor, ze spaceships.'

'They're all locked in the *Neverness,*' said Mike confidently. 'Think of it as a kind of prison, we're quite safe.'

'Hey, maybe all kinds of things have slipped in there, like planes and ships from the Bermuda Triangle,' suggested Carmen.

'Does that mean our father could be inside this place too?' asked Anna eagerly.

'Take no notice sis, it's all a load of twaddle.'

'William, you can't deny that things have disappeared, we've seen it with our own eyes,' said Carmen. 'No doubt you've got a theory of your own though.'

'Yes I have, actually. Umm, I think that perhaps this *SAR* contraption causes things to disintegrate. Yes, it vibrates them until their atoms fall apart and things just appear to disappear. Yes, that's it! In fact, I think it's downright dangerous and we should ban Muffton from experimenting. He might unwittingly cause the atoms to reassemble and then those nasty spaceships will come back and get us. So, no more experiments, understand?'

'You don't know what you're talking about. Anyway, you've got no right to tell me what to do.'

'It's far too risky.'

'Don't be stupid. We can take a vote if you like.'

'Mine goes with Mike,' he said without hesitation.

'Well I'm against it I'm telling you!' snapped William. 'All those who agree with me, raise your hands.'

In the end it was a very close result, with Carmen casting the deciding vote in favour of the experiments continuing.

'Bloody cheek,' said Mike, unlocking the lab door. 'They wouldn't have stopped me anyway. I'd have moved out.'

'I'd have come with you. You know, there are plenty of nice places just a stone's throw from here…well, we wouldn't want to be too far from the girls, would we?'

'Not really, well apart from Anna. Did you see that resentful look on her face when she voted against me?'

'Don't worry about it.'

'I won't. I'll just get on with my work. I couldn't care less.'

The following morning when he woke, the tiredness had gone and he felt much more optimistic. Now that their problems were over, he saw no reason why they couldn't resume some sort of normal life. Looking in the mirror, he hardly recognised himself. It was about time he had a shower and shave. Over the last couple of days, personal hygiene hadn't exactly been his top priority.

'Morning William,' he said, entering the kitchen.

'Ah, there you are you layabout. I've already finished a work of art and what have you done? Nothing!'

'It's only half ten, what's the matter with you?'

'My lawn, that's what's the matter. It's in a terrible mess. Ruined one of my paintings. I'll never be able to hang that now, not with that burnt patch in the middle.'

'You've burnt a hole in one of your paintings?'

'No, no, the lawn. That melted dome thing doesn't help either. It's totally ruined the aesthetic balance of the classical er...er...intricacies of my building. I want you and Muffton to clear it away, and don't go dumping it in the grounds either, get rid of it properly.'

'We were going to do that anyway. Mike said he might be able to salvage some parts from the kit.'

'There's nothing for him in there, not unless he needs a large supply of carbon. It's all charred to oblivion.'

'A bit like your toast then,' he said, pointing to a column of black smoke.

'What? Damn, now you've ruined my breakfast as well.'

'It's your own fault, you should have been watching it instead of staring out of the window. What are you looking for anyway?'

'Keeping an eye out in case they come back.'

'They've gone, William.'

'They might send more...then they'll find us and kill us.'

'I shouldn't worry about that, Mike's going to freeze the stratosphere again.'

'He can't, can he? The kit's all burnt and it's going to take forever to get a new one made. Face it Ogroid, we're finished.'

'Look, even if they do send more ships, it'll take time. We don't even know where they came from, it might have taken them years to get here. If I were you, I'd calm down, nothing's going to happen... Here, I've cut you some more bread...hmm, quite nice this, who made it?'

'Carmen. Personally I prefer white. This brown stuff doesn't toast well, it's so crumbly you can only cut thick slices. That's why it gets jammed in the toaster.'

'Where are the girls this morning anyway?'

'Playing tennis.'

'What, gone to a club somewhere?'

'No, the courts here.'

'You've got tennis courts?'

'Yes, what did you think was behind that very tall hedge at the back of the workshop?'

'Nothing, I just thought it was a very tall hedge.'

'The entrance is around the other side. There's an archway cut through. Got a bit overgrown, but Anna and Carmen sorted it out. Yes, there are two lovely courts...and a pavilion. Father was keen on his tennis. He was a good player! Never managed to take a set off him. Actually, while we're on the subject, did I tell you I was specially chosen to be a ball boy at Wimbledon?'

16

'No?'

'Yes, father got me in. I can remember as if it were yesterday…getting changed into my little green outfit in the public toilets…'

'Public toilets? Didn't you have changing rooms?'

'No, no, things like that are just for the players. No, everyone else has to use the toilets.'

'So, did you see anyone famous?'

'As a matter of fact I did. Lucy Buttercluck… Fiona Dank-Fritters… I would have seen a lot more if that damn window hadn't steamed up. Oh yes, very good memories… You know, it was such a thrill to be out there on Centre Court. The crowd mumbling between points…the stark silence just before they served. Yes, I remember taking up my position at the net with the other two ball boys…'

'Other two? There are usually *only* two.'

'That's what the umpire said. Anyway, they removed one of the boys and the match began. It was all going so well, but then at the end of the third game some idiot marched over and dragged me off court. I think it was the father of the ball boy I was competing against, jealous of a very good catch I'd just made. Yes, beat him to that one, skinny little twerp!'

'I'd like a game actually. I'll go and get changed.'

He stood in the hallway practising his shots, the racket making a satisfying swoosh as he hit an imaginary ball. He hadn't been able to find an entirely white outfit, so had dressed in his beige holiday shorts and a yellowish-white T-shirt. At least the headband gave him a professional look. Just as he was lunging for an especially tricky half volley, the girls came back, obviously having finished.

'Morning Victor, what are you up to then?' said Carmen.

'Oh, I was just going to join you.'

'We were playing tennis, not badminton.'

'Yeah, I know…this is the only racket I could find.'

He could hear the girls giggling as they climbed the stairs. Feeling put out, he decided to go to Dellfield and visit his old house.

He pulled up outside and considered driving straight off again, but then talked himself into taking a look. Putting the key in the front door, he tried to push it open. He'd forgotten to cancel the newspapers before going on holiday and the mound that had built up on the floor prevented him from squeezing inside. Going through the back entrance, he went into the hall, scooped everything up and carried it to the kitchen. He began sifting through to find his mail. There were mostly bills, along with a couple of nasty letters from his bank manager. His credit card statement also made sorry reading. He'd overspent on the holiday and would have been in real financial trouble if he'd had to pay it all off. Still, none of that mattered any more, so he casually dropped everything into the waste bin. He turned his attention to the newspaper on top of the pile. It was the last issue of *The Daily Wonder* ever to have been printed, dated Friday the thirteenth of August 2049. As usual the headlines were nothing special, so he thumbed through looking for something more interesting.

'Hello, what's this?'

PRODUCT RECALL FOR THE SPRING-LOADED ROTARY MT!

The distributors are recalling the above product due to safety issues. Anyone in possession of this item should return it to the place of purchase for a full refund. Please note, this only applies to the Spring-loaded Rotary MT, all other products in the Rotary range are unaffected.

'Hmm, that name rings a bell.'

He turned the page and was faced with the horrific sight of a middle-aged woman dressed quite inappropriately, trapped inside a rotating washing line.

DEATH TRAP WASHING LINE CLAIMS EIGHTH VICTIM!!

Mrs Sogsworth of Hitsfield Mortimer had a lucky escape yesterday when she became the eighth victim of the Spring-loaded Rotary MT. The fire brigade were called and it took them several hours to free her. A spokesman for the fire service said, 'She was an extremely lucky woman. It was a nice calm day and had it been at all windy, we could have been faced with something very nasty indeed.'

'I bet!'

Mrs Sogsworth was taken to hospital and treated for shock. She was later discharged and gave us a full account of what happened. 'I'd been using the washing line for several weeks and had no problem with it before. Yesterday was a different matter though. I had an unusually large amount of washing, due to an elderly relative staying. As I hung the sheets over one of the rearmost lines, there was a loud snap and I found myself suddenly snatched up into the air with these arms and lines wrapped around me all tight. The more I struggled, the worse it got. I was screaming for half an hour before my neighbour found me. You know the rest of the story.' The Health and Safety Executive have issued this statement, 'This device is dangerous. It can go off without warning, just like a giant mousetrap. Perhaps that's what MT stands for?' We at The Daily Wonder disagree. We think MT stands for Man Trap!

'Damn, it's really bugging me, *Rotary MTs*? Where have I heard that before?'

In a bizarre twist, the Army have expressed an interest in buying them. Colonel Raymond Whimpsey told our reporter, 'They would appear to be an excellent anti-personnel device, especially if we were to use them in suburban warfare.' However, a secret source has provided us with some disturbing information. It appears that these Rotary MTs originally came from the Army! Thousands were disposed of through a Government Auction, relabelled as washing lines, then sold to the unsuspecting public. The Government has denied this. The police have today also issued a warning, 'These devices are dangerous and should not be approached. If you see one, phone our MT hotline immediately...'

'Yes, I remember now! There's a stack of them on that Army lorry Mike and I recovered from Fritsbury.'

He went upstairs and dragged an old leather suitcase out from under his bed. It was full of odds and ends, mostly from his childhood. He took his prized conker and let it dangle from the tatty piece of cord. It still looked shiny and new even though it was nearly twenty years old. It had been a record breaker, defeating no less than one hundred and eighty-nine others. The fact that it had been cast from lead and hot-coated in an authentic coloured plastic probably had something to do with it. The ordinary ones had always cracked too easily and this one had been much more reliable. He then came across his small cigar tin full of foreign stamps and the hand puppet with a papier-mâché fish head, which he remembered scaring the girls with at his first orphanage. There were also several copies of his favourite childhood comic, *Mystery and Magic Weekly*. Closing the lid, he took it to his van and placed it on the passenger seat. He felt a pang of nostalgia for the old days, but it didn't last. He had much more to look forward to now, more than at any other time in his life.

Chapter 2

They'd decided on a general fancy dress theme for the party, but he still didn't know what to go as. He sat on the lawn with his dogs enjoying the sunshine, trying to think of an idea. He held his face to the sun and closed his eyes. All he could see was a fluorescing bright red through his eyelids.

'I know, a vampire!'

'Pardon?'

'Oh, hello Mike. I was just thinking about the party.'

'I'm going as a grandfather clock. I'm making it from cardboard. Are you going to make your own costume then?'

'No, I thought I'd nip over to *Driftwood Film Studios* near *EcoWorld*. They made *Bloodsuck Hotel* there a couple of years ago.'

'Oh yeah, I saw that. I liked the bit when the vampire jumped out on that bloke from the dumbwaiter shaft.'

'Brilliant, wasn't it? So, do you want to come?'

'Nah, I've got to work out how to make the clock face.'

Returning with his outfit later that morning, he drove slowly up the driveway enjoying the heavy shade provided by the avenue of trees. As he got closer to the house, he spotted someone lurking at one of the landing windows and quickly realised it was William, still surveying the sky.

'Shit, he's seen me. Now he'll come down and delay me trying it on.'

By the time he'd got out of the van, William was upon him.

'Where have you been and what's in that bag?'

'It's my costume for the party.'

'I've got an outfit too. Found it in father's wardrobe. He was keen on fancy dress, although now I come to think of it, I can't remember there being that many fancy dress parties here. So, what are you going as?'

'You'll have to wait and see. It's a surprise.'

'It had better be good. I don't want you turning up in that stupid magician's cloak.'

'What are you wearing then?'

'Not telling. It's brilliant. The girls will be falling over me. I'll probably get off with Danii. I'm going to ask her out on a date. Anyway, enough of that. I just came to tell you that the lawn's getting a bit long. Be a good chap and cut it.'

'When?'

'Now.'

'No, do it yourself. Come on, out of my way, I want to go upstairs and get my outfit ready.'

'Selfish toad, Ogroid!'

He spent much of the afternoon parading in front of the mirror, occasionally making adjustments to the cloak with safety pins. He wasn't very happy with the quality of the fangs, so he took a mould of Wolfie's teeth and made some new ones from plaster. When they were dry, he added a little bit of mustard to yellow them and then a layer of varnish for the final touch. They looked very realistic and didn't at all distort his mouth.

He'd been hiding near the stairs in the main hallway for about twenty minutes. William normally fetched some wine at about six o'clock and today was no exception. He pushed his fangs into place, followed him down the cellar steps and lurked in a dark corner waiting to strike.

'**Whaaa!**'

'**Ahhhhh! Help! Oh my God, help!**'

'Calm down, it's only me.'

'Victor, you idiot! Oh, my poor little heart. You're such a moron, you really are. I could have died just then.'

'It was only a joke.'

'Jokes are meant to be funny. You really shouldn't tamper with the unknown. In fact, I wouldn't be surprised if the ghost of Poffington Hall gets you for messing around in his territory.'

'What, this place has got a ghost?'

'Yes, a very nasty one actually, and it'll get you. It doesn't like smart arses.'

On the day of the party, he spent several hours experimenting with theatrical make-up until he was satisfied that no one would recognise him. At seven thirty he went down to the ballroom where quite a large group had already congregated. He made his way to the buffet table to join Danii and Carmen.

'Hello Victor. Nice costume.'

'Thanks. I like yours too…and yours Danii,' he said, looking them up and down. 'Umm, what are you?'

'Air hostesses.'

'Oh right… I like the hats. What gave you the idea?'

'I saw a photo in a magazine,' said Carmen, searching her bag. 'Here, look.'

He took the picture and studied it.

'Bloody hell, that's the same plane we've been using!'

'We got the uniforms from a clothing museum,' added Danii. '*BEA* was an airline company from the last century.'

'Last century?'

'Yes, almost a hundred years ago.'

'Where's William?' he asked, scanning the room.

'Over there, helping the sisters.'

'Nadesche has this idea for an evening of silly games,' said Danii. 'Could be fun.'

William was busily counting a line of chairs next to the stage, dressed as an airline pilot. He rather suspected that the outfit was part of a feeble plan to get Danii interested. He cast his eye around to see what some of the others were wearing. Mike looked quite cumbersome, especially with the dangling pendulum, but at least he'd had the sense to paint the numbers and hands onto his face. Gina was dressed as a sexy nurse, so he immediately tried to think of a suitable ailment that she could attend to after a few drinks.

'Hmm, is Xenia supposed to be a car mechanic? Those overalls look like mine. Yes, the same burnt patch on the left arm from when I set fire to myself. Shit, I hope she hasn't gone through the top pockets.'

During a bored moment in the workshop, he'd taken a scrap of paper and listed each of the girls, giving them marks out of ten for looks, shagability and so on. In the end he'd expanded the list to several sheets and if remembered correctly, it encompassed some fairly dodgy areas. If it got into the wrong hands his reputation could be damaged.

'If the worst comes to the worst, I'll move out. Hang on…she's wearing the red ones, they don't have top pockets. Phew, thank God for that!'

'Ah, there you are Ogroid,' said William. 'Nadesche wants to play *Musical Chairs* and we needed help with the setting up. Thanks to your skiving tactics, I've gone and pulled a muscle in my back. Selfish, so selfish!'

'That plane we've been using is a hundred years old!'

'So?'

'Well, don't they have a shelf-life?'

'Look, plenty of old cars used to turn out for the London to Brighton Rally, didn't they?'

'Yes.'

'There you are then, perfectly safe. Come on, we're about to start.'

When the music began he shuffled along the line of chairs to the end, did a neat turn and plonked himself down immediately it stopped. He was dismayed when Sazoa went for the same seat a little too late and landed on his lap, ripping her tight riding breeches in the process. She was dressed as a ringmaster, which he thought was unsuitable because the crotch bulge was rather prominent. Suddenly they were off again and Anna swiped away a chair. This time Stefan fell onto his lap.

'For God's sake, keep still.'

'Ooo, sorry. It's just that it's all so exciting.'

'Just stop fidgeting... *Damn, I should have joined the line between the girls. What is he wearing? Looks like William's lederhosen. Horrible, all tight with those lily-white thighs... Oh fucking hell, that's one of his balls poking out of the side! Urrgghh, it's all squashed...and it looks like he shaves them. Hang on a sec...* Excuse me Stefan, you shouldn't still be sitting here, you're out! Get off me! Come on Mike, where's the music? Let's go, let's get moving!'

For the next game, Marco announced his own version of *Blind Man's Buff*. With everybody blindfolded and milling around the ballroom floor, the object of the game was to find your partner by touch only, no talking allowed. He'd been paired with Serge, so he'd already decided to keep his blindfold off and lurk in a corner. As he suspected, Marco was taking full advantage and was going around feeling low. He then noticed that William was fortuitously bumping into the girls, one after the other, having a good grope. He was sure that William was cheating, but it would be difficult to prove and wasn't really worth stopping the game to make a scene about. Deciding to go out for a while, he was just heading for the door when someone crashed into him.

'Oh, it's you. I suppose that puts us out then?'

'You know it is me from ze garlic, non?' said Serge, lifting his blindfold.

'Umm, yeah, something like that.'

'Ze fang is good, I like.'

'Oh, thanks.'

'Dog merchant.'

'*Bloody cheek!*' he thought.

He leant against one of the great marble pillars in the hallway, pulled a joint from his pocket, then rummaged around for a lighter.

'Yeah, he can get stuffed.'

'Talking to yourself Victor?'

'Oh, Carmen...umm, couldn't find my lighter...got it now,' he said, holding it up for her to see. 'Want a drag?'

'No thanks. I'm just going to get some more bottled water. One of your fangs is missing by the way.'

'Is it? Shit, I hope I haven't swallowed it.'

'Don't worry, I'm sure it'll turn up.'

Back inside, a three-legged race was well under way. Incredibly, William was out in front, dragging Stefan along like a rag doll as if he just wanted to get the ordeal over with. Having crossed the winning line, William immediately untied his leg and headed for the drinks table. Sazoa was standing close by, struggling to release herself from Serge. Someone had obviously been over-zealous with the ties. He was glad that he'd missed out on that particular game and went to get himself a drink.

'William, don't planes suffer from metal fatigue or something?'

'I don't know, but I have to tell you I'm getting Ogroid fatigue, so bugger off! Oh look, we're out of red.'

'Oh, I was just going to have a glass,' said Sazoa, giving up with the knot.

'Never mind, I've got plenty stacked in the hallway. Got Anna to bring it up earlier. Perhaps you'd like to accompany me and select a bottle or two?'

'Ooo, how lovely.'

He helped himself to a beer and watched them link arms. Serge was now trying to untie himself from Sazoa and was dragged along on all fours as she moved off.

'Nobody invited you!' snapped William.

'Non, you cannot go wiz 'er. Not before we 'ave cut off zis zing…'

'I don't think that's any of your business, Serge.'

'Non, ze legs, zey will not part.'

'Ooo, has he been pestering you Sazoa? Go away, you nasty French pervert!'

The tie finally fell loose and Serge stuck a finger up, cursing heavily at William.

'Victor, can you 'elp?' said Xenia, appearing with Nikki. 'We cannot undo it.'

'Yeah, everybody's having problems. Umm, are those my overalls?'

'Oui, I 'oped zat you would not mind.'

'I don't, it's just that I normally keep a modelling-knife blade in the back pocket.'

'Oh, I will see.'

'Umm, I'd better do it. You might cut yourself.'

'Go on zen, 'ave your fun,' she said, sticking her bottom out towards him.

'Umm, right. No…no, nothing there, damn,' he said, pausing with his hands still in position.

'Pervert!' said William, returning with Sazoa. 'What are you doing anyway?'

'Helping Xenia.'

'Helping yourself more like.'

'She can't get herself untied.'

'So you thought you'd just fondle her arse, did you?'

'No, these are my overalls. I was feeling for a knife blade, that's all.'

'Zank you for trying to 'elp, we go to ze kitchen.'

He sat on the stage with a bottle of malt whisky, dangling his legs over the edge. He had been looking forward to this party, but now felt a bit of an outsider. Mike was engrossed in a conversation with Carmen and William had his hands all over Sazoa, looking for a reaction from Danii.

24

'*Damn, why can't I get myself a girl? Hmm, I could get Gina to tend my imaginary ailment.*'

He slid off the stage and sidled over to her.

'Hello Gina...umm, I've been having some pain in my upper leg recently, I was wondering if you could take a look for me, maybe give me a massage with that special oil?'

'Not now Victor, I play a game wiz Stefan and Marco.'

'It's really hurting. Can we go to your room later?'

'Non, I do not zink so. I must go.'

He walked over to the workshop, thinking that no one would miss him. He fiddled about tidying some shelves, then emptied a washing up bowl full of oily nuts and bolts onto a workbench intending to sort them out. After staring at the mess for a few seconds, he couldn't be bothered and scooped them back in with one movement of his arm. Going outside, he practised swooshing his cape to show off the red lining and then ran across the lawn with his arms outstretched, trying to take off. Feeling giddy, he sneaked into the ballroom and resumed his seat on the edge of the stage. Almost immediately, William came striding over.

'Listen Victor, I was having a nice walk around on the roof garden with Danii earlier...'

'Good for you.'

'Yes, aircrew always hang out together...probably be joining the *Mile High Club* soon.'

'So you've asked her out on that date then?'

'No, not yet, I'm building up to it. Make her jealous by flirting with some of the other girls first. These things have to be planned carefully. Anyway I got distracted, I noticed that the plants and shrubs were all looking dry. In fact, they're so dry I want you to water them.'

'Do it yourself.'

'I can't, my back's painful after moving all those chairs. Look, if you won't do it they'll die. The leaves will drop off, then they'll mould and I, or Danii for that matter, could skid. She could go flying.'

'You wish.'

'Just do it. You'll be doing Danii a favour too.'

'What's he trying to get you to do now?' said Mike, coming over with his arm around Carmen.

'I want the tubs watered on the ballroom roof, that's all. Actually Muffton, you can help him. It's a lovely view from up there, you'll enjoy it.'

'Yes,' said Anna, joining them. 'It's quite a drop, careful you don't fall. William, can I have a word in private please?'

In the early hours, most of the survivors were sprawled around the sitting room. The hallway lights flickered on and off several times and he noticed through the crack in the door that someone was lurking just outside. William then jumped into the room with his arms in the air, wearing a pair of purple velvet knickerbockers and an Elizabethan ruff; his eyes were bulging and his nostrils flared. Altogether it was a very ugly sight.

'**Whhhaaa!** Whhhaaa…and spit upon the thigh of a toad and cast its shadow into a pit of doom! Ogroid, you're the toad.'

They watched in silence as William pranced back out into the hallway, where he again flickered the lights before banging the door shut.

'What do you think could be wrong with him, Victor?' asked Danii.

'I've never been able to work that out.'

The girls had suggested clearing up the ballroom before going to bed and his job was to collect all the empty bottles. He staggered up the steps onto the stage, but tripped. Grabbing the curtain to break his fall, there was a loud clatter as it all came down on top of him. He heard a collective gasp and the room fell silent. As he lifted his head from the mounds of material, he saw Sazoa bent over a table. William, who had changed back into his pilot's uniform, was standing behind her with his trousers at half-mast.

'She's fainted, that's all,' said William, quickly dressing himself. 'Sazoa, Sazoa, are you all right?'

The next morning he woke with his tongue stuck to the roof of his mouth and a throbbing pain behind the eyes. Splashing his face with cold water, he swallowed a couple of aspirins and went down to the kitchen.

'Morning Mike.'

'Hi Victor. You look a bit rough.'

'I'll be all right when I've had some coffee.'

'Here, I've just made some.'

'Thanks… You seemed to be getting on well with Carmen last night. Where is she?'

'She went off with Danii about an hour ago. Haven't seen William yet though.'

'He's probably having a lie in.'

'Let's water those tubs, that'll wake him.'

'I did it last night, set a sprinkler going.'

'What, in the dark?'

'It was getting light by then. Thought I'd get it out of the way.'

'How did you get up there, through his room?'

'No, by ladder.'

'Well, if you're ready we'd better go and start work.'

They were sorting out some materials in the workshop when a van pulled up outside.

'Hello boys,' said Carmen, coming in with Danii. 'Just wondered if you'd been along the motorway recently?'

'Umm, no,' said Mike. 'The last time was when you sent us to clear it before our holiday.'

'You ought to see it now. That weird growth is getting really wild. Something's going to have to be done about it…and I don't mean a quick trim down the sides either. It'll have to be taken back ten metres from the edge of the carriageway into the fields, otherwise we're in danger of losing our main route to London.'

'Sounds serious. We'd better take some flame-throwers, then bulldoze it afterwards.'

'Yeah, don't worry, we'll start first thing tomorrow,' he said. 'Anyway, what have you two been doing?'

'We've been to a cheese wholesaler. Would you mind unloading the van for us?'

'No problem. Just park by the front door, we'll do it after lunch.'

He considered rolling some of the larger cheese wheels into the house, but thought better of it in case he got told off for being unhygienic. Instead he put as much as he could onto a low-loader and pushed it through to the cold store, where Carmen was organising the shelves.

'Where's William then Victor, is he still in bed?'

'No idea.'

'He's probably too embarrassed to come down after last night.'

'Oh yes, I forgot about that. I'd better go and see if he's okay.'

He trotted upstairs, pressed his ear to the door and knocked loudly.

'William?'

'What do you want?'

'Are you okay?'

'Wait a minute.'

William stood glumly in the darkened doorway wearing his pyjamas.

'We were getting worried, haven't seen you all day.'

'Feel a bit depressed. Can't see the point in getting out of bed when the weather's like this.'

'What are you talking about?'

'The rain. It's lashing down.'

'What do you mean, it's a beautiful day out there.'

'What?'

William went across to the French windows and pulled the curtains. Water pounded on the glass, running down like a river.

'You idiot Ogroid!' said William, pressing his face against a pane. 'It's a hose-pipe!'

'Shit, I thought that clip needed tightening. Sorry, it must have shot off.'

'I've wasted a whole day because of your incompetence? If that roof has leaked, I'll strangle you! Now clear off, I want to get dressed.'

Downstairs, he glanced around the ballroom, but couldn't see any puddles so resumed the task of unloading. As he wheeled the next batch through the kitchen, he noticed that Carmen and a few of the others were sitting around the table having a chat. He decided to take a break himself and joined them for a coffee. Suddenly it went quiet as William walked in.

'Hello. Where have you been then?' asked Danii.

'Don't ask, I'll just get in a temper again.'

'Have you got an explanation for your performance last night?' asked Carmen.

'Oh that. I would have thought it was quite obvious, a moment of thespian inspiration. Did you appreciate it?'

'Not really, no.'

'I'm surprised at you Carmen. Uncultured, the lot of you.'

'I think we must be talking at cross-purposes. I was referring to what we saw on the stage.'

'Oh, I might have guessed. I've already explained that. Sazoa was feeling sick and flopped over a table. I was just helping her when everything came crashing down around my feet.'

'Yeah, including your trousers!' he taunted.

'My belt buckle broke! Really, you lot are perverted. Think what you like, I don't care. Now then, listen everybody. I'm inviting you all to an art exhibition. I've set the date for Thursday the first of September, so you'd jolly well better be there.'

'Will it be paintings that you've done, or works by famous artists?' asked Carmen.

'They're all by me.'

'Are they oil or watercolour?'

'I don't know, does it matter? Gloss, I think.'

'What are your subjects?'

'Things…umm, the house and lake mostly, if it's any of your business. Anyway, you'll see for yourselves soon enough.'

'Come on then,' said Carmen, getting up, 'there's work to be done.'

'Ooo goody, a trolley of fromage! Danii, why don't you show me where it's kept?'

Five minutes later he was just carrying the last wheel inside when William blocked him in the kitchen doorway, elbowed him in the ribs and pushed aggressively past. The cheese dropped to the floor and William viciously stamped on it with his heel before charging off. He crouched to inspect the dent.

'Did William just do that?' Carmen asked, coming to take a look.

'Yeah, he's in a real bad mood. What's upset him now?'

'Danii told him off for mauling the cheese.'

Later that evening he was in his room wondering what the truth about William and Sazoa really was, when he got a sudden pain in his abdomen. He realised that he hadn't been for about five days and sat on the toilet for some considerable time.

'Arrgghh! Fuck, that's a big one! Oh no, what's that? I must have caught tapeworms from the dogs! Wait...phew, it's only that fang I swallowed. Right, when I've finished I'll give it a quick rinse under the tap and put it in the matchbox with the other one.'

Over the next ten days he spent quite a lot of time in the workshop, fiddling around with a couple of classic cars he'd picked up. Mike was usually locked away in his lab, while William rushed around in his artist's smock and beret, in a highly emotional state.

'Where's Muffton, I haven't seen him in ages?' asked William, as they sat around the kitchen table for lunch.

'He's busy working on a new project,' he replied.

'New project? What about the replacement *SAR* generator?'

'Yeah, he's doing that too.'

'Good. Tell him to hurry up with it.'

'It's a really interesting lab he's got, isn't it?' said Carmen.

'He's shown you around then?' he asked.

'Yes, well, I've been taking him the occasional snack.'

'Has he shown you his plans for the *PooP* machine?'

'For God's sake Ogroid, we're eating,' complained William. 'Can't you talk about it afterwards? Damn stupid project name anyway.'

'I can't say I'm surprised though,' said Anna. 'He always did talk a load of shit.'

'Ha, ha, very good that, sis, ha! Oh, do you think you could cut my meat into smaller pieces? It's awkward for me trying to use this knife.'

'What happened to your fingers anyway?'

'Nothing.'

'That blood-soaked hanky looks unhygienic, why don't you let Carmen dress it properly?'

'Yes, let me have a look...'

'Oh, do stop fussing. Now then everybody, I know that you're all pretending you've forgotten about my exhibition, but I'm glad to say it's set up, ready and waiting. I've even prepared a delicious buffet and there are some very palatable wines to sample. So, if you'd all like to hop in your cars when we've finished, you can follow me into the city. Oh, Victor, before you go and get changed perhaps you could load a small generator into my *LandFido*. I want to get the spotlights on. My pictures can be better appreciated that way.'

'What do you mean, before I get changed?'

'Well you can't go dressed like that.'

'I thought I was excluded?'

'I'm letting you off, count it as a special favour.'

The gallery was modern, with minimalist décor. The clean lines were broken by William's crookedly hung paintings, all draped in different coloured and patterned sheets. It looked like a decorator had set up, rather than an artist.

'Here we are then. You will notice that my work is still covered. It's my intention to reveal them as we go, because this will give you time to absorb the enchanting qualities of each piece without being distracted. Well, that's enough talk, I welcome you all to my wonderful exhibition, *William, A Stroke of Genius!* Now then, before you look at my paintings I want to inform you that I've written some poems, so I hope you appreciate them. This first one is called *Ode to Poffington*. Here goes. One, two, three... *Oh, thy walls and windows are sturdy, my house since last Thursday...*umm, it's longer than that I know, but I needed a rhyme. Sorry, I'll start again. *Ode to Poffington... Oh, thy walls and windows are sturdy, my house since last Thursday. I love thee Poffington without shame, from the time your doorway I first came.* There, what do you think to that then?'

'Rubbish!' he shouted. 'It doesn't even make sense.'

'You pleb Ogroid, poetry doesn't have to make sense,' said William condescendingly. 'Carmen, stop that childish giggling, and you Muffton. Right, now we've ascertained that none of you are cultured enough to recognise the value of verse, perhaps you'll be more comfortable looking at pictures.'

The first one was of a chicken. It was a basic outline, without detail or perspective. The next painting was of a house, with a window in each corner and a curl of smoke coming from the chimney. He wouldn't have guessed that it was Poffington Hall, except that the name had been added across the bottom in big, black capital letters. There was a bemused silence as they were ushered along. It seemed that everyone was lost for words.

'All the animal pictures you've just seen were painted from memory, you understand. Now then, over here I have a special collection of landscapes from my more outwardly mobile, expressive period. You will notice that I've experimented with views other than those of Poffington and the lake.'

'Look Mike, you can see the numbers showing through,' he whispered.

'What was that Ogroid? I hope you're not criticising my work again. Remember, I did you a special favour in allowing you to come along.'

'No, I only said I didn't know you'd painted such large numbers. Well, apart from those on the car roofs,' he said, to more stifled giggles.

'I only did that so I could spot them easily from the air. Now then, the quantity I've created is directly related to the effort I've put in. Look and learn Ogroid, if you worked hard you might be able to achieve greater things. Not in art of course, but in something altogether more bland, bead-stringing for example. Right, if you'd all like to move into the bar, you can help yourselves to the buffet and have a glass of wine. I shall circulate amongst you so you have the opportunity to tell me which paintings you want to purchase.'

He was feeling quite hungry and eagerly went in search of food. The buffet consisted of two large platters of cheese and pineapple kebabs. Huge cubes of cheddar covered in dirty thumbprints had been pushed onto skewers, interspersed with tiny chunks of pineapple. He picked one up and estimated that it weighed about half a kilo. A severely hacked cheese sat on the end of the table. His eyes followed a trail of blood to a bundle of soggy kitchen towel, which had been discarded amongst the crumbs on the floor.

After the last of the wine had been consumed, everybody wanted to leave. William was a little cross at not selling more of his work.

'You're all missing the bargain of a lifetime. No more takers then? ... Right that's it! You've missed your final chance, the sale's over. Now then Anna, I'll have your two paintings delivered to your room for free, but in exchange I'll want those diamond cufflinks grandfather gave you just before he went completely potty. You know he mistook you for me, don't you?'

'Oh, all right, but I'm keeping the duelling pistols, you're not having those.'

'Well, that was different, wasn't it?' said Stefan, coming over with his arm around Marco. 'We were just saying to each other that we ought to have more social events.'

'Yes, but what? I really don't think I could stomach an evening of William on the violin.'

'I don't even play the violin, Carmen,' objected William. 'How silly you can be sometimes! No, no, I'm more of a trumpet person.'

'Ooo, I've got an idea,' said Marco. 'We could go ten-pin bowling. Does anyone know if there's an alley close by?'

'Yes! We used to go every week in London,' agreed Stefan excitedly.

'Actually, there's one over at the RAF base. I could probably get it up and running quite easily,' he offered.

'Stupid idea,' scoffed William. 'Who in their right mind would want to do that? What about going on an archaeological dig, or brass rubbing in the local church, or...'

'It sound like shit,' Serge interrupted.

'Couldn't have put it better myself,' said Carmen.

'It does all sound rather boring,' said Danii. 'Actually, I'd love to go

31

ten-pin bowling. Our orphan group used to play at least once a month.'

'Oh, *ten-pin* bowling,' said William. 'Sorry, I thought we were talking about that stupid bowling the French do.'

'And why is zat stupid?' asked Gina.

'Umm…well, it's just balls knocking into each other.'

'Ooo,' exclaimed Marco, 'perhaps we could do that instead?'

He spent much of the next week at the RAF base. It didn't take long to get the bowling alley sorted out, but he wanted to have a good snoop around the hangars. Some days he just felt so bored that he acted on any idea that came into his head. He was hoping it wouldn't be long before Mike was ready to go into the *Neverness*, as that could be something to really get their teeth into. Even William was keeping a low profile, he'd been locked away in the reference library all week with a *Do Not Disturb* sign hung on the door.

He was sitting at the kitchen table making a list of his top one hundred favourite female celebrities, when William came in looking very excited.

'Victor, I've come up with a brainwave for an outing!'

'What's that then?'

'A river-punting picnic.'

'It sounds stupid. We'll all fall in.'

'No, no. We take the punts upstream and find a grassy bank.'

'I don't think so.'

'Okay then, what about this… A hypnotic evening on Magdalene Bridge with William Smargle? You set up floodlights, I hypnotise people from the crowd and get them to do silly things.'

'Like what?'

'I don't know…umm…oh, forget it. Er, bell ringing in that tower on Magdalene Bridge? We can pretend it's May Day and jump in the river.'

'You can if you want.'

'The trouble with you Ogroid, is that you're a killjoy. You have no spirit of adventure. Right, the punting picnic it is then. I firmly believe in the idea and I've already prepared a poster all about it. There's a space on the bottom for people to sign up. I'm sticking it on the fridge door.'

'Stick it where you like.'

'I'm adding my own name at the top of the list, that way they'll see I'm serious about it. The girls will be falling over themselves to get into my boat. Yes, they'll all be grabbing my pole most probably. Now then, I'm setting the deadline for Sunday. If people haven't got their names down by then, it'll be too late, they'll jolly well have to stay at home. Right, I'm off to join the girls on the tennis court, give them a bit of forewarning about the picnic.'

After William had left the room, he went over to have a look at the notice.

OUTING ON WEDNESDAY 14 SEPTEMBER
Everyone is invited to sign up (below, left) for William's Punting Picnic!
Meet at 12.30 sharp on the steps of Magdalene Bridge.
Sign up NOW to avoid disappointment! (Deadline Sunday)
3 to a punt max.
Bring own hampers, champers and blankets.

'Hmm, doubt if anyone will be interested in that.'

He toyed with the idea of spying on the girls' tennis session, but decided against it because William would be hanging around and that would spoil it for him. Instead he opted to tidy up the workshop. He hadn't been in there long when he heard a commotion outside. Gina came running through the doors in a terrible panic.

'Quick Victor, quick! Zare 'az been an accident!'

He rushed out after her and saw Danii and Carmen propping William up from either side as they dragged him along.

'Can you help, he's too heavy?' shouted Danii.

'What on earth's wrong with him?' he asked. 'Why's his face all red, is he drunk?'

'He was heckling us and by sheer fluke Carmen hit the ball straight into his mouth.'

Just as William's legs were collapsing, he dashed forward into Danii's place, taking most of the weight. Nikki and Nadesche were jumping up and down in horror as he manhandled William through the door and pushed him into a chair.

'We can't get it out, it's jammed behind his teeth,' Carmen explained.

'Urrgghh...urrgghh!' gagged William.

'He's trying to say something,' said Danii.

'No, he wants to write it down,' said Carmen. 'Quick, get a pen.'

He thrust a pencil into William's hand and found a scrap of paper. William seemed on the verge of passing out and his head rolled around loosely as he wrote.

'What does it say?' she asked.

'I can hardly read it. Er, qu...quick? Yes, quick...quick tra...track?'

'No, it's an instruction. Quick, tracheotomy! He can't breathe!'

'Can't he?' he said, pinching William's nostrils together just to make sure. 'Oh right. Pass me that modelling-knife Gina.'

The girls all turned away as he sliced into the tennis ball and wriggled it free.

'**Idiots!**' choked William. 'I nearly suffocated. Useless, the lot of you!'

At breakfast the following morning William had gone into a sulk when Carmen said he had looked like a pig with an apple stuck in its mouth, but it had all been forgotten now they were on their way to the bowling alley. They drove past the broken barrier and followed the grid of roads through to the entertainment centre. He was pleased that everybody was impressed with the neon *Lightning Bowl* sign flashing away on the roof.

'Should be in for a few strikes tonight then, ha ha,' joked Marco.

'Ooo, this is fab! We're going to have such fun. I've waxed my balls and everything,' added Stefan.

'Oh no, I hope they're not going to change into their shorts,' he thought, following them inside.

'Okay, we need to pick the teams and it just so happens that I've got an idea,' said Marco. 'If we divide into four, the winners can play each other in the final.'

'Ooo, good idea,' said Stefan. 'Me, Marco and Sazoa on one team and we'll play against Serge, Nikki and Nadesche. Mike, you take Victor and Carmen and play against Danii, Anna, Gina and Xenia.'

'What about me?' asked William.

'Oh yes, forgot about you, big boy. Umm, let's see…'

'Join us William,' said Carmen.

With the teams sorted, he went back outside to fetch the refreshments and proceeded to set it up on a table while the others helped themselves to bowling shoes.

'William, you're up first,' said Mike, sitting at the console.

'Oh, do I have to? Okay then, where are the mallets?'

'Mallets? You bowl them idiot. Haven't you played before?' he asked.

'Yes, of course I have, but I think I'm muddling it up with a variation of croquet that father invented.'

'Just get on with it.'

William picked up the largest bowl he could find and lugged it onto his shoulder.

'Difficult to get under your chin, isn't it?'

'Just bowl it, will you?'

William hurled the ball from chest height like a shot-put and it crashed down, trickling into the gutter on the neighbouring lane.

'None,' said Mike, entering the score.

'I want another go.'

'Okay, but roll it this time. Look…look at the way Serge just did it.'

William took another bowl and examined it.

'This one's no good, it's got holes in it.'

'Yeah, try putting your fingers in them,' he said, raising his eyebrows to Mike.

'Ah, I see… Oh no, damn thumb's stuck now. Help!'

'Stop panicking, you can bowl with your other hand. Come on, you're holding up the game.'

They sat down for drinks at the end of the match, which Danii's team won easily. When the others had finished they came over to join them.

'Ooo, still stuck is it?' asked Stefan. 'I could give it a tug for you.'

'Oh, would you?' said William.

'You weren't putting your fingers in the hole correctly. I could give you some private lessons if you want.'

'Another time perhaps, I'm feeling a bit exhausted. Now then, if you could just hold the ball in the palm of your hand while I get myself positioned properly...yes, that's it. You know, it was actually quite good for balance.'

'Still didn't get anything down though, did you?'

'There's no need to be snide, Stefan, I did my best. Oh look, it's nearly there. Grip it a bit firmer, then give it a quick pull.'

'Pervert!'

'Shut up Ogroid and bugger off! You're always sticking your nose where it's not needed.'

Getting his morning coffee, he was surprised to see William looking so cheerful after the fuss with the bowling ball last night, although he was walking a bit strangely.

'What's the matter William, crapped yourself?'

'Don't be stupid! You're only going to put me in a bad mood if you carry on like that, so you might as well shut up. Now then, let's see who's coming on my punting picnic, shall we? ... Oh no. Oh dear, this can't be right.'

'How many have you got?'

'Four.'

'Who are they?'

'That bloody Stefan, his sidekick Marco, Sazoa and Serge. Give me your pen, Victor.'

'You're not adding my name.'

'No, no, stupid, I'm crossing mine off...there! They can do what they like. We can have a nice quiet day at home without them.'

'I thought you were getting on okay with Stefan?'

'No I was not! Well, I did give him a chance, but he blew it.'

'What, did something happen then?'

'No, of course not.'

'What then?'

'Nothing. Oh, you know after we got home last night and that ball was still stuck on my thumb?'

'Yes,' he replied, beginning to regret asking.

'Well, Stefan took me up to their room so he could pull it off.'

'That sounds dubious,' said Danii, coming into the kitchen.

'I'm talking about the ball, the bowling ball!'

'Whatever,' she replied, taking a couple of cartons of juice from the fridge. 'We're playing tennis, see you later.'

'Yeah, bye Danii...so William, what happened?'

'Well, that's the strange thing, I can't remember. I recall sitting on his bed eating a large bag of curry-flavoured crisps...he came out of the bathroom with a giant pot of Vaseline...hmm, it's all blank from there. The next thing I remember is entering my own room and the bowl had gone.'

'Why are you so annoyed with him then?'

'He just grabbed my arse outside the library, didn't he? Bloody cheek, taking liberties like that...and he'd borrowed *Hypnotism for Beginners* for a week without signing for it. How on earth am I meant to keep track of all the books if nobody signs for them? Gave him short shrift, I can tell you! And as for groping me, I'm not standing for that kind of behaviour, especially when my bottom feels so sore this morning. Hmm, must have been those crisps. So, what are you up to today then?'

'Staying out of Stefan's way for a start. Actually, I think I'll get out and about. Pick up a few more classic cars for my collection.'

'Look Victor, I don't want my grounds looking like a car park.'

'No problem, I've got a secret place for them.'

'Where?'

'If I told you that it wouldn't be secret, would it?'

'Oh, do what you want, Anna's going to help me in the cellar with some cataloguing.'

That evening he lay on his bed looking at the ceiling, feeling bored. A month had passed since that fateful night when the spaceships had arrived. Although he was relieved that Mike's equipment had dealt with the situation, he was left feeling that it had all been a bit of an anticlimax. He just didn't have enough excitement in his life.

'Hmm, I could go up to the lab and see how the PooP machine's progressing.'

He leapt off the bed and was just putting on his shoes when there was a series of knocks on the door. It was the secret code.

'Come in Mike,' he called. 'Hi, I was just on my way to see you.'

'It's ready, it works!'

'Are you sure?'

'Yeah, I can make things disappear! They reappear the moment I cut the power!'

'How do you know they aren't suspended on the other side?'

'Because I sent a mug of *hot* coffee in for two hours, it was stone cold when it came out! I'm going to call it *TransPooP*, what do you think?'

'It's got a certain *ring* to it I suppose. Can I see it in action?'

'Yeah, it's all set up, raring to go.'

Inside the lab, he examined the device sitting on the bench directly in front of them. It was the size of a tea tray and had dozens of conical coils set around the edges.

'What happened to that other machine you were working on, the one I saw last Christmas?'

'I lost it…disappeared and never came back.'

'This new one's a bit small, isn't it?'

'It's just the prototype. I've already designed the full-size kit, I'm going to start building it tomorrow.'

Having witnessed various objects disappear, then reappear, Mike was direct with him.

'When it's ready, I'll need you to volunteer to try it out.'

'Oh, I don't know about that. Send William in.'

'He'll never agree, will he? Too much of a coward.'

'Do you think it's safe?'

'We could send the cat in first if you're worried.'

'Or we could get William drunk. He won't know what's going on.'

Before going to bed, he paced up and down his room considering *TransPooP*. He couldn't believe he'd agreed to play guinea pig. The idea of using William still appealed, but Mike had emphasised the need for a sober account of what was on the other side. As he tried to reassure himself that it would be okay, he was distracted by another knock on the door.

'Who is it?'

'Me.'

'Oh William, come in.'

'Right Victor, I want to go on a little trip.'

'Have a nice time.'

'No moron, you and me. It's the trip I was planning before all that nonsense with those spaceships.'

'Oh yeah. Where was it you wanted to go?'

'Berlin and Monte Carlo. Hans and Helga will be our first port of call though. I've told the girls that's where we're going.'

'Do I need to ask what for?'

'Some very special wine. Two separate collections consisting of more than two hundred bottles of pure gold.'

'When are we going then?'

'As soon as you've serviced the plane.'

Chapter 3

'Hmm, nice clear day…perfect for flying,' said William, pulling up next to the plane.

'What's that?'

'What?'

'That mess on the side, just below the cockpit. It wasn't there yesterday when I finished servicing the engines.'

'I did it after you'd gone. It's a picture of Danii. Naked I know, but quite artistic, don't you think?'

'Did she pose for you?'

'Of course not, I just used my imagination.'

'What's that bit dangling down?'

'The paint ran.'

'It looks more like Sazoa.'

'Look Ogroid, I hope you're not going to go on about that, because if you are it's only going to make me irritable. How was I to know? Anybody could have made the same mistake.'

'Has Danii seen it?'

'Don't be stupid! When would she have seen Sazoa naked?'

'No, has she seen the painting?'

'Of course not, so no blabbing.'

He spent a good hour pumping fuel, keeping a watchful eye on William who was becoming increasingly agitated.

'I've finished.'

'Good.'

'What's up, having second thoughts about flying this thing?'

'No. It's just that we're going to be sitting ducks for those spaceships.'

'They've gone William, how many times do I have to tell you?'

'Okay, but I think we'll fly especially low today. Better safe than sorry.'

The engines of the old Dakota spluttered into life and they bumped their way to the end of the runway. Just for a change they decided to head south, then follow the M4 to London. Flying over Heathrow, he spotted several airliners crashed and burnt out on the runway. There were more in the fields surrounding the airport. He then remembered William's fancy dress costume.

'You haven't been trying to fly jets, have you?'

'No, it's wreckage from when this thing first happened, just like all the cars and lorries. I even saw crashed trains when I went up north searching for paperwork. Hmm, you've given me an idea though. I want you to find me a flight simulator. One of the really big ones on hydraulic legs. I could practice whenever I wanted then. Yes, I firmly believe that jets could be the way forward.'

'I don't.'

'What was that?'

'What?'

'A rattling noise. There it was again! It's coming from the port engine. Go and take a look.'

'No way!'

'I'm telling you there's something wrong with that engine! You must have forgotten to tighten some nuts during the service. It'll drop off and we'll be killed.'

'It's on the wing, you idiot! You'd have to be mad, or desperate to go out there, and I'm neither.'

'You're wearing your parachute, aren't you? If you fall off, I'll land and pick you up.'

'Parachute?'

'Yes, I never fly without one. Look, nice and compact, fits on this special belt.'

'Why didn't you get me one?'

'Why should I have to do everything for you all the time? Oh listen, it seems to have stopped now. Count yourself lucky. Hmm, I'm starving, what have we got to eat?'

'Nothing.'

'What's in that sandwich box down by your feet then?'

'That's the medical kit… Look, plasters, antiseptic cream…oh, and a pack of sixteen aspirins.'

'Right, that's eight each, unless you don't want yours.'

'You're not having mine, I'll probably get a headache later. Anyway, you can't eat pills to stave off hunger.'

'Yes I can! I've done it before many times, so did father. Now give me that tube of antiseptic cream, it'll help them slip down.'

Landing at Hamburg they took a hire car from one of the parking lots and followed the signs for the town of Grossensee. After driving for nearly ten kilometres, he unzipped the breast pocket of his new flying jacket and handed over the scrap of paper with Hans and Helga's address.

'We should be nearly there now,' he said.

'Yes, looks like straight ahead at the crossroads. This little map he's drawn is actually quite helpful. Keep following the road around the edge of the lake…yes, this looks good.'

'Nice out here, isn't it?'

'Not as nice as Poffington. Okay, take a left in about a kilometre. Hans should live in the second house on the right.'

'I hope they're still there, they could have moved by now.'

Slowing up by a large detached house, they turned into the driveway and stopped in front of a rickety looking garage. The place was in silence. He walked over to the front door and pressed the bell. It didn't ring. Returning to the garage, he peered through the glass, shielding his eyes to get a better look.

'The camper van's here. At least we know they made it home.'

'Hans! Helga! Are you there?' shouted William. 'Hello, anyone home?'

'Let's try around the back.'

'There's nobody about, we might as well go.'

'Hey look, it's our old breakdown truck. They must still be here. **Hello! Hans, are you there?**'

'Hallo,' called a voice from an upstairs window.

'You're not Hans. Where is he? What have you done with him?' asked William accusingly.

The window closed and the stranger disappeared from view. They waited expectantly, unsure of what was going to happen next. Then the back door opened and the chap came out to meet them. A pretty girl stood warily in the doorway, watching intently.

'So, you are ze Engländer zat Hans is speaking of, ja?'

'Yes, we are the Engländer,' he said, holding out his hand.

'But you know, zat goal in ze Vorld Cup in 1966, it vos never crossing ze line! You are cheating!'

'Even so, we did score another, so it wouldn't have altered the outcome anyway.'

'Nein, nein, zare vos peoples on ze pitch! Ze referee must be stopping ze game. Vee are vinning zat Vorld Cup!'

He couldn't believe he was in an argument about something that had happened half a century before he was even born. Nevertheless, he couldn't let it go.

'Nonsense, look…'

'I am finding zat cup und I am grinding off England's name und putting on Germany's instead.'

'You'll have a long journey then, it's in Brazil.'

Just then a familiar voice called from the direction of the garden. It was Hans.

'Herr Victor, Herr Villiam! I am vondering ven you vill come to see us. I see you are already meeting Jürgen. Zat is his girlfriend Hilka standing in ze doorvay. Vee have found zem on ze vay home from Calais. Vee also have a chicken und it is laying eggs. Vee are keeping it in ze garden vis ze donkey.'

'You've got a donkey?'

'It is belonging to Jürgen. Oh ja, vee have also two mice und one snail.'

'Good job Serge didn't come with us then,' said William.

'Come, you can see him ven you are vanting.'

Grazing in the garden was a sad looking donkey with large floppy ears. They walked over to a neat stack of flowerpots and Hans pointed to one lying on its side. He peered in and saw the snail hanging upside down.

'Vee are feeding it und it is not running avay.'

'And the mice?'

'Ah, zey are in ze rafters. Vee are seeing zem only occasionally.'

'How do you know there are two?'

'Because one is black und one is vite. Come inside, Helga vill be so pleased to see you.'

They followed Hans into a rustic kitchen where Helga was putting on her apron.

'Herr Villiam, Herr Victor! Velcome to our home. Please be sitting. I vill make tea und somesing to eat.'

'How are you?' asked William.

'Zings vos a little difficult in ze beginnings, but vee are getting on vell now zank you. You are meeting Jürgen und Hilka?'

'Ja, zey are already meeting Jürgen,' said Hans. 'So, ziss is Hilka.'

'Pleased to meet you,' he said, stepping forward to shake her hand. 'And I'm William.'

'Don't push, you nearly knocked me over!'

'Get out of my way then Victor, you're blocking me!'

'Push me again and there'll be trouble!'

The girl just smiled and turned away.

'Hilka is not speaking English,' explained Hans.

'So, the donkey's yours then, Jürgen?' he asked.

'Ja, vee see it ven vee are valking to find ze peoples. Hilka und I are not driving, vee are cities peoples. Ze donkey is gut for carrying our zings.'

'Will you be riding it to Brazil?'

'Vot?'

'Vee are finding Jürgen und Hilka in Hamburg,' Hans interrupted. 'Zen vee are talking und drinking, zen vee are inviting zem to stay vis us for ze night. Now zey are living here.'

'How nice.'

'Oh ja, Herr Victor. I am not vanting you to zink zat I am stealing your vatch ze last time vee are meeting,' said Hans, going over to a cupboard. 'So, I have for you ziss tray of vatches. I am also making you ziss clock.'

He was overwhelmed. The tray was full of exquisite antique watches. The clock however, was made of wood and when he opened the door on the back, he could see that all the cogs and workings were wooden too.

'It does not keep such gut time, but it is vorking.'

'How does the spring operate?'

'Zare is a zick piece of green villow connected to ziss ratchet. Ze pressure on ziss lever is keeping it ticking, ja? You must vater ze villow two times each day or it is stopping because it is no longer springy. Oh ja, I am forgetting somesing...'

Hans went over to the cupboard again, rummaged around and returned with a piece of wood the size of a baseball bat, which had a square hole cut in one end.

'Ziss is ze key.'

'It's a bit big, isn't it?'

'It must be so because ze villow is difficult to stress. I vill show you.'

Hans placed the clock on the floor, trapped it under his foot, put the key into position and began leaning on it. A strained creaking noise came from within the casing. Undeterred, Hans continued pressing until the ratchet snapped into place.

'It's ticking! Well, clonking.'

'Ja, it is a little noisy, but it is ze first I have made you understand. I vill make ze ones in ze future more quiet, you vill see.'

Hans set it down on the table and they watched as it jiggled its way across the surface. The creaking noise was getting more prominent, rather like a ceiling beam just before it collapses. The sound was so terrible he began backing away. Then it stopped.

'Now vee must vind again. I am not so strong you understand, but you are bigger, so you can stress it more, zen it is going for longer. Oh ja, zare is also a cuckoo coming from zese doors. I make it in memory of my Grossvater.'

'Oh, was he Swiss?'

'Nein, he vos cuckoo. Ja, it is not vorking so vell at ze moment. Perhaps ven it is going for a day or so, it vill appear.'

'Er, that's great Hans, thanks. I'll put it in the car.'

He came back into the kitchen to hear Helga in the middle of a story as she poured the tea.

'Ja, und I have been vorking vis ze vicker for some time now.'

'You've met a vicar?' he asked.

'Nein, nein. Vicker. Basket veaving. Ziss tea cosy is made from vicker. Come, I vill show you all ze zings I am making. Vee can see ze house at ze same time. Vee are killing two birds vis one stone, ja?'

They shuffled behind Hans and Helga up the creaky staircase and entered a bedroom.

'Und zese are sleeping socks.'

'Wicker socks?'

'You like? I am making for you ven you are vanting.'

'Ja, zey are very comfortable,' said Hans. 'A little noisy ven you are getting up in ze night maybe, but very comfortable.'

After the tour of the bedrooms, he stuck his head around the bathroom door. He didn't like the look of the wicker toilet seat at all.

In the evening they had a tasty vegetable stew and he mopped up the juices with Helga's excellent home-made bread. He liked it because of the strong smell of yeast and it was quite different from any other he'd had.

'Superb, thanks Helga.'

'More vine Herr Victor?'

'Yes please,' said William, thrusting out his glass. 'Well Hans, that was a nice present you gave Victor earlier.'

'Oh ja, Herr Villiam, I am forgetting,' said Hans, reaching for a bottle on a nearby shelf. 'I have for you ziss vine. It is old, but gut I zink. I am replacing for ze bottle I am drinking before, ja?'

'Look Victor, 1989 Glühwein. That makes it *Mauer* vintage, excellent!'

'And it's in a nice wicker bottle holder.'

'It is gut for ze vinter, ja?'

'We had a bad winter last year, how was yours?' he asked.

'Vee have snow, very high. It is lucky zat vee have gut supplies of food und fuel. Vee vos unable to go out for some veeks.'

'It was the same for us. We had drifts covering the upstairs windows.'

'Ja, it vos terrible. Vee have flooding aftervards. Vee make preparations for ziss year already.'

'Vell, I zink it is almost sleeping time,' said Helga. 'Herr Villiam, you can take ze sofa und Herr Victor, ze room next to Jürgen und Hilka.'

The moment he sat down to pull off his shoes, he knew it was going to be a problem. The bed was made of wicker and creaked remorselessly with every movement. There was no room to lie on the floor, so he just tried to keep as still as he could.

An hour later he was still awake, wishing he had been offered the comfy sofa. In between the fidgeting and the less frequent moments of silence, he could hear William snoring away without a care in the world. Then began the noisy rhythmical creaking from next door. Jürgen and Hilka obviously had a wicker bed too and he realised it was just the beginning of a very long night.

In the morning, he struggled to keep his eyes open as they stood beside the car ready to leave.

'Vee are seeing you again soon, ja?'

'Yes, I suppose we could drop in from time to time,' he said.

'Oh ja, vee have one more present for you,' said Helga, handing him an egg box. 'Zare is only two, but vee like you to have zem.'

'Excellent,' said William, snatching it away. 'It's ages since I've had an egg.'

'Vell, enjoy! Auf Wiedersehen!'

William tucked the box under the passenger seat, then leaned across to blow the horn as they went down the drive.

'Careful Victor, you nearly crashed into that tree.'

'Get off the steering wheel then…and stop pressing the horn!'

'Steer straight. I don't want to have to eat scrambled eggs when I could have nice fried ones.'

'Look, it's one egg each. You're not having them both.'

'I know, but it's made the trip really worthwhile, don't you think?'

'Yeah,' he replied, letting out a huge yawn. 'Oh God, I hardly got a wink of sleep last night. My bed was made of wicker, Jürgen's too.'

'You didn't go in there, did you? Pervert!'

Back at the airport, the cool breeze revived him as he prepared for the next leg of their journey.

'Come on Victor, put some effort into it. We'll be here all day.'

'It's hard work. I've already pumped three hundred and fifty-seven litres. Why don't you take a turn?'

'I'd pump that handle twice as fast as you if it wasn't for my back. Just get on with it and stop complaining.'

Soon they were flying east towards Berlin. The view from the cockpit didn't change as the undeviating motorway cut through the thick pine forests and large flat fields of the countryside. Eventually, the great metropolis appeared on the horizon. William rummaged around in a bag, produced a street map and opened it across his knees.

'Hmm, now which airport shall we use, there are so many to choose from? *Ip dip…*'

'For fuck's sake William, just land!'

'Hold on then, we're going in.'

He stood on the runway looking for suitable transport. Unfortunately the only vehicle in sight was a luggage train. It had six cages attached to the tractor unit, two of which were full of bags. He crouched down and examined the linkage to see how they unhooked.

'No, no, Victor, leave them in place, they'll be perfect for transporting my wine.'

'What about these suitcases?'

'What about them?'

'We don't want to take them along as well, do we?'

'It really doesn't make any difference. Now stop fussing and let's get going.'

They set off across the tarmac at a steady ten miles an hour.

'Can't this thing go any faster? Put your foot down.'

'It's reached top speed already. Look at your map and tell me which direction to take.'

'Now then, it's called the Grünewald. Hmm, looks quite nice, a lake surrounded by forest. Turn right out of the airport and follow the motorway south.'

The house was very impressive and had a large brass plaque fixed to the wall by the entrance, bearing the name *Herr Brocklebunce*. He opened the decorative iron gates and drove up the tree-lined driveway. Looking for a way inside, he decided to climb through a small side window. It turned out to be a downstairs toilet, so he had a pee and then went to open the front door.

'What kept you?' said William, looking impatient. 'Come on then, let's see what he's hiding. We shouldn't find any rubbish here.'

He followed William down into the cellar and shone his flashlight around the racking. It was surprisingly small, but immaculately laid out.

'Oh my God, I don't believe it!' William exclaimed, plucking bottle after bottle. 'I'm taking the lot. I can't bear to leave any of this behind. Get cracking, we're cleaning this place out.'

It took him two hours to load everything into the cages. Exhausted, he flopped onto the tractor seat to catch his breath.

'Excellent!' said William. 'All we've got to do now is get down to the Med avoiding the Alps. It'll be safer if we take the long route, I don't fancy flying between mountains, do you?'

'Not really, no.'

'It's too late to start the journey this afternoon.'

'Yeah, it'll take ages just to get back to the plane.'

'Right then, we might as well stay the night here. We can have a snoop around these other posh houses.'

After searching the neighbouring property, he found himself a nice old clockwork toy collection under one of the beds. There were weird looking cars and trains, and even some ridiculous chunky robots that could only march stiffly in a forward direction.

'Are you going to play with those bloody things all night?' said William, pulling his head out from under his sleeping bag.

'You're jealous because I found them first.'

'Oh, just put them away.'

'I'm only seeing what each one does,' he said, unwrapping another piece from the disintegrating brown newspaper.

'All these whirring noises are giving me a headache.'

'I've still got my pills. They're yours for two gold coins.'

'How did you know I'd got gold coins? Have you been snooping?'

'Yes, I looked in that pouch when you went to the toilet. Now do you want to buy my pills, or not?'

He awoke with the chilly dawn, made a cup of tea on the camping stove and woke William by jabbing his foot with a knitting needle he'd found on the arm of the sofa.

'**Ouch, ouch! Idiot!** I'll be limping all day now. In fact, my foot is so bad that I can't be responsible for looking after those eggs in case I fall and smash them. I'm going to have to risk making you *Egg Monitor* when we land in Monte Carlo.'

'Oh, just shut up and get dressed. I'm ready to leave.'

Without saying much, they made the slow journey to the airport. Following the roadmap, they flew south-west for Nürnberg, on to Stuttgart and then west to Strasbourg. The flight was quite pleasant and he was absorbed with all the new scenery. Shortly after landing in Monaco, they drove past the picturesque marinas and gazed at the mass of luxurious yachts.

Eventually, high up on the hillside overlooking the sea, they found the spectacular villa that belonged to François Malinguerer. After carrying out an extensive search of the premises, it became apparent that the wine wasn't there. William tore into all the paperwork he could find.

'Yes, a result! Here's a letter from *Banque de Rothsquerque* in Geneva. Something about a cooled safety deposit box he's hired. My French is good enough to know that's where it'll be, in the vault. Oh, how careless, he's written the box number on the bottom, two…one…nine. So, it's off to Geneva then.'

'Geneva? But it's surrounded by mountains! You said yourself you didn't fancy flying through the mountains. We could crash and be stranded. We'd end up having to eat each other.'

'No, no, it'll be okay. In the morning we'll retrace our steps to Lyon and follow the Rhône valley all the way. There, what about that for a plan? I was always good at geography, knew it would pay off one day. Right, cook those eggs up then, Victor.'

'I can't, I left them in the plane.'

'Brilliant, you've fouled up. I should never have put you in charge. They'll be bad before I get to eat them.'

'It.'

'What?'

'It. One egg each, remember?'

The sound of William snorting woke him a little before six. After a mug of coffee they set off for the airport. His arms and back were aching with all the manual refuelling, but he reasoned that it was at least keeping him fit. Soon they were in the air heading for Lyon, where they banked right for Geneva. Flying up the valley, the plane continually rolled from side to side as William tightly copied the course of the river.

'For God's sake, can't you just cut across the corners? I'm feeling really queasy with all this meandering.'

'We'll get lost if I do that. It's far better to keep the river in sight.

There's something wrong with this plane, I'm telling you. I've been pulling back on this stick for hours just to keep us at a stable height. My arms hurt. Still, I'm glad to see that you managed to get the dashboard clock working.'

'That's the altimeter, idiot! We're climbing!'

'I know, I know! It's just that this stick feels as if it's been over-tightened...and why in God's name do you keep sniffing your fingers like that? Pervert!'

'It's pine resin off those logs I used for the fire last night...here, smell.'

'Get your fingers out of my face! Look, nasty smudge marks all over my goggles now. It'll be your fault if we crash.'

As the expanse of Lake Leman stretched out before them, William prepared for landing. Luckily the airport had a variety of vehicles close at hand and they set off for the city centre in a shuttle bus. There was a tourist information office in one of the squares, so he popped in and took a street map in order to locate the bank more easily.

The entrance was heavily shuttered and the solid old building looked impenetrable. He scrutinised the ornate façade, wondering how to get in. The evenly spaced arched windows were well out of reach. He hurled a brick up at one, but it just bounced off.

'What hope do we have if you can't even break a pane of glass? Sometimes Victor, you're useless, you really are.'

'Okay, let's look for a plant hire.'

They found a vehicle with a hydraulic arm and helped themselves to a multitude of other equipment. He aligned the cradle against one of the windows, drew it back a little, and then rammed it into the glass.

'Useless, utterly useless,' said William, grabbing the remote control.

'No, hands off!' he said, snatching it back. 'I'll try hitting it full pelt.'

He swung the arm around as far as it would go, then let it fly. There was a terrible *clang* as the cradle snapped off and fell to the ground.

'Brilliant, just brilliant.'

'Okay then, I've got another idea. I'll ram it head on.'

He swivelled the arm so that it was positioned over the cab roof, reversed out into the road and centred himself on his selected window. With the jousting pole at the right height, he lurched forwards with wheels spinning and bounced up the kerb. The end smashed through the glass, but he braked too late and careered through the wall amidst a cloud of dust and flying bricks.

Inside, they stood behind the service partition looking around at their options. A sledgehammer proved useful on each door, until they found the one that led to the vault. At the bottom of the steps some heavy-duty iron gates blocked their path.

'Get the cutting gear Victor, you'll never hacksaw through those.'

'Sure, no problem. We'll soon be in.'

With the gates dismantled, he wiped his brow and stood in front of the vault door, assessing its size. It was some three metres in diameter and had hinges the size of mooring posts.

'You'll have to blow it,' said William casually.

'Blow it? You could use two tons of dynamite on that and it would still be standing. Nothing else would though.'

'How are we going to get in then?'

'How should I know? I'm Victor Ogroid, mechanic, not a hardened bank robber.'

'You must have some idea.'

'We could fetch a mini digger and jack-hammer, try and get through the wall to the side.'

'Oh, this is unbearable. My wine is sitting only a few metres away and I can't lay my hands on it. You'll have a nice reward if you can get in for me, a nice reward indeed!'

'Hang on. It doesn't have any external means of opening, does it? No combination dial or keyholes.'

'So?'

'Well, that must mean it's got an internal electronic opening device, set to open at specific times. If we rig up a generator, we can wait until morning and see if it opens by itself. We can spend the night here, lay our sleeping bags on the floor.'

'Okay, let's go and find one then before the light goes.'

The second the power came on, the alarms went off. It was deafening. Their first instinct had been to run and they'd already made it out onto the pavement before they remembered there was no one around to catch them. It took him a good fifteen minutes to smash down all the bells and sirens while William helpfully supervised.

After a very uncomfortable night, they sat glumly staring at the vault. Already two possible automatic opening times had passed, but the door remained locked. He was hoping for third time lucky and listened expectantly for a *clunk*.

'Three, two, one and...'

'Fuckety fuck, it hasn't worked,' complained William. 'Now what are we going to do?'

'Umm, I've just had a thought. What day is it?'

'Saturday. Bugger, we're going to have to wait until Monday.'

'No, there must be a control panel somewhere. Let's try the manager's office.'

'Okay, but get a pan first and fry those eggs, I'm really hungry. I can't believe we forgot to have them last night. Must have been all that panic with the alarms. Still, glad about it now though. Right, I'm nipping off for a pee, we can crack on after we've eaten.'

He pulled the frying pan from his overnight bag and set it on top of the camping stove. It was dry and he knew the eggs would stick badly without any oil. There was nothing else to hand, so he rubbed his finger down both sides of his nose and smeared the grease over the bottom. By the time William returned, the eggs were cooking nicely and when he served them, they slipped straight out.

'Mmm, delicious,' said William, licking the yolk off a mouse mat. 'Yummy. Mmm, did Helga give us some butter as well?'

'No, why?'

'They just seemed quite buttery, that's all. Why couldn't I have had the ashtray? Some of my yolk has run off the edge of this mat onto my trousers.'

They found the control panel just inside the manager's door; it was flashing a message.

Error. Power failure. Enter new access code.

'Result!'

'But we don't know the code,' moaned William.

'It says enter the new code, moron. I'll make one up. Umm, one, one, one, one, one, one... Right, now what?'

Enter date, time and opening parameters.

'Right Victor, it's Saturday the twenty-fourth of September 2050, nine twenty-five exactly.'

'My watch says nine twenty-three.'

'Well it's wrong. It would be more accurate to use that clock Hans gave you. Set it to open at nine thirty.'

'Just shut up. I'm setting it for ten o'clock.'

They waited with baited breath as the minutes ticked towards the hour.

'Three, two, one and... Bah, you're useless Victor. You've botched it.'

'No, you'll see,' he said, staring confidently at his own watch.

'I'll just have to face it, my life's ruined. I'll never have a good wine collection now. You'll suffer for this, Ogroid.'

'Be quiet. Three, two, one and...'

Right on the dot there was a heavy *clunk* followed by some whirring noises and the door slowly swung open.

'Bloody hell!' said William, sounding genuinely surprised. 'Come on then, get busy.'

They walked into the main thoroughfare of the vault.

'Victor, look at all this money!'

He sniffed a pile of crisp banknotes, but quickly became distracted by a stack of glittering gold bars.

'I want a crate of that!'

'No, we're meant to be looking for my wine, let's get on with it.'

49

'I don't care about your wine. This gold is beautiful, I'm having some.'

He stacked ten crates onto a trolley and started wheeling it out.

'You'd better get ten for me as well. I suppose it is quite nice after all.'

He craftily loaded an extra crate to keep himself ahead and went out to the shuttle bus. When he returned, he found William fidgeting in front of the safety deposit boxes at the far end of the vault.

'So William, how on earth is an entire wine collection going to be in that tiny box? It'll hold three bottles at the most.'

'He'll have spread them around. You don't keep all your eggs in one basket, do you? We'll probably find the keys to the other boxes inside this one. Prise the door off then.'

He was having trouble because it was so tightly fitted. The gap wasn't wide enough to insert anything that would gain sufficient leverage. He resorted to using the jack-hammer, but became frustrated when it wouldn't make any impression.

'You should have looked for the key at the house. I've been struggling with this for nearly an hour. William? ... William? ... Typical. Yeah, you have a nice sleep while I bust my guts.'

The sound of the pickaxe echoed through the vault as he swung it full force at the tiny door.

'Stop that you idiot! Stop it! You'll break them!'

'Ah, so you're awake then? Sorry, there's no other way. Now keep back.'

Within seconds the door fell to the floor. There was nothing inside except a scrap of paper, which William snatched up.

'Oh look, it's written out in three languages... *To whom it may concern. If you're reading this note then I'm glad to say you won't find my wine here, so hard luck.* Signed François Malinguerer. Damn him! I'll never get it now. Might as well hang myself.'

'Well, that's that then. I'm off home.'

'No, we've got to go back to Monte Carlo. It must still be hidden in the house.'

'Okay, *you* go back, I'll find a van and take my half of the gold.'

'How will you get across the Channel, clever dick?'

'I'll take a boat.'

'You'll sink and drown.'

'Look, I've probably sailed more boats than you. Don't forget I worked in a boatyard.'

'Selfish, that's what you are, utterly selfish! You'll pay for this Ogroid, preventing me from getting my wine.'

'What are you moaning about, you're still going home with plenty, aren't you?'

'Suppose so. Anyway, the girls will finally realise that you've lost your mind when they see you take all that gold into the house.'

'You've got just as much as me! Besides, I'm not taking it into the house.'

'Where are you going to put it then?'

'In the workshop attic.'

'Hmm, good idea. You might as well put mine up there too.'

He was looking forward to sleeping in his own bed that night and felt relieved to be in the air on the final flight back to Oxfordshire. Once they were following the motorway to Paris, he was able to relax and quickly dozed off. When he woke, he stared vacantly at William.

'What are you looking at?'

'Not much.'

He focussed on the top of William's head, trying to unnerve him. He wondered how many minutes it would be before he got a reaction.

'For God's sake, why do you keep looking at my hair?'

'I'm not, I'm looking at your bald patch.'

'I haven't got a bald patch!'

'It's all shiny. I've seen more hair stuck on a toilet brush.'

'Well, yours looks like a pubic mound!'

The rest of the journey went smoothly and they landed without mishap. Once home, he stashed away the crates of gold and joined Mike in the observatory. He was just recounting the trip's main highlights when William came thumping up the stairs, looking pleased with himself.

'Well, it's all been laid down in the lower cellar. Anna's been helping me. That passageway is filling up nicely...down one side anyway. It would have been better if you'd let me get Malinguerer's stuff though.'

'I hope you're not going to go on about that.'

'But it's so frustrating. I could almost smell it. It's there somewhere. We'll have to go back and look for it.'

'Will you?'

'*TransPooP* is coming on in leaps and bounds,' announced Mike.

'*TransPooP*?' scoffed William. 'What's that, a doggie litter bin emptying service?'

'It's short for *Transportation to Places of other Parallels.*'

'Well, it's crap and I don't want anything to do with it.'

'Nobody invited you, did they?'

'What a waste of time. You're as bad as Victor with his gold.'

'Oh, have you got some gold?'

'Er, yeah, only a few crates though. Thought it could come in useful one day. What's more, it just looks and feels so nice...really silky.'

'Pervert!' accused William.

'You've got ten crates as well!'

'I only got it to use as doorjambs. Nice, shiny, decorative doorjambs.'

'Yeah, right.'

He slept most of Sunday morning and woke feeling energetic. The weather was crisp and sunny, so after a shower he put the dogs into the van and drove to Woodswell Park for a long walk. By the evening he'd caught up with everyone's news and was starting to feel restless. Mike had disappeared into the lab and he ended up alone in his room, aimlessly fiddling about. As he lay on his bed, he couldn't stop thinking about the gold bars. He liked the idea of building a collection and considered where his next stash could come from.

'I know, I'll rip off my old bank!' he shouted, sitting up. 'Teach those arseholes a lesson. Yeah, *Recteller Bank* is getting done over again…this time by the front door.'

Within minutes he'd got the whole thing worked out.

'I'll do the job alone and make my getaway in that old Jag I got from the film studio. I'll do it tomorrow night, when everyone's asleep. Right, in the morning I'll drive to the RAF base and pick up my motor…hide it in the barn next to the workshop. Hmm, must make sure it's got fuel…put the dynamite in the boot…pack a crowbar, cutting equipment…'

The next day went without a hitch and he waited patiently until two in the morning before making his move. He threw the rope ladder out of the window and climbed down onto the gravel below, confident that nobody had heard him. After a flash of inspiration, he stopped off at the washing line and removed a pair of tights. He got an extra kick imagining that they were Danii's. He then sprinted across the ornamental garden to the east wing and hid on the corner. Noting that the house was still in darkness, he trotted down the steps onto the lawn and made a dash for the barn. He was relieved when the Jag started first time and then drove slowly to the main gates, only turning on the headlights once he was on the open road.

Parking in a side street, he took his robber's kit and walked towards the bank. The doors blew off easily and he stepped through the swirling dust into the lobby. He flashed his torch across the staff photographs hanging on the wall. Their stupid faces stared back at him. They had always been obnoxious and he loathed them.

'*Ruud van der Seagull*, Wank Manager. *Sandra McDuck*, bitch. *Wendy Dells*, bitch. *Fiona Pickbottom*, bitch. *Ellen Crokeswattle*, fucking ugly and a bitch. Oh look, even the cleaner, *Paula Jones*. Looks like a man in drag. What a bunch of twazzers!'

He took the mallet from his kit bag and smashed them to pieces. On the way home, he felt more satisfied with what he'd done to their photos than he did with the small stash of gold coins he'd taken from the vault.

He decided to move his gold from the workshop while he still had the cover of darkness. Taking the wheelbarrow from the stable block, he got to work. After several trips, he had all the crates piled beneath his bedroom window. Tying them to his belt with separate lengths of rope, he climbed back into his room and hauled them up, one at a time. He prised one of the lids off and marvelled at the smooth gold bars. They were beautiful. He considered where to hide it all and eventually locked everything in a disused cupboard in his bathroom.

Chapter 4

'Did anyone hear that boom last night?' asked William, spooning a heap of marmalade onto his toast. 'Sounded like an explosion.'

'I didn't hear anything. You probably dreamt it,' he said dismissively.

'Actually, I thought I heard something too,' said Danii. 'About three in the morning?'

'Perhaps it was thunder.'

'Or maybe we had the same dream Danii?' said William, flashing her a smile. 'When people are really close they tend to have the same dreams.'

'Hmm…no,' she said. 'It probably was just thunder.'

'I've got some shocking news,' said Marco. 'Somebody's stolen my tights from the washing line! Put them out last night, now they've gone.'

'Could have blown off,' he suggested.

'Why do you think I rinsed them in the first place love?'

With freshly washed hair, he unlocked the bathroom cupboard and checked on his gold reserves.

'Hmm, I haven't got nearly enough…and the banks around here will never be holding any serious quantities. I'll have to go to London.'

The image of those tights wouldn't go away, so he washed his hair a couple more times and then went downstairs to look for Mike. William was hobbling across the hallway clutching his leg.

'What's up with you?'

'I've gouged my fucking knee. Some idiot left a wheelbarrow sticking out of the hedge by the walled garden.'

'Are those the same trousers you wore on the Monte Carlo trip?'

'Yes, why?'

'You haven't sponged that egg off yet.'

'Oh no, so I haven't,' said William, picking at the yellow streak with his nail. 'Mmm, shame to waste it.'

'Don't eat it…urrgghh, you're disgusting! Have you seen Mike?'

'Carmen said he went to work early…probably wasting his time on that stupid poo machine.'

He took the lift directly to the lab and rattled the padlock to get Mike's attention.

'Ah Victor, you've come just at the right moment, *TransPooP* is ready!'

'What about freezing the stratosphere, have you done that yet?'

'No, that can wait. This is much more interesting.'

It didn't look at all like he'd expected. It consisted of a short platform with high sides that curved inwards. An old leather armchair had been fixed in the middle.

'Right, this is the *SDD* box, next to the seat. You just put this special foil suit on and connect yourself to the box with this jack plug. The suit will then conduct the *SDD's* energy and keep you from being suspended. It's essential you stay in the unit. If that jack plug comes out, you won't be protected, so beware. I've also fitted some oxygen tanks behind the seat because there probably won't be any air on the other side. There should be enough for three hours.'

'Are you sure this is going to work? What if something goes wrong?'

'Stop worrying, you'll be a pioneer.'

'As long as I don't end up like Sir Vivian Cleaver.'

'Oh yeah, I remember him…sunk to new depths in his home-made submersible. Wasn't it just two metal spheres welded together?'

'That's right. He had to be rescued from the Tonga Trench by a remote controlled sling. When he finally surfaced the press dubbed his craft *The Cleavage*.'

'Anyway, nothing can go wrong. I've been extremely thorough with the testing. Don't tell anyone, but I sent the cat in. It seemed to quite like it.'

'The cat? When?'

'Yesterday. It worked *purrfectly*.'

'You know that Nikki was searching everywhere for her?'

'Yep.'

'How could you tell it liked it?'

'I just told you, I heard it purring. I've installed this two-way radio inside the helmet.'

'Oh, that's good. Look, why don't we send in a video camera instead?'

'Tried that, the signal gets corrupted and nothing records, it's just a fuzz.'

'So, you'll be able to get me out at a moment's notice?'

'Yeah, it's going to be okay.'

He put the suit on and climbed in. Mike fitted the brass goldfish bowl helmet over his head and opened the oxygen valve.

'Is this the helmet from that diving suit Serge gave you for Christmas?'

'Yeah, it's come in useful after all.'

'It smells of cat.'

'Sorry about that, it was the only way I could think of restraining it with an air supply. Now then, whatever you do, don't get out…and keep your seat belt done up. Don't fret, you'll come back the instant I cut the power.'

'How long are you sending me in for?'

'Ten minutes. If you want to come out before that, just say.'

He took a big gulp as the machine started. His fingers dug into the arms of the chair and he now wished he hadn't volunteered. Everything began to go fuzzy and in a green flash he entered a kind of dream world. The light was hazy and soft. A green-tinted mist hovered all around, seeming to fluctuate and fluoresce in an ever-changing state.

'Wow, it's bucking frilliant!'

'What? What can you see?' came Mike's voice through the headset.

'Everything! Looks like everyone's in here! Animals too, firds and bish…oh, and the spaceships!'

'Can't quite make out what you're saying. Firds and bish?' questioned Mike.

'Yes! It's like being on the surface of another planet. My watch seems to be ticking more slowly. Everything's mifting in drow slotion. The light's all weird and there's a maint fist everywhere.'

'A maint fist?'

'It's difficult to move. I'm making slow progress by paddling my arms.'

'Good job nobody can see you. It must look really naff.'

'Ooo, a naked woman! She's got her back to me…brunette…quite slim…trying to get around the front…nearly there, yes…oh no!'

'What? What is it Victor?'

'Mary huff. Horrid, old and wrinkly. I think I'd like to come out now.'

In an instant, he'd returned to the lab. It was like magic.

'That was brilliant! Show me how to work the controls and go in yourself.'

'You seemed to be talking gibberish.'

'What do you mean?'

'First you said *bucking frilliant* and then things like *maint fist*.'

'Maint fist…faint mist. Bucking frilliant…hey, the effects of crossing parallels must distort speech into spoonerisms.'

'Who's Mary Huff though?'

'No idea, never heard of her.'

'Oh well, it doesn't seem to have done you any harm. Get the suit off, I'll give it a go.'

He received a thorough briefing about the controls and then helped Mike get ready. He felt more confident now he was pressing the buttons and watched in amazement as Mike disappeared.

'Wow, it's mucking farvellous!'

'Who? Have you seen somebody you know?'

'No… Wait, there's a poup of greople drifting towards me.'

'Shall I get you out?'

'No, not yet… I don't recognise any of them… Unbelievable! Now there's a shock of fleep…oh no, wait, they've disappeared into the mist.'

'Hang on, I'm bringing you out.'

Suddenly, Mike was back in the lab.

'I can't believe it actually works! It's brilliant! Right, send me in again.

This time though, I'll touch something, see what happens.'

Mike disappeared in another green flash.

'How's it going?'

'Good. I've got some old bid in front of me... I'm reaching out for her. She's solid. Ooo wait, there's a shimmering green light flowing over her...she's starting to move! I don't like it, get me out!'

Mike reappeared and hurriedly twisted off the helmet, gasping for air.

'That was freaky, her moving like that.'

'Hey, perhaps she was acting out whatever she was doing the moment she disappeared.'

'That would make sense. It's weird in there, isn't it? In a state of constant flux.'

'Yeah, there doesn't seem to be a right way up either. It's like being upside down no matter which way you turn. Do you think we should tell William about it?'

'Not yet. Let's get him drunk like we said and send him in for a laugh. He won't know what's going on.'

As they sat around the dining table that evening, the girls complained that the lines marking out the tennis courts had become badly faded. William promised to help them immediately after supper.

'Mmm, that was delicious. Right, I'll find the keys to the pavilion, then you can get straight on with it in the morning. I wonder where they could be? I haven't seen them in a long time.'

'We can help you look if you want?' he offered.

'Umm, yes okay. I think they could be in the study somewhere. Excuse us then girls, we'll get searching.'

'So William, how's the wine collecting going?' he asked, as they left the dining room.

'Oh, fine thanks Victor. Picking up the odd bottle locally.'

'Have you got anything that's drinkable, but not too valuable?'

'What on earth are you talking about? Wine doesn't have to be expensive to be drinkable.'

'Perhaps you could give us a tasting?' said Mike.

'Well, I must say I'm pleased that the pair of you are showing some signs of culture at last. No time like the present, let's do it now.'

They'd been in the cellar for half an hour, but because they were only allowed to take small sips, their plan was failing. William wandered off down the racking looking for something special.

'This is hopeless,' whispered Mike, 'and he's boring me to death with these vintage stories.'

'Let's go to the workshop for a smoke.'

'Great idea, we can get him stoned instead. Load a bong with that Nepalese stuff.'

He shivered and turned up the collar of his jacket as they walked towards the workshop. It was a reminder that the long hot summer was drawing to a close.

'I'm not sure if this is a good idea, it'll taint our palettes.'

'What's the matter William, never had a bong before?'

'Of course I have. I once had two at the same time. Hello, where's that old wreck come from then?'

'It's a Jag, my new smoker.'

'I'm not sitting in the back with you two, so you can forget that for a start.'

'I didn't know you had that,' said Mike, going to have a look. 'They've got massive boots, these things.'

'Er, don't bother Mike, it's locked I think. I don't have the keys on me.'

'No, it's open, look.'

'God, you're right, they do have a big boot,' said William. 'What's that? Hmm, there's something quite heavy inside this old rag...'

'It's probably just the jack,' he said, trying to snatch it away. 'Put it down, you'll get oil on your clothes.'

'What the hell is it? ... It's a gun! Look, the barrels are all sawn off. It's totally useless.'

'I got the car from the film studio, it must have already been in there.'

'Oh, and there was me thinking that you'd become a yardie, ha! Get rid of it, it's lowering the tone.'

He packed a special mix into his largest bong and asked Mike to give him a hand to reposition it so they could all sit around comfortably.

'You do the honours then William,' he said.

'Yes, I'll be in charge.'

William opened a box of matches upside down and spilt them all over the floor. After a lot of fumbling, there was some huffing and puffing, followed by a loud bubbling sound. He looked on in bewilderment as the contents of the bowl shot out in a jet of water.

'Idiot! Suck, don't blow!'

'No need to get nasty, I was just unclogging the pipe.'

'It wasn't blocked. Oh, give it here. I'll sort it out.'

Eventually they dragged William to the house in a semi-conscious state and propped him up against the front door. He glanced inside the hallway and was relieved to see that the coast was clear. Bundling William into the lift, they arrived in the lab undetected.

'Hold him up Victor, I'll get the suit.'

'He's really out of it, he'll miss it all,' he said, helping to get William's arms into the sleeves.

'Let's soak a cloth in cold water and slap him across the face before we jam the helmet on his head.'

'Good idea.'

Leaving William unattended, they padlocked the lift and trotted down the turret staircase, only to be intercepted by Anna in the library.

'Isn't William with you, Victor?' she asked, deliberately ignoring Mike.

'No. Perhaps he's in the cellar?'

'He's not...and he's not in the study either. Did you find those keys?'

'What keys?'

'The pavilion keys.'

'Oh yes. No, sorry, we didn't.'

They collected the dogs from the Winter Garden and escaped into the fresh night air. An hour later they returned to the lab.

'Standby for *Goggles* re-entry,' said Mike, flicking the switch.

'Yep, here he comes... Oh good, he's semi-awake. Right, let's get him out of the suit.'

'He's wriggling too much. Hold him down while I pull his helmet off.'

'Hello? What are you doing in there?' shouted Danii, as she repeatedly knocked on the door. 'Mike? Victor?'

'Pull his helmet off?' he whispered to Mike. 'Why does she always turn up at moments like this?'

'Victor, are you in there?'

'Yes! Umm, just a minute!'

'What are you doing?'

'Nothing...why?'

'We're still looking for William. Are you going to open this door?'

'Can't! In the middle of something!'

'Have you seen him?'

'Who?'

'William!'

'No sorry.'

They waited until her footsteps had receded down the hallway.

'What on earth is she going to think we were doing?'

'Relax, I don't think she heard,' said Mike. 'Come on, help stand him up. If they catch us on our way down, we'll just say we found him drunk in a corner.'

Getting dressed the next morning, he wondered if they'd gone too far with their prank. He was worried that William might have recalled what had really happened, and braced himself as he entered the kitchen.

'Morning Victor,' said Danii. 'I'm just making toast, do you want some?'

'Oh, please. So, how's it going then William?'

'Fine. I was just telling the others about my strange dreams last night.'

'Really?'

'Yes, I saw father floating on the sea in his catamaran and those spaceships were hovering over him.'

'How odd.'

'Yes, everything was green. I was deep-sea diving and God knows what else.'

'Deep-sea diving?' asked Mike. 'Have you done that before?'

'No, but I'd be good at it. Don't forget I learned to snorkel at a very young age. Hmm, that dream seemed incredibly real, but I was quite disorientated when I woke up, almost like I'd been drugged.'

Just then he caught Mike's eye and desperately wanted to laugh. He choked and his coffee siphoned from his nose back into the mug.

'Really Ogroid! Your table manners get worse every day.'

'No they don't.'

'Hello, what's that then?'

'What?'

'That over there...on my grandmother's prized Welsh dresser.'

'It's the clock Hans gave me. It seems to be going quite well now, must have loosened up a bit.'

William walked over, picked it up and shook it.

'It's rubbish, get rid of it.'

'It's not doing any harm. Stop shaking it about like that.'

Without warning the barn doors burst open and a larger than normal cuckoo flew out.

'**Aaaggghhh! Aaaggghhh!**' screamed William, staggering backwards with the sizeable clock dangling from his nose. '**Aaaggghhh!**'

'Quick Victor, help him!' shouted Anna.

'Don't move, I'm coming.'

'Get it off me you idiot! It's a trap, not a clock. Aaaggghhh, that hurts!'

'Anna, get some tissues to soak up the blood. Hold still, I'll prise its beak apart and...'

'**Oww, oww! Ouch!** ... Oh my poor nose.'

'Oh good, I don't think it's broken.'

'It feels broken, idiot!'

'No, the clock, it's still in one piece.'

'Get it out of my sight this instant, before I smash it to a pulp!'

'Come on, let's get you to the surgery,' said Anna. 'I think Carmen's in there, let's see if she can stop the bleeding.'

William had calmed down by teatime, although the dressing seemed a little over the top; Carmen had swathed his face completely in bandages, leaving him peering through a small slit.

'Hmm, I'd rather like a game of croquet. Yes, croquet on the lawn.'

'Croquet? It's a bit slow, isn't it?' he replied.

'Look, I've been pecked. I don't want anything too vigorous. In any case, a bit of fresh air will probably do my nose good. Go to the shed and fetch the gear then Ogroid, otherwise it'll be dark before we've started.'

'Count me out, I'm going to the lab.'

'You're playing Muffton and that's final! Now then, there seem to be a few people missing, so find them. Check the salon first, they're probably all in there.'

Everyone stood in a huddle looking bored, while William paced up and down the lawn indicating where he wanted the hoops set. Once play commenced, William took an ungainly swipe at the ball and the mallet head flew off, hitting Mike in the testicles. The game was disbanded and Carmen helped Mike inside for some unspecified treatment.

'William, let's take a walk around the grounds instead,' he suggested.

'Umm, yes, all right.'

'We can cut through the orchard… How's your nose feeling then?'

'Throbbing, but I suppose there are always people worse off than yourself, Mike for instance. Hmm, that must have hurt.'

'He'll be okay. That clock's locked away in my room now, you'll be pleased to know.'

'Good. Oh look, those apples are nice and juicy. Go up and get me one.'

'Stand back, I'll throw a stick and knock some down.'

'No, I want a picked one, not one that's all bruised.'

He reluctantly climbed into the tree and edged his way along the branch towards a big red apple.

'No, no, I want that one…higher up to your right. Yes, yes, keep going…that one there!'

It was just out of reach. He shimmied along a bit more and stretched out his arm. He could just touch it with his fingertips and with one final lunge he had it in his grasp. He twisted it off and tossed it down, but then noticed that William wasn't looking.

'Watch out!'

Just as William turned, the apple hit him squarely on the nose.

'Ouch! You idiot, Ogroid!'

Walking back to the house, the bloodstain in the middle of the bandages got bigger and bigger. By the time they'd reached the surgery William looked like an extra in a horror film. The bandages were sagging with the weight of blood, making it look worse than it actually was. However, William still insisted on staying in bed for the next two days to recuperate, and the house was very quiet.

Taking his dogs around the grounds for a mid morning walk, he spotted Serge fishing on the far side of the lake. Curious, he went over to see.

'Caught anything yet?'

'Non.'

He moved aside to give Serge room to cast, but accidentally kicked the tackle box. Hooks and floats were strewn everywhere.

'Er, sorry about that.'

'Dog merchant.'

He gathered the items up and sat down on the bank to watch. Serge started reeling in, but the rod was almost bending in half under an immense weight. He thought that it was probably a piece of burnt out paddleboat from the party disaster in July.

He was reminded of the day he'd taken William fishing for his first, and as it turned out, last time. He'd got William set up and then stood back to watch him cast.

'Bugger, the weight has swooshed around the tip of the rod! This equipment is useless, utterly useless!'

'Wait a minute, I'll untangle it for you.'

After several repeat performances, he'd had to cut away most of the line, and by the end of the day there was almost nothing left. William had been reduced to hovering the tip of his rod a few inches above the water, with a hook tied to the little bit that remained.

'Ooo, got something! Got something!'

'Get it to the bank, quick!'

'Oh no, I've caught a snake! Help, it'll bite me!'

'It's an eel you idiot, just land it.'

'Oh my God, help! It's all coiled around my leg!'

'Stand still, I can't do anything with you dancing around like that!'

In the ensuing struggle William had fallen to the ground.

'Help! Help! Oh my God, help!'

'Hang on, I'm just trying to prise the hook out.'

'Hurry up! It's constricting the blood flow to my leg, it'll be all withered!'

'Stop pulling on the rod then, it's creating too much tension.'

Suddenly the hook was free, but the line had been so taut that it twanged and caught William's nose, snagging the inside of his nostril.

'Aaaggghhh! Aaaggghhh!'

'Hold still, I'll get my fishing knife.'

In the end he'd had to use a pair of snips because the barb had gone in so deep.

'You idiot Ogroid! Take me to hospital. My fucking nose is all gouged!'

Before they'd got to the hospital, they'd nipped into a pub for a couple of drinks and had ended up getting legless. Out in the cold night air, they'd felt the need for food and had joined the queue at a kebab stall, engrossed in reminiscing about their skiing holiday with Bunty Junipers. Twenty minutes later they were at the head of the queue.

'Two kebabs please,' said William.

'No kebabs, sorry.'

'No kebabs? Okay, what have you got then?'

'Weasel, Russian Sauce or Kedgeree P.I.'

'I don't fancy any of that. I'll just have a bag of chips.'

'No sir, we don't do chips. You can get your snacks over there.'

'Don't do chips? Pah! What sort of catering establishment is this?' William complained.

'I'm selling tickets for the films that are showing tonight. Come on, what will it be?'

'What's going on Victor, how did we get in here? What were they again?'

'Weasel, Russian Sauce or Kedgeree P.I!' said the woman impatiently.

'I don't care, they all sound as bad as each other. You choose Victor.'

'Two for Russian Sauce then please.'

They had just sat down when the lights dimmed. The film was really good up to halfway, which was when they'd been asked to leave. They hadn't been noisy with their snacks or anything like that; it was because William had been caught loitering in the ladies toilets.

'I thought it was the men's.'

'The lady said you were standing there fiddling with your zip,' the manager said sternly.

'I was looking for the urinals, couldn't see them anywhere.'

'You urinated in the hand basin in front of her.'

'I thought it was a bloke. You saw her yourself!'

'Okay, I'll let you off with a warning this time. You're lucky I'm not calling the police.'

By the time they'd got to the bus stop William had forgotten about his nose; for months afterwards though, he'd pretended to be in agony whenever he'd sneezed or got angry and flared his nostrils.

He looked over to see that Serge was still furiously reeling in, dragging the heavy object closer to the bank. When it finally surfaced, it looked like a dead body all covered in weed. He nearly turned and ran before he realised what it was.

'Hey, it's that *Android Sister* from the Christmas show!'

'Merde, zis beech. I do not forget.'

Serge dragged the android by the ankles a few metres up the bank and started to kick it. He decided to fetch a wheelbarrow and when he got back, the lifeless robot was still getting a beating. He tried to pull it away, but found himself in a tug of war situation, which he eventually won when Serge slipped and fell into the lake. Quickly manoeuvring the android into the wheelbarrow, he headed for the lab.

'Ah, Victor, stage two, we're ready to roll!'

'What, you've finished rigging up the retrieval device?'

'Yeah. All you have to do is make your way over to what you want to retrieve and fix this clip to it.'

'Or her.'

'What?'

'Or her. We can get some tasty birds.'

'Girls will have to wait. We need to do a lot more research before we bring people out. So, shall we give it a trial run?'

'Okay, but I need a hand with something first. Serge found the missing *Android Sister* in the lake.'

With the robot safely stowed in a cupboard, he got himself seated in the module. Mike handed him a cable, which looked suspiciously like a jump lead.

'Remember, nothing big and no people. Just get something small...and static.'

'Static?'

'Yeah, something that wouldn't have been moving too much when it disappeared.'

He quickly returned with a chicken.

'I could have got more, but I'll need a sack or something. Fish as well. We'll have to set some tanks up...fresh and saltwater.'

'Good idea, then we can put them in the lake and take the others down to the sea.'

'Give me that bag, I'll fetch some more chickens.'

The next day he and Mike skipped breakfast with the others and fried some eggs and bacon on a camping stove in the workshop. They'd hidden the chickens in the barn because there weren't enough eggs to go round.

After another successful retrieval session, they were making their way carefully down the stairs with a barrel loaded onto a porter's trolley.

'What have you got there?' asked William, interfering.

'Nothing,' he replied.

'Nothing? It's full of water. Look, it's dripping all over the carpet.'

'Stop fretting, it'll dry.'

'There's something in there. What is it?'

'Fish, if you must know.'

'Fish?'

'Yes, we caught them.'

'What, in the lake? I didn't think there were any left. Let me see... Hmm, these are all sea creatures. Prawns, mullet, mackerel. Are we going to eat them? I could have a Smarglesboard.'

'A Smarglesboard? What the hell's that?'

'Had one on a ferry to Hamburg once. Really nice it was. Lots of fish. Don't know how they knew my name though, but then again I was travelling first class. So, where did you catch them? Have you been going to the seaside without me?'

'They came from the *Neverness*,' said Mike proudly. 'We can bring back anything we like.'

'What, all that twaddle about the *Neverness* isn't twaddle after all? Ooo, this is brilliant! Are there any people in there?'

'Yeah.'

'So we could get some girls? Some girls for me!'

'Most probably, yes…eventually.'

'Excellent, excellent! Let's get started right away!'

'No, we need more practice. As I've explained to Victor, we have to be sure what we're dealing with first. Anyway, we can't just start bringing strange girls into the house.'

'Oh, stop fretting Muffton, we'll keep them a secret.'

'We'll get found out.'

'I'm sure William's right on this one, Mike. It'll be okay, you'll see.'

'Hmm, now where can we put them?' asked William.

'We're taking them to the sea,' he said.

'No, no, the girls! Let's see…in the cellar? No. Umm, somewhere off the premises would be better. I know, we can set them up in a house of their own, but not too far away. Don't want a lot of driving every time I want a shag. Got fed up with that before.'

They left William muttering to himself and carried on outside to load the drum into the van. It seemed like a lot of effort for thirty or so fish, but they knew they had a duty and drove straight off for the coast. William was looking out for them when they got back, eager to begin.

'Come on you two, I've been waiting hours.'

'We'll just get some beers, see you up there in five minutes.'

As they rounded the corner, he could see William impatiently fidgeting about outside the lab.

'Oh, I'm so excited! Come on, hurry up. What's it like?'

'You'll see for yourself in a minute.'

Mike unlocked the door and William pushed his way inside.

'Where is it then?'

'There… What do you think?'

'It's crap. I was expecting something like the *Tardis*. At best, this looks like a stumpy canoe. Are you sure it works?'

'Of course it does. Now get this suit on and when you're in there don't get out of the chair…and don't fiddle with anything either.'

'Don't know what you mean Muffton.'

He glanced at his watch. William had been gone for about half an hour and it was apparent from his enthusiastic commentary that for once he was impressed with Mike's work.

'Oh, this is brilliant!' said William, stepping out of the module. 'Listen you two, we're going to have to keep this a secret from the girls.'

'Why?' asked Mike.

'They'll want to be in on it.'

'Well, they already know I'm working on it, don't they?'

'I'm only asking you to keep quiet until we've got some nookie sorted.'

'Fine. Okay, we'd better see if we can bring a large animal back before we take it any further.'

'Me, I want to do it!'

'Umm…might be better if Victor goes.'

'No, I'm going!'

'All right, but don't get anything dangerous,' warned Mike. 'No lions, bears or crocodiles or anything like that.'

'Or snakes,' he added.

'Right, let's get on with it,' said William, putting the helmet on.

'Are you sure you're up to this?' asked Mike.

'Of course I am, now send me in!'

After a quick briefing on how to use the clip, William disappeared and was almost immediately on the radio.

'Got something! Ready to come out!'

He looked on in amazement as a sheep appeared behind the kit. It instantly went mad, knocking over chairs and butting into tables.

'Why on earth did you get that?' he asked.

'I don't know.'

'Get hold of it quick, it'll do untold damage!' shouted Mike, grabbing a handful of wool.

After a lot of disruption, they managed to topple it onto its side.

'Get it into the lift,' said William.

'No, the stairs, it'll have to be the stairs. We can't get into the lift from here any more, I've welded the door up.'

'Why did you do that? I don't remember giving you permission to go welding up my doors.'

'I did it yesterday. It's far too dangerous for people to have free access.'

'You are a bloody nuisance Muffton. Come on then, let's get it out. If it craps on the carpet, you're cleaning it up.'

By the time they'd struggled to the first floor, Danii and Carmen were on to them.

'Where on earth has that come from?'

'And more to the point, what were you doing with it upstairs?' added Danii accusingly.

'Mike's equipment works!' said William.

'Pardon?'

'His *SDD* equipment! We can get into the *Neverness* and bring things back.'

'It's a bit hit and miss at the moment,' said Mike, playing it down.

'Yes, we don't know what's coming out next. You girls had better stay away from the lab, there might be snakes and spiders,' said William, gripping on to the sheep.

'Hey, this is fantastic!' said Carmen. 'Do you think that you'll ever be able to control it?'

'It'll calm down when it's set loose in a field.'

'Not the sheep, you idiot. I mean in choosing what you can bring back?'

'Oh right. Umm, a long way off yet I think, don't you Mike?'

'Yes, much more research to be done before we've got control over that aspect.'

'Is this why you're wearing that silly shiny suit, William?' asked Danii.

'Of course it is. You don't think that I'd normally choose something like this, do you?'

'So, what else have you got?'

'Some chickens,' said Mike.

'Have we?' said William, looking puzzled.

'Yeah, we're hoping to get some chicks soon too.'

'Feathered chicks,' he said, trying to cover for Mike's nerves. 'They've laid a couple of eggs, but we need a cockerel to umm...'

'Hmm, seems quite hopeful, this device,' said Carmen thoughtfully. 'I'll have a chat with you later Mike, you can tell me all about it.'

As Danii and Carmen walked away, William looked alarmed and stood shaking his head.

'Why do they always interrogate us when we're trying to have fun? Hmm, we could have a problem, we're going to have to move the kit.'

'I agree,' he said. 'It'll be far too risky sneaking girls downstairs with them hanging around... Hey, why don't we use the workshop? We can build a cage as well...stop the retrievals escaping.'

'Brilliant Victor! Oh I say, this is exciting!'

'Come on,' said Mike. 'Let's get this sheep outside before it gets dark.'

The following morning he began work on the cage. Mike dismantled the equipment and then ferried it over on a trolley. The first they saw of William was when he popped into the workshop just before lunch.

'Almost done then?'

'Yeah. Close your eyes a minute.'

'Oh goody, have you got a present for me?'

'No, I'm welding, you'll get arc-eye.'

'I thought I was getting an egg. You kept those chickens a secret. I demand an egg!'

With the cage finished, Mike began setting up and made a few modifications to the retrieval device. The connecting clip was now attached to a rod instead of the original cable, creating a fixed distance between the unit and the retrieval, guaranteeing its appearance safely behind bars.

'Right, I'm having first go to get a girl,' demanded William.

'No,' said Mike. 'I think we ought to monitor that sheep for a week. Make sure it doesn't develop signs of instability or fall ill.'

'For God's sake, I can't sit around staring at a sheep for a week. I want a shag I'm telling you!'

'I think Mike's right. We can continue bringing things out though, so we won't be wasting time.'

'Oh, okay,' conceded William, 'but I'm going to have to borrow your bicycle pump, Victor. Bring it to my room after dinner.'

The rest of the week was spent rescuing all kinds of animals, which they released into the paddock behind the stable block. In fact, the whole thing had become quite addictive, taking up every waking hour.

When the sheep showed no signs of abnormality, they became more confident and recovered two horses. Gina and Anna were especially keen on riding and agreed to look after them. He felt pleased that the recent opposition to Mike's experiments had softened, and with all these other distractions going on, perhaps the girls wouldn't notice when they started to retrieve people.

'I want my turn before we pack up for lunch,' said William. 'You know how I love my Sunday roast. I'll be too full to put the suit on afterwards.'

'You've just come out,' he argued. 'Look, you're still wearing it.'

'Oh, so I am.'

'It's my go now.'

'After that Victor, we're packing up. I need to give everything the once over,' said Mike.

He donned the suit and secured himself in the device. Before he knew it, he was swimming around in the green mist looking for something different.

'Ooo, I've mound a funkey!'

'A mound of funky?' questioned Mike.

'Yes, I'm bringing it back.'

'Do we want it?' William's voice shouted in his ears.

'Yes, now get me out!'

Suddenly he was in the workshop.

'Bloody hell, he's got a monkey!'

'What in God's name do you want with that? It looks naughty, it'll have to go back,' grumbled William.

'Don't be stupid, it's harmless. I'm keeping him as a pet.'

'It'll be swinging from the chandeliers and generally wrecking the place. It'll bite people, we'll get germs and die.'

'I'll keep it in my room.'

'It'll smell of monkey poo.'

'I'll build it a cage and clean it out regularly, stop fretting.'

'Right, I'm shutting the kit down,' said Mike. 'Don't worry William, you can get yourself a pet another time.'

'I don't want a pet, I want girls. I'm getting impatient, when are we going to get some? Surely we've had enough practice by now?'

'What do you think Mike?' he asked, trying to keep hold of the fidgeting monkey.

'Well, I think we've proved the kit's safe and reliable, but it's still bothering me about having to keep secrets.'

'We'll have to, won't we?' said William. 'They'll only spoil our fun.'

'So then, let's get it straight,' he said. 'We'll get ourselves loads of attractive girls…real stunners!'

'I like it, I like it a lot!' drooled William.

'Yeah, it'll be a bit like the *Babeboards* we had at the pub, but this time in the flesh!'

'Ooo, I can get some prostitutes!'

'Why? We can have any girl we want.'

'But what if they don't fancy us?'

'They'll have to shag us because there won't be anyone else for them to do it with.'

'Oh, I've just had a thought. Dildos! We'll have to collect up all available dildos and hide them. It just so happens that I've got a list of every UK sex shop up in my room. I'll do the local ones as a matter of urgency, then see to the others at a later date. The important thing is that those dildos don't get into the wrong hands. So then, are we clear about the overall plan?'

'Okay,' said Mike reluctantly. 'We can try recovering our first human next time we go in. By the way, I've had an idea. We can get a canoe paddle, it'll help us catch up with our prey.'

'Shit, why didn't we think of that before?' he said. 'All this time we've been paddling like crazy with our arms.'

'Where are we going to put these girls anyway?'

'Hmm, let's see now. There's a lovely country hotel not far from the *Ark* site, a converted manor house. Father nearly bought it actually, just before he went missing. No one will ever find them there.'

'Sounds perfect,' he said. 'We'll take a look tomorrow. Get it up and running like a proper hotel.'

'They'll need a water supply,' added Mike. 'We'd better take one of those tankers from the Army camp.'

'Yeah!' he said enthusiastically. 'Get it all kitted out…electricity, food, condom machines, that sort of thing.'

Chapter 5

He saw a large wooden sign bearing the name *Forest Lodge* and turned into the driveway.

'Wow, look at all that red creeper growing over the front, it looks fantastic!'

'Yes, father always had a soft spot for this hotel. The gardens have been beautifully landscaped, although it's looking rather overgrown now.'

'Did you say it used to be a manor house?'

'Yes, original Cotswold stone. It's got twelve en suite bedrooms, plenty for you-know-what. There's also an indoor swimming pool and a small gym. Hmm, next time you're in town Victor, pick up a dozen or so leotards and bikinis. Leave them scattered around the changing room, I'm sure they'll get the idea.'

'The girls will kill us if they find out,' said Mike.

'They won't though, will they? Not unless you blab.'

The hallway had a flagstone floor and was tastefully furnished with a large antique desk and some comfy looking sofas. Through a doorway to his left was the lounge and directly opposite he could see the restaurant. They went under an archway beneath the broad wooden staircase and found themselves in the bar. A large conservatory had been added to the rear, where an old well featured in the centre of the floor.

'Well done, this is really nice,' he said, as they wandered around.

'Thank you,' said William smugly. 'I always knew I'd make a good hotelier.'

'Let's rename it *The Babehouse.*'

'*The Babehouse*? Yes, yes, I like that! Now then, there's a lot of work to be done, so I suggest you two make a start. I'll just check the wine cellar before I go searching for dildos. Oh Victor, I'll need to take your van, unless you want to run me home?'

'Run you home? We've just got here. Oh okay, we'll unload the tools and unhook the trailer. You'll have to pick us up later though.'

By early evening the hotel was almost ready; they'd filled the water tanks, got the generator going and even tidied a few bedrooms.

'Right Mike, all we have to do now is light the boiler.'

'Where is it?'

'There must be something in the basement, let's go and see.'

They entered a dark, damp room and switched on the light.

'What the hell is that?' asked Mike, as they gazed at a large crustaceous object hanging on the wall. 'Keep back, it might be an alien chrysalis.'

'Umm, actually I think that *is* the boiler.'

'It looks like a stalagmite.'

'Yeah, it must have been leaking for years.'

'It's totally encrusted. We'll have to chip some of this crap off...'

'No, don't touch it, it'll probably fall apart. Let's try and light it with one of these long matches.'

To their surprise, the gas ignited first time. After waiting for the system to heat up, they were greatly relieved to find that all the bathrooms had hot water.

'Right, shall we help ourselves to a glass of brandy from the bar while we wait for William?' he suggested.

'Yeah, where's he got to? He should be here by now.'

'Let's sit in the lounge, it's quite nice in there.'

After waiting for half an hour, he took a glossy magazine from the coffee table. He stared at the cover for several minutes before realising it was *Forest Lodge*. He skimmed through the classifieds.

'Listen to this Mike. *Furberry Limited, London, Paris and Stroud. Send us your furry animal and we will convert it into a fashion accessory of your choosing.* Jesus, how did they get away with it? Oh, here's another. *Frumpbuster. We come to you and throw out your wife, then install a nice new younger one.* Is that legal?'

He threw it into the inglenook and looked around for something to do.

'He's not coming, is he?'

'Doesn't look like it. Let's take the short cut over the hill past the *Ark* site.'

Back at the house they found William in the cellar, engrossed in updating his wine catalogue.

'Where did you get to then?' he asked.

'What? Oh yes, I was just about to come and fetch you. How did you get on?'

'All done, everything's working. We can start moving girls in whenever we like.'

'Excellent!' said William, rubbing his hands together. 'So immediately after dinner we're going fishing! Ooo, I can hardly wait, sex on demand, brilliant! Oh by the way Victor, the rear of your van is bursting with dildos. I've left it parked by the workshop.'

'My van? I thought you were just using it to drive home to collect your *Fido*?'

'I didn't know how many I'd find. As it turned out the *LandFido* would have been too small.'

Over dinner the girls were watching them with interest as they scoffed their food much faster than normal. He began to wonder if they'd been followed to the hotel earlier, but dismissed the idea and decided he was just being paranoid. They took it in turns to make excuses to leave the table and met up in the workshop.

He felt lucky because he'd won the toss and would be the first to go in. Scrambling into the suit, he took a final swig of beer and put the helmet on. He floated around in the *Neverness* for several minutes looking for something of interest.

'Hey, I've got a couple of real basty tirds in sight!'

'Basty turds?'

'Yes, real basty tirds. They're floating...they look delicious!'

'Bring him out Mike, something's wrong,' he overheard William say.

'There's nothing wrong!' he called. 'They're floating right in front of me.'

'He's gone mad. Get him out.'

'Tell William to stop panicking, I'm okay... I'm nearly within reach now. There are four photographers surrounding them...they're holding hands.'

'The photographers are holding hands?'

'No, the girls. Wait a sec, I recognise them! It's Indala and Pershia, the supermodels. We've hit the jackpot, get me out!'

Inside the cage, the models stood looking puzzled.

'Hello there,' he said, smiling as he stepped out of the module.

The two girls turned to each other, pulled a face and then stared back at him without saying a word.

'Right then,' said William, taking charge. 'We know who you are, so we'll start by introducing ourselves and then we can explain what's happened.'

'What's going on? Just a second ago we were being harassed by the paparazzi outside our flat. Where the hell are we?' asked Indala.

'First things first, girls. My name's William and this is Mike, oh, and that's Victor. Now then, this might come as a bit of a surprise but...'

They took it in turns to chip in with details about the situation and as the minutes went by the girls seemed to be getting more and more agitated.

'What? Everyone's gone? Fuck it!' said Pershia. 'We'd just announced our lesbian relationship to the press. It was going to earn us a fortune with all the stories.'

'Not to mention the photos,' added Indala.

'Ah, I see. Just a little money-spinning ruse then?' said William.

'No, we really are lesbians,' said Pershia.

He was getting stressed and had a sick feeling in his stomach, which he hadn't experienced since childhood. It was all going wrong and he struggled to get a grip.

'They're lesbians,' he whispered, 'they're not going to be interested in us.'

'Don't worry Victor, it'll be okay,' said William. 'Now then girls, I've got a lovely country hotel not far from here, you can stay there for now. I've actually done a lot of the work myself. It's even got hot and cold running water…and electricity.'

'The toilets work too,' he blurted. 'They're connected to a septic tank, so they shouldn't back up or…'

'Yes, that's quite enough about that, Victor. Now then, we'll drive you over there straight away and you can get settled in. It's getting late and I'm sure you'd like to take a hot bath and have an early night.'

'What time is it?' asked Pershia.

'Nearly ten thirty.'

'I want a Chinese,' she said.

'Umm, Pershia my dear, there aren't any Chinese restaurants left.'

'I'll have steak and chips then.'

'So will I,' added Indala. 'I want it rare and the chips mustn't be at all soggy.'

'I want mine well done…and I want mushrooms, lots of mushrooms. Not canned, freshly picked…and freshly squeezed orange juice with ice made from pure mountain spring water.'

'I'll see what I can do.'

'You'll see what you can do? There will be trouble if I don't get it how I like it, understand?' said Pershia aggressively.

He watched William escort them to the *Fido*. He could tell they were going to be somewhat difficult; Pershia in particular was a real bitch. He beckoned William over for a quiet word.

'We should have sent them back. We don't stand a chance.'

'Stop fretting Ogroid. They'll soon come round when they realise they've got no audience.'

'I doubt that very much. How on earth do we go about getting lesbians to shag us?'

'We could dress up as girls ourselves. Get them interested and then…'

'You can if you want. Hey, what about banning lesbianism? I am in charge after all.'

'Yeah right, how would you police it?' said Mike sarcastically.

'Fit cameras in their room?' suggested William.

'No, it's not decent.'

'What about that periscope I saw you with, Victor?'

'We're not stooping that low to get our kicks,' he said. 'Not yet anyway. Hmm, we could get some dodgy mags, leave them lying around the lounge.'

'They'll just start fancying the women if we do that.'

'No, idiot! Magazines with blokes in. Displaying dongers and things. Show them what they're missing.'

'Oh, I see. Yes, that might be the suggestion of the week Victor, well done! I'll get started on that in the morning. Now then, you two had better sneak into the kitchen and get their food cooked.'

'We can't cook it in there, the girls will be on to us in a flash,' Mike pointed out.

'Just grab the ingredients then. You can cook it at the hotel.'

'Good idea.'

'By the way, the biggest room is above the swimming pool, put them in there,' he said.

'Well that's a lot of good, how do I get to it?'

'Turn right at the top of the stairs. It's the door facing you at the bottom of the hallway.'

He was up earlier than usual and went down for breakfast feeling somewhat apprehensive. As he passed the salon door, he could see Marco cutting Gina's hair and Sazoa busily doing Nikki's nails. He was surprised at just how much was going on and wondered if it was always like this.

'What are you boys up to these days then? You all look a bit agitated,' said Carmen, loading the dishwasher.

'I've been running some important tests with my equipment just lately,' said Mike defensively.

'Made any progress with those chicks you were on about?'

'No!'

'We need a cockerel, still haven't found one yet,' he said, covering for Mike. 'We're just concentrating on getting them laid…the eggs, that is.'

'Yes, we could do with more eggs,' Carmen agreed, giving him a quizzical look. 'And why are you looking so red in the face William?'

'No reason. Been getting out and about a bit, it's probably all the fresh air.'

He wondered if they were under suspicion. He'd never been good at evading awkward questions and felt glad that they weren't directed at him.

'Victor, why's your van full of dildos?' asked Danii.

'Huh!'

'Ooo, I'd love to stay and hear your excuse,' said William, 'but I've just got to nip down to the cellar…'

'They're his,' he said, pointing at William. 'He borrowed my van, he put them there.'

'Is that true?' asked Anna.

'Ha! Umm, yes. Er, it was going to be a surprise for everybody.'

'I sincerely hope not,' said Carmen. 'So, what did you have in mind?'

74

'Yeah, come on William, we can't wait to hear this,' he taunted.

'Okay then…umm, I was intending to enter myself…'

'I don't think this sounds at all savoury,' said Danii.

'If you'll just let me finish, all will be revealed…thank you! Right, as I was saying, I was intending to enter myself for the *Turnip Prize* this year. Heard of that, haven't you? Yes, I'm going to stick all the dildos together to make one big penis. It'll be called *Willy of the South* and I'll get first prize.'

'I wouldn't be at all surprised,' said Carmen. 'Hey, it'll be a prize dick, made by a prize dick, winning a dick of a prize.'

'You're just jealous because I've got all the dildos.'

After breakfast they drove to Woodswell in the van and parked up in the Market Square.

'So, you're not intending to make this *thing* then, William?' he asked.

'Of course not. Made that up to get us out of an awkward situation. By the way Victor, you might want to sort through that pile of gay magazines I put outside your bedroom door just before we left.'

'What? Gay magazines? We need pictures of straight men, you idiot! Why didn't you tell me after breakfast? You're fucking useless, if the girls see them they'll think *I'm* gay!'

He was fretting as he stared vacantly at the old wooden well. What were they doing here this morning? Why did everything have to be so complicated? Getting himself together, he sliced through the padlock with some bolt cutters, lifted the lid and peered down into the blackness.

'Did you hear those stories about all those kids falling in?' asked Mike. 'That's why the council locked it up. Going down at the rate of three a week at one time.'

'Yes, I was one of them,' said William glumly. 'That nasty bully Ricky Buttings and his gang pushed me in. Got wedged halfway down. It tapers towards the bottom, you know. I was stuck for six hours. Still, got them back…one at a time.'

He opened the van doors and began emptying the dildos out of their packaging into a shopping trolley.

'You two start dropping them down.'

'Okay, then tomorrow I can return the empty boxes to the shops,' said William. 'Hmm, quite a cunning plan that Victor, I like it. They'll be *really* frustrated when they don't find anything inside. Yes, they'll be gagging for it!'

'Yeah, thought of it last night.'

'Right, once we're finished we'll go to *The Babehouse* and see what's going on.'

Inside the doorway to the lounge, they found the two girls locked in a catfight, rolling around on the floor screaming at each other.

'Quick Victor, go and get your video camera,' said William.

'No, there won't be time, I'll miss all the action.'

They watched in delight as the girls clawed and pulled at each other's inadequate clothing while scrabbling to grab hold of a hairbrush, which was gradually being pushed further and further away. He stood open-mouthed hoping he'd get to see something, but somehow all the interesting bits remained covered. Exhausted, the girls burst into laughter and flopped flat out on their backs.

'Oh look Indala, it's the three hoteliers,' said Pershia, standing up to face them. 'Now listen to me, something's happened to the water.'

'What's wrong with it?' he asked.

'Nothing comes out of the tap any more and the toilet won't flush.'

'But we only filled the roof tanks yesterday, there was enough for a couple of months.'

'Indala left the tap running all night. What are you going to do about it?'

'Umm, I'll get a water tanker and refill them, but you must be more careful because…'

'Because what? Because you can't get proper running water in your own hotel? Indala, give me that list. Right, let's see… The telephone doesn't work, the television doesn't work, there's no room service…'

'That's because…'

'Be quiet, I haven't finished! The quality of food is poor and I doubt that a pig would even eat it. That steak was so chewy my jaw hurt.'

'And the chips were still partially frozen,' added Indala. 'I was sick in the night.'

'The mattress on our bed is too soft, the curtains smell and there are signs of mould around the windows,' Pershia went on. 'There's a stain on the toilet seat and not a sign of complimentary soap or shampoo anywhere.'

'Not to mention the pubic hair I found in the shower.'

'It could have been one of your own,' said William defensively.

'We don't have any,' said Pershia.

'Ooo,' they said in unison.

'The sheets aren't made from Egyptian cotton and I'll sue if I get a rash. Also, my toothbrush is the wrong colour, I always have a green one. Something needs to be done about our clothing situation too. We've only got one pair of knickers each and they're soaking in the basin.'

'Ooo.'

William started coughing and thumped his chest, then fell to the floor all floppy, like a puppet with cut strings; he led on his back between the girls, one eye rolling around in its socket.

'The only clothes we've got are the ones we're standing in,' said Indala, ignoring what had just happened. 'It's outrageous, we never wear the same things twice. Get a selection of clothes sent over immediately!'

'You, you down there, get up!' said Pershia, kicking William.

'Umm, I'm just having a little rest. I've got a weak heart you know. Felt a bit wobbly there for a second, but I'm sure I'll get a view of it... I mean get over it.'

'Oh, I'm fed up with this, I want to go home to London.'

'I'll drive you,' offered William, continuing to lie there.

'This is a stinking, low class hole! What sort of hotel has condom machines fitted outside the bedroom doors? There's nothing for us here.'

'There's nothing for you in London either,' he reminded her.

They ignored him and walked outside. William scrabbled to his feet and brushed himself down.

'Look, why don't you and Mike walk home, I'll get straight off with them.'

'You wish.'

He tentatively approached the models who were standing with their arms folded high across their chests, staring into the distance.

'Well, goodbye then Pershia...and you Indala,' he said, offering his hand. 'It was nice to meet you.'

'Yeah, bye,' added Mike.

They pretended not to hear.

'Come on then girls, hop in,' said William.

'No, *you* bring the car to *us*!' snapped Pershia.

'I don't have to...'

'Do as I say!'

'Er sorry, but you don't understand. I don't have to because *this* is it,' said William, pointing at the van.

'Ha, you can't be serious? We don't want people seeing us in that shitty thing. Order us a limo at once.'

'I'll have to go and fetch another vehicle then. Why don't you wait inside, I'll only be ten minutes.'

'Hurry up about it!'

He felt quite relieved as they climbed into the van. If the models could be dumped off in London, they could start afresh and put this bad luck behind them. Things could only get better from here.

'I can't wait to see the back of them. They're real bitches,' he said.

'Yeah, why are they so horrible?' asked Mike.

'We haven't got a limo, what am I going to do?'

'Your *Fido* should be good enough. Oh, I've just thought of something. Ask them what date they think it is. We need to find out exactly when they ended up in the *Neverness*.'

'Good idea Victor,' said Mike, 'and we should keep notes about where people were when they disappeared too, see if there's any pattern.'

'God, even moaning about the colour of their toothbrushes,' said William. 'You did well remembering to give them one at all, I'd say.'

'We didn't. We just cleared out all the clothes and tidied the bed, we completely overlooked the bathroom.'

'Urrgghh. You mean…'

'Yeah, and they were pensioners,' said Mike. 'Found their false teeth on the bedside table.'

'Right, we're here. I'll drop you two by the workshop. I need to nip up to my room for a cap and bow tie. You can tell the girls I've gone to fetch more papers to do with the Poffington court case if they ask. You might as well get rid of the mags now Victor, we won't be needing them any more.'

'Shit, forgot about those.'

He was horrified when he turned the corner into his hallway and saw three huge piles of gay porn magazines blocking his bedroom door. He came out in a cold sweat, praying that nobody had seen them. He quickly dragged them inside and covered them with a sheet.

After lunch he ventured back into the *Neverness*. He was sure he'd spotted Sheil the Aussie babe singer, but couldn't paddle fast enough and eventually lost her in the mist. He was really annoyed about that. On his next turn however, he recovered two stunning actresses, Natasha Hussom and Nicole Wupper. Their last memory was of being at a restaurant together in London, and they thought it was still Friday the thirteenth of August 2049. They were quite confused about the new situation.

He sensed that Mike seemed uncomfortable about the presence of yet two more celebrities in the workshop, so he volunteered to take them straight to the hotel. After seeing the state the models had left their room, he quickly closed the door.

'Umm, that one's not ready. I think there are a couple free at the top of the stairs,' he said, leading them away.

'It really doesn't matter. It's not forever, is it?' said Nicole.

'What do you mean?'

'We'll be leaving tomorrow. We have to look for our boyfriends and families,' said Natasha.

'Oh yeah, of course,' he said, wondering why no one could grasp the situation they were in.

He and Mike were hanging out in the workshop when they heard the *Fido* come up the driveway. They went to the house and found William flopped in a chair just inside the hallway, looking extremely harassed.

'Bad news, they're over at the hotel again, they didn't want to stay in London. I was about to leave them outside their pad when Pershia grabbed the ignition key and dropped it down her top.'

'Did you try to get it back?' he asked.

'Thought about it. Anyway, they were really shocked that there was nobody to fuss around them. Made me drive all over the place. Photo studios, agents' offices, venues here, there and every-bloody-where. Then they realised the only form of attention they were likely to get was from us and announced they were coming back. They made me carry all their bags down from the flat. They were on the first floor and it took me six trips, made my legs turn to jelly. Then they wanted to go shopping. Oh dear, I'm so tired.'

'Did you remember to ask them what day they thought it was?'

'Oh yes. They seem to think it's still August 2049.'

'So, they must have disappeared on Friday the thirteenth too,' said Mike. 'That probably means everybody is in the *Neverness*.'

'We don't know that for sure,' he said, 'we've only found people from London so far.'

'True.'

'Terrible day, terrible,' moaned William. 'On top of all that I promised I'd arrange for them to get their hair done.'

'Why did you do that?' he asked.

'To shut them up of course.'

'Did you see anyone else at the hotel?'

'No, I just dropped them outside. Here are their food orders by the way,' said William, passing Mike a folded sheet of paper. 'Why would I have seen anyone else?'

'Because Natasha Hussom and Nicole Wupper are there, that's why. We got them this afternoon as replacements.'

'Oh dear, this is getting out of control. Now we've got four to look after. We're going to have to send them all back. They're too high maintenance, these celebrities. We need prostitutes.'

'Nah, it'll be okay. The actresses seem quite nice in comparison.'

'Let's see what food they've ordered then,' said Mike. 'Chicken Kiev and chips with fresh strawberries, vanilla ice cream and meringues for pudding. Where the hell are we going to get fresh strawberries?'

'And what's chicken Kiev?' he asked.

'Just boil up some chicken in vodka, that'll do,' said William.

'Right, that's solved, but what about the strawberries?'

'Open a tin and hope for the best.'

'Hope for the best? They'll be all soggy.'

'We could put them in the freezer for an hour, that'll harden them up,' suggested Mike.

'Ooo, good idea. Actually, that sounds like it could be quite nice. Make me a bowlful while you're at it,' said William.

'We'd better get them in the freezer now. What about the meringues though?'

'You won't be able to make those. Just say they're out of season and give them a wafer instead. Now listen, after we've eaten I'll have to sneak into the salon and pick up the hair-do kit.'

'What, aren't you going to get Marco to do it?'

'Don't be stupid, he'll blab. No, no, going to do it myself. I'm pretty certain they won't want anything fancy…probably just the usual fuss and blow job.'

'That sounds a bit unsavoury,' said Danii, coming into the hallway.

'Blow dry, I mean blow dry!'

'What are you three up to then?'

'Just thinking about getting my hair done, that's all,' said William, brushing a strand over his bald patch. 'What's it to do with you anyway?'

'Okay, calm down,' she said, raising her eyebrows.

They stood and watched her go upstairs. William waited until her door closed before breaking the silence.

'Good, I think we got away with it. Right, let's go over the plan one more time. During the meal try and act normally… Victor, why do you keep staring at the ceiling like that?'

'No reason.'

William looked up to see what was interesting him so much. High above their heads, Jappa was swinging from chandelier to chandelier.

'Oh really, that thing is the limit! I knew this would happen!'

'Jappa, Jappa. Come on down. Come on, Jappa.'

'Jappa? Pah! What sort of name is that? … Oh, hello there Serge.'

'Urgh, what you look at?'

'Been fishing again? Caught anything yet?'

'Non.'

Without warning Jappa dropped down onto Serge's head and a terrible scuffle ensued.

'Merde! It is a menace, zat monkey of yours.'

During dinner he pretended to need the toilet and slinked off to the kitchen to pack the food, then left the bags outside. When he returned, he could see Jappa vigorously picking his nose.

'For God's sake Victor, do we have to have that wretched thing at the dining table? It's putting me off my supper. Look, look, it's eating one as we speak.'

'Leave it alone, it's perfectly harmless,' said Danii.

'Anyway, I 'ave seen you do ze same, William,' said Gina.

'No I do not! Just a pain in my nose. Massaging it, that's all.'

'From ze inside, I 'ave seen. It is disgusting, a boy of your age.'

Jappa then surprised everyone by flicking something towards William, chattering loudly when it landed on his plate.

'Oh, that is going too far!'

'I know, it must have been fully four metres,' he said.

'Anyway, why is it dressed in that stupid jacket and bow tie?'

'I think he looks really sweet,' said Danii. 'Where are you getting these clothes from then, been raiding a toddler's shop?'

'No, they're from a special outlet near Banbury.'

'You've been driving to a monkey shop?' scoffed William.

'It's for circus supplies actually.'

'You're going soft in the head. Pah! Making journeys to circus shops, indeed.'

Mike helped carry the dirty plates to the kitchen while he collected the hidden bags of food and kept watch for William outside the salon. A few minutes later they met up on the driveway.

'Have we got everything?' asked Mike, as they piled into the *Fido*.

'Yeah, no worries,' he replied.

'Hmm, you'd better start boiling that chicken as soon as we get there,' advised William. 'I've got a feeling it'll take some time.'

They arrived at the hotel to find the models sitting in the lounge, looking completely bored.

'It's about time, we've been waiting hours! We've changed our minds about chicken Kiev. Indala wants special fried rice and chips and I want a baked potato with mozzarella cheese topping and chips.'

'Baked potato and chips, are you sure?' said William.

'We can have chips with everything, it helps us lose weight. It's the new *ChipAway* diet, don't you know anything?'

'Er, see to that Victor, will you? Still having the same puds though, yes? Good. Now then, I think it would be best if you have your hair done in the conference room, why don't you follow me?'

'Baked potato and chips are easy,' he said, watching them leave the room, 'but how do you make special fried rice?'

'No idea. We'll have to make something up.'

Five minutes later, they'd just got the kitchen equipment on when William burst through the swing doors, wearing a baggy floral shirt open to the waist and tight velvet trousers.

'Well, what do you think?'

'Umm, why the black frizzy wig?'

'So they won't know it's me, of course. They think they're getting it done professionally. Now then, I need two tablecloths, I forgot to grab the gowns in my haste. Oh, do you have some scissors as well?'

'You're not going to *cut* their hair, are you?' he gasped.

'Got to. They've just shown me pictures in a magazine, it looks do-able.'

'Help yourself to anything you need, we're off to pick up supplies for their new food orders.'

'We'd better find out what Natasha and Nicole want first,' said Mike.

'No, we'll give them the chicken. Let's get it on the stove before we leave.'

The frozen chicken sat inside a large pot, the bottom barely covered by the litre bottle of vodka.

'Stick the lid on, let it steam,' said Mike.

Arriving back with the additional ingredients, he arranged them neatly on a worktop.

'Right, first things first,' he said, getting organised. 'Open a couple of beers, they're in the freezer bag.'

'Okay, I'd better get the strawberries out too.'

'So…frying pan and a spot of oil.'

He lit a gas ring, turned the knob to maximum and stuck the pan on top. He slurped some oil into it from a container next to the stove and took a swig of beer.

'Oh no, the strawberries are frozen into a block!' exclaimed Mike. 'They look like a resin paperweight. Why did you put them in water?'

'William said they'd be more succulent that way.'

He took another sip of beer and did a loud belch. Just then William came in, looking worried.

'Pudding bowl, I need a pudding bowl.'

'What for?' he asked, emptying the box of rice into the hot oil.

'It's all going wrong. It's a good job there are no mirrors in there.'

'What's up?'

'They both want their fringes level with their eyebrows. I've cut them several times and they're still crooked. I need an edge to follow…ah, perfect, just like the one Nanny Muttlecroft had.'

As William left, he turned his attention to the smoking pan.

'Shit, it's all sticking to the bottom. Quick Mike, pass me that fish slice.'

'Urrgghh, it looks horrid. Why isn't it swelling up?'

'Don't know…it's all going black.'

'Oh, I've just remembered something. When you make rice pudding you add milk, that's what's wrong.'

'There's a carton of long life in the bag, tip it in. I'll try and scrape this gunk off the bottom.'

The instant the milk entered the pan, a large cloud of steam engulfed the kitchen and hot oil splattered everywhere.

'Ouch, ouch! My arms feel like they're being stung by a thousand bees, ouch! Quick, get the extractor fan on Mike, I can't see a thing.'

'Where is it?'

'I don't know. Feel for a switch by the door.'

The lights went out.

'Shit! I can't find it again now, wait a sec…'

In the darkness, the sound of a dishwasher started up, followed by a blender and then a noisy convection oven. Finally the lights came back on.

'Oh look, it seems better now…just needs to settle,' he said.

'It's oil floating on milk, where's the rice?'

'In a clod on the bottom, it'll be okay once we've strained it. Now, get those potatoes in the microwave and put the chips in the oven.'

'Should I wash them?'

'Umm, nah. Pick the lumps of mud off first though, we don't want any complaints. Now then, we need something to add to the rice to make it special. Mike, when we've had a Chinese, can you remember what they put in it?'

'No, I've never paid that much attention. Bits mostly. Look in the cupboards, see what there is.'

'Hmm, there's a can of sweet corn…and some brown sauce. This is going to be really nice.'

'Let's finish it before we judge it.'

'How long did you program the microwave for?'

'Fifteen minutes.'

'Is that all? We'd better give them an extra ten, then we can nip out for a smoke.'

Just as they were about to go outside, William ran in looking frantic.

'Quick! When is a fringe not a fringe?'

'What have you done?'

'Technically, they've got what they asked for. I've had to redraw their eyebrows higher up their forehead, but women do that, don't they?'

'How high?'

'Quite.'

'William, how high?'

'Well, they just touch the stubble on the hair-line, but I've drawn them thicker to reduce the gap.'

'Stubble?'

'Yes, took off a bit more than I intended. What shall I do?'

'Have you cut the back of their hair yet?'

'No.'

'Good. Just cut a chunk off each, you can stick it on a strip of tape and glue it across their foreheads.'

'Brilliant Victor! Now then, do you have any kebab skewers? It's just that the picture they've shown me has got a bun with chopsticks stuck through it.'

'There are some skewers in the drawer over there, but we haven't got any buns. We were just nipping out for a smoke, are you coming?'

'Umm, no thanks. I need to keep my concentration, don't want any slip-ups.'

The sound of the microwave pinging brought them back in. The large pot containing the chicken smelt of burning, so he lifted the lid and looked inside.

'Shit, the vodka's evaporated and the chicken's stuck to the bottom,' he said, holding the pot upside down. 'Get the plates ready Mike, I'll try and get it out.'

'It looks all rubbery on top, are you sure it's cooked properly?'

'Of course it is, look, it's black underneath. Get the potatoes out and then strain the rice for me. Save the milk juice though, it'll make a nice sauce.'

'These potatoes have gone all small, they look like walnuts.'

'Doesn't matter, just take the biggest one and bung that mozzarella cheese on top, then stick it under the grill. Hmm, these chips look good,' he said, pulling the tray from the oven. 'Let's eat a few.'

Just then William came striding confidently into the kitchen, wearing a very tall chef's hat.

'It's worked! I cunningly glued the picture from the mag onto the hand mirror, they didn't even notice it wasn't their own face staring back at them. I've dimmed the lighting in the restaurant too.'

'Why are you wearing that hat?'

'I seem to be on a roll, so I thought I'd take it through. Is it ready then?'

'Yeah, nearly. Just waiting on the melted cheese. The rest is on the trolley. Okay, it's starting to bubble…that'll do. Hmm, looks nice, better taste a bit.'

He put a fork into the runny cheese and lifted it to his mouth. It had drawn a string nearly a metre in length, which got longer as he tried to pull it free. His arm began to stretch towards the ceiling, but still it kept coming. He climbed on a chair, and then onto the prep table with the fork high above his head. By this time the string was two metres long and he considered the only way out was to start eating. He'd already munched halfway down the giant strand when he stopped and glanced over at Mike and William, who were watching in disbelief. He realised that he probably looked stupid, but the cheese was quite tasty, so he carried on chomping. His face was practically in the potato when he eventually bit the end off.

'What in God's name is wrong with you, Victor?'

'I don't know. It just seemed to get out of control.'

William approached the trolley and cast his eye over the plates.

'On second thoughts, you cooked it, you take it in.'

'No, it's okay William, go ahead.'

'I've changed my mind.'

'Why?'

'Because it doesn't even look like food. In fact it looks poisonous.'

'It's not that bad. Okay, I agree that the chicken could have turned out a bit better…'

'Look, I don't want anything to do with it!' snapped William, viciously kicking the chef's hat under a table. 'You'll just have to take it in yourselves. I'll meet you outside.'

'Oh, okay then.'

'You'd better warm the engine, William,' said Mike.

'Yes, be ready to leave…and have the doors open for us,' he added.

Chapter 6

In the sober light of day he knew they were in big trouble. Immediately after breakfast, he called a crisis meeting in the workshop.

'By now they'll have seen themselves in the mirror. They're going to kill you, William.'

'Oh, it wasn't that bad. Anyway, I was in disguise, they won't know it was me. It's more likely they'll be dead from that slop you served up.'

'Dead? They might have been sick again, I suppose.'

'That chicken wasn't cooked properly, anyone could see that.'

'The models didn't have the chicken, did they?'

'Let's face it,' said Mike, 'we're all in trouble.'

'Hmm, well you two had better go and investigate, I've got work to do in the cellar.'

'No way! You're not wriggling out of this one.'

'Well, let's just abandon them.'

'Don't be stupid, they'll come looking for us. The girls will probably bump into them on the road or something. We'll be in the shit.'

'We'll all have to go over together then,' conceded William. 'I'm sure we can bluff our way out of this. After all, they're not the brightest.'

As they drove slowly to the hotel, it proved quite easy to butter William up and persuade him that he was the best person to handle the situation.

'Yes, always did fancy being an ambassador… Right, we're here. Leave this to me.'

He nervously followed behind Mike as William led them into the hallway.

'We want a word with you,' growled Pershia.

'Who, me?' said William, trying to look innocent.

'Yes, where's that imbecile who fucked up our hair?'

'Gone. Up gone and left. Can't find him anywhere. We think he was an impostor. Why, is there a problem?'

'We're going to sue. Our fringes dropped off in the shower and there are big chunks missing from the back. We had to cut these meat skewers out too!' she said, waving them dangerously close to William's nose. 'They'd been glued in! It's outrageous!'

'It doesn't look that bad my dears. I'll tell you what, a bit of luck this, actually…a top stylist has just moved into the area, I'll get him to come and do it properly for you. How does that sound?'

'We'll kill you if he doesn't turn up! You've got an hour. Come on

Indala, we'll have to wait in our room, we can't be seen in public in this state.'

The models ran for the stairs just as the actresses were on their way down. Pershia shrieked, covering her head as she ducked past.

'My God, what's happened to those two?' asked Nicole. 'Were they in some kind of accident?'

'Yes, I think so,' said William. 'They won't say exactly what it was, but I'm going to help them. I must say it's good to see you both looking so well. Now then, is there anything I can do for you?'

'Yes, is there a car we could borrow?'

'Of course, I'll bring one for you later.'

'We'd like to set off after lunch. Well, lunchtime. Naturally we won't be eating anything.'

'I understand perfectly.'

Once home, they headed directly for the salon. Luckily Marco was alone.

'Hello old chap, how are things going then? Look, we need to ask a favour, but it's a secret, understand?'

'Ooo, I like secrets. Go on then, what is it?'

'How would you like the opportunity to do the hair of supermodels?'

'Are you pulling my...'

'No, this is serious. Maybe some actresses too.'

'Where have they suddenly sprung from then?'

'Never you mind. Now do you want to do it or not?'

'Hmm, suppose it would look good in my portfolio. Could pick up a bit of hot goss as well.'

'Good. Get your stuff and meet us on the driveway in fifteen minutes, and don't say a word to anyone.'

Marco loaded a variety of bags into the *Fido* and sat in the front next to William.

'Now then, I'm going to have to blindfold you.'

'Ooo saucy, I like games. I was only saying to Stefan the other day that we need more stimulation.'

'What are you doing, Muffton? You're meant to be driving the car for the actresses. Get out.'

He sat in the back listening to Marco chatter on as William drove them to the hotel. He was still feeling anxious and wondered just what they'd got themselves into.

'Right we're here, you can pull that scarf off now,' said William.

'Ooo, a nice country hotel. It reminds me of when Stefan and I first got together.'

'Why don't you save that story for your customers? Go on in then, Victor will bring your kit.'

Inside, the models were impatiently pacing up and down the lounge in a rage, with their heads wrapped in towels.

'Hello girls! This is Marco, he's going to rectify your hair. Still no sign of that impostor though, but rest assured, we'll find him.'

'When you do, you're to hand him over to us, is that understood?' said Pershia, prodding William's chest with her finger. 'And you two, are you the ones responsible for that pigswill of a meal?'

'No,' he said. 'It seems that the hairdresser and chef were in cahoots. They've been running amok locally.'

'Now then darlings,' said Marco intervening, 'we'll have you looking beautiful again in no time. I'd just like to say that I *adore* both of you, I'm your biggest fan. I was at the fashion show in Milan. You were *fab*, knocked the spots off everyone!'

'Well, it's nice to finally meet somebody who knows what they're talking about,' said Pershia.

'Come on then my dears, let's slip you into some gowns, then you can choose your hair extensions.'

'Do it in the conference room,' ordered William. 'It's just through there.'

'Thanks love, see you later. I'll need at least four hours.'

'Oh hello,' said Nicole, suddenly appearing. 'Natasha and I are ready to leave.'

'No problem,' said William. 'Your car's waiting outside, it's the black saloon.'

'Thanks. So, we'll be on our way then.'

After the actresses had gone, they stood in the hallway wondering what to do.

'Four hours, just for hair?' said Mike.

'Yeah, mad,' he said. 'Hey, I've got a brilliant idea! Why don't we go into the *Neverness* and find a chef?'

'Oh yes!' exclaimed William. 'He can live-in and do all the cooking from now on.'

As they drove to the workshop, he felt relieved that they'd be able to offload some of the responsibility for looking after the models. It would also leave them with more free time, so they could search for girls they actually stood a chance with.

'Okay then, it's all ready,' said Mike, starting the kit. 'Who wants first shot?'

'Victor, you go in.' said William. 'I've got a terrible acid stomach. It's all this stress.'

'Well go and get some tablets then,' he said, zipping up the suit. 'And be quick because we'll need to do an interview.'

It wasn't long before he spotted a middle-aged man wearing kitchen whites, clutching an egg whisk. He thought this was a good indication of culinary expertise, unless the chap was some kind of deviant.

'Good afternoon,' said William.

'Who are you? What am I doing here? Help!'

'Steady on old chap. Now listen, you've been in a state of suspended animation and…'

'Help! Help! Let me out, help!'

'Send him back.'

William reluctantly put the suit on, rubbing his stomach and belching loudly several times as he stepped into the module. Soon they were questioning another prospective candidate. The interview seemed to be going well.

'Excellent!' exclaimed William. 'Can cook, can drive, stable disposition. French, but speaks good English.'

'Oui, it all sound good for me,' said the chap. 'No more paying ze tax or trouble wiz ze police.'

'That's right, and you can have anything you've ever wanted.'

'What about ze sexy women? Do you 'ave any?'

'Send him back.'

'Okay…there he goes,' said Mike. 'Well, that was interesting because he was in France when he disappeared.'

'Yeah, where's Pont d'Ouilly anyway?'

'It's a small town south of Caen,' said William. 'Used to stop off there with father occasionally.'

Mike had been inside for quite some time and still they hadn't heard from him.

'Are you all right in there?' he asked.

'Yeah, wait…Got one, got one! Cut the power Victor, I'm coming out.'

The chef looked dishevelled and weary as he sat in the cage. They watched him fumble around in his pockets before lighting a cigarette.

'Hello,' said William.

'What's going on then? What have I been arrested for this time?' said the man, blowing out a plume of smoke.

'We'd better explain, something strange has happened.'

'Oh aye? Somebody dead from food poisoning again?'

'He seems perfect,' whispered William, before turning to readdress the man. 'No, this isn't a police cell. Actually, things are a lot different now. I'm in charge and I'd like to offer you a job.'

'Oh aye?'

'Yes. It's in a small hotel, very exclusive. Clients are top celebrities, no rubbish.'

'Oh aye?'

'Are you up to the challenge?'

'Aye.'

'We'll pay you,' he said, chipping in.

'And give you accommodation,' added William.

'Can I have free drinks at the bar?'

'Yes, you'll have to pay for nothing.'

'I'll do it. When do you want me to start?'

'Tonight. So, what's your name then?'

'Ernest.'

'Ernest, good.'

'No, Ernest Glugg.'

'Excellent. Right, we'll take you straight over and you can get stuck in.'

'What time does the bar open then?'

'Whenever you want, you'll be running that too.'

'Are you from Manchester?' he asked.

'Aye, but I move around a lot for work. I'm living in Lincoln at the moment.'

'Do you know what date it is?'

'Aye, my birthday, the thirteenth of August.'

'Oh, Happy Birthday! Okay, let's go, we'll fill you in on what's been happening on the way.'

By the time they'd finished showing Ernest around, Marco was ready to be taken home.

'How did it go then? Happy now, are they?' asked William, as they pulled out of the driveway.

'Ooo, I've never seen such a mess. I'll have to attend to their hair on a regular basis to get it into shape. Still, now that I know where they live, I can stop by whenever I want.'

'Bugger, forgot the blindfold. Look Marco, you're not to tell the girls a thing, understand? We're relying on you to keep this a secret.'

'Ooo, I don't know about that. This is quite a coup for me. Anyway, I've already promised them a manicure with Sazoa.'

'You're to keep your mouth shut! I'll be watching you like a hawk!'

Once home, they followed Marco into the sitting room where several of the girls were watching a film.

'You'll never believe this, I've just met Pershia and Indala!'

'Shut up idiot,' hissed William.

'What?' asked Danii.

'Pershia and Indala, the supermodels! I've just done their hair! Ooo, Stefan will be so jealous, and it's going to look brill in my portfolio.'

'What are you talking about?' asked Carmen. 'Oh, it's something to do with you three, isn't it?'

'Don't know what you mean,' objected William.

'So, where have these girls come from then? Did you find them on one of your trips?'

'Sort of.'

'Come on, out with it!'

'Er…'

'Mike, perhaps you'll tell us then?'

'Umm…they came from the *Neverness*.'

'The *Neverness*? So, you can selectively recover *people* now?'

'*Selectively* might be a bit of an overstatement,' lied William. 'It's all a bit hit and miss at the moment.'

'This is incredible.'

'Yes, fancy it being two supermodels that came out first,' said Danii.

'Coincidence, that's all.'

'Does anyone want to see the photos?' said Marco, reclaiming the girls' attention. 'Here we are, Indala, Pershia, oops, thought Stefan had deleted that one!'

They started slowly backing away as Marco continued to skip through the pictures stored in his camera.

'Wait zare you boys, we 'ave a few questions,' said Gina.

'Oui, where 'ave you 'idden zem?' asked Xenia.

'Yes, where are they?' added Danii.

'They're at *The Babe*…'

'*Forest Lodge*,' interrupted William. '*The Bay Tree*, if you remember Mike, was the other hotel we considered. Yes, they're at the *Forest Lodge*. We were going to surprise you with them later.'

'Is zat so?' said Gina.

'Yes. We decided a few days in quarantine would be best. You know, just in case they've got anything nasty.'

'You've all been wearing biological suits then, have you?' said Carmen. 'Idiots. If they have got anything, it's too late.'

'Let's go to the hotel and meet them,' said Danii. 'They do know we exist, don't they?'

'We might have hinted at it,' said William sheepishly. 'Actually, we recovered two actresses as well, but they've gone to London.'

'What are zey called, 'ave we 'eard of zem?' asked Xenia.

'Might have. Natasha Hussom and Nicole Wupper.'

'Yet two more famous and beautiful women,' said Danii. 'Not such a coincidence after all!'

'You boys are getting out of control,' said Carmen. 'First there's a sheep in the house…*upstairs*. Then you're driving around with a van full of dildos, now you've got a secret horde of girls!'

'Oui, you are acting so strange,' said Gina. 'And what are you planning to do wiz zose ten crates of gold 'idden in ze workshop?'

'Yes, what next?' asked Carmen. 'Burying treasure chests in the lawn perhaps?'

'We've got a bloke as well,' he said defensively. 'He's a chef.'

'A celebrity chef?'

'No. Damn, we should have thought of that.'

After taking directions, the girls immediately left for the hotel. He wandered across the room, turned the television off and flopped down in an armchair.

'*Ten* crates of gold?' asked William.

'Yeah, I moved mine.'

'Where to?'

'Not telling.'

'Well I don't care because I've got an idea.'

'What's that?'

'I'm going to get a treasure chest like Carmen suggested. Get loads of jewellery…diamond rings, exquisite earrings and bracelets.'

'What for?'

'You have no imagination, do you Victor? To buy favours from the celebs, of course. Sapphires, emeralds…give them a pearl necklace.'

'Getting a bit ahead of yourself, don't you think?'

'Hmm, it's a good job you didn't put that new *Babehouse* sign up.'

'It's still in the workshop, we were going to do it tomorrow.'

'Well you'd better get rid of it. Burn it, we can't use it now.'

While they were tending the bonfire Anna pulled up, scowling as she wound down the window.

'Very nice, if you like that sort of thing.'

'It's not our fault,' objected William. 'It's the equipment. It's got a bias towards females, but Mike thinks he knows what's wrong with it.'

'Yes, it needs tweaking. Should be able to sort it out…eventually.'

'The models are up at the house, by the way.'

'Why?' asked William, sounding surprised.

'Because they wanted to see where we lived,' she said, starting to pull off.

'Hmm, we'll have to produce more blokes or we could be in trouble,' said Mike, as the car disappeared.

'Yeah, only goofy blokes though.'

'What?' said William.

'They'll have to be goofy, so they don't fancy them.'

'Really Victor, that's the last thing we need, more like you. We'd better get back to the house, God only knows what could be happening.'

In the hallway, Marco was busily introducing the models to everyone as if they were old friends. William immediately wrestled control of the situation by suggesting he conduct a guided tour, and whisked them away to look at the Winter Garden. He followed the group around, all the time thinking what a mess it had become. Everybody now knew about the hotel, the models had been nothing but trouble and he seemed further away from a shag than ever.

'Now then, these are the main stairs. Take a look at the magnificent chandeliers as we ascend to the first floor. The bedroom doors were all salvaged by father from Windsor Castle after that ghastly to-do back in the thirties.'

'Oh Indala, this is so much nicer than the hotel,' enthused Pershia, as she opened Gina's door. 'Hmm, I like this room, I think we'll move in here.'

'Pardon?'

'Oh look, a pretty little French girl. Are you the maid?'

'Non, I am not! And zat is my room and you are not 'aving it!'

'Look darling, I am Pershia and I can have anything I want!'

'Not any more you cannot! Zings are different now and you and your friend will 'ave to learn 'ow to cook and clean, and 'ow to survive wizout your big egos!'

'How dare you speak to me like that, you're just a French person!'

'Get out of my room zis minute, you 'orrible piece of shit.'

'Come on Indala, I won't stay in the same house as that little tart! Driver, we're leaving!'

'Do not call me a tart, you beech! Get out, get out! Merde!'

'**Driver, come now!**'

He watched William run after them and felt relieved that it had ended without bloodshed. Meanwhile, everyone wanted to know more about the *Neverness* and Mike was bombarded with questions.

'So, how many can you recover in one go then?' asked Stefan.

'Just one. *TransPooP* is quite small at the moment.'

'Have you seen any nice boys in there?'

'It's hard to see anything at all.'

'What is it like zen?' asked Nikki.

'Dark...very dark.'

'And creepy,' he added. 'You have to feel your way around, you never know what you're going to lay your hands on next.'

'Ooo, perhaps I could have a go?' joked Marco. 'I like to do a bit of delving.'

In the morning they had a conference out of earshot of the girls and decided that they needed more help at the hotel. Getting the chef had been a stroke of genius, but they could also benefit from someone to take care of the cleaning.

'Right, a chambermaid it is then,' he said. 'No reason why she can't be young and tasty though, is there?'

He took his time, aware that this could be a real opportunity for him. He returned with a stunner. She was tall and altogether quite slim, except for a nice pair of large, but well-proportioned boobs. She seemed less well groomed than the models and he hoped that she'd be more down-to-earth.

'The girls aren't going to like this,' whispered Mike, shaking his head.

'Stop fretting, she's a chambermaid, that's all. They probably won't even notice her.'

As the interview progressed, he realised that she was just his type and he could be in with a real chance.

'So Jasmine, you're from Luton and you've been working in an airport hotel?' confirmed William.

'Yeah, that's right.'

'Excellent, excellent. So, I think I can safely say, welcome to our club!'

'Ooo, thanks,' she said excitedly.

'I'll get you unhooked.'

'No, I'll do that William…'

'Stop pushing Victor, I'll do it!'

'No. I found her, so I'm doing it!'

'Oh, do what you want. Pervert!'

They escorted Jasmine across the lawn to the house. He wasn't worried about the girls' reaction because they'd be presenting her as part of the hotel staff, so the fact that she was attractive shouldn't arouse suspicion.

'Ooo, a bit like playing millionaires this, isn't it?'

'Umm, you'll be living at the hotel actually,' he said. 'Don't worry though, it's really nice.'

The girls weren't very enthusiastic about their latest acquisition, so they decided it would be best to get Jasmine to the hotel without delay. After a few drinks, they left her in the bar chatting with Ernest and returned home.

'What's the story then?' he asked, as they accelerated up the driveway.

'What do you mean?' said William.

'You saw the look on their faces, we're in trouble.'

'Oh, stop imagining things. You're nothing but a prophet of doom.'

'No, I think Victor's right on this one,' said Mike. 'Anna looked as if she was about to erupt.'

'Oh, take no notice of her. Leave it to me, I'll deal with it.'

As they entered the sitting room, he immediately picked up on the frosty atmosphere.

'So zen, let us see what we 'ave so far,' said Xenia. 'Five beautiful girls and one ugly chef.'

'Yes, look here you three,' said Anna. 'We demand that you get us some good-looking men. We've prepared this list of celebrity hunks.'

'We don't need more men,' protested William.

'Especially men with big egos,' he added. 'Anyway, those models are lesbians, they don't count.'

'You 'ave to get some men. It is always more girls for you to chase,' complained Gina.

'That isn't fair,' said William defensively. 'We only got that Jasmine girl because she was a chambermaid. She's there to look after the models, that's all.'

'Yeah, right,' said Carmen sarcastically.

'The actresses have gone as well,' he threw in, 'so they can't be counted either.'

'Anyway, if we did get more men, things could get difficult,' continued William.

'How?'

'Well you know how stroppy men can be, they could revolt and...'

'Oh, do shut up William,' said Anna.

'Oui, it is just excuses all ze time wiz you boys,' said Gina.

'Look, we're in control of this equipment, not you!' snapped William. 'We decide, so there!'

'Okay, if that's the way you want it, we'll stop providing your meals, see how you like that!' said Anna. 'I'm sure they'll oblige you at the hotel.'

It was quite late when Jasmine brought their food out. They quickly realised that Pershia had turned her into a personal slave and was ordering her around in an obnoxious manner. They'd originally tried to sit with the models, but were embarrassingly shooed away and had to retreat to another table. The actresses still hadn't returned, so they ate their steaks in an unusual silence.

The standoff continued for the next three days. They spent much of the time locked away in the workshop attic getting more and more wrecked, only venturing out to drive to the hotel for food. They were quite taken aback when Gina came over to negotiate. However, they took full advantage of their position and issued her with a list of demands in return for allowing more men to join their numbers. She went away to discuss it with the others and returned an hour later with a compromise.

'Non to ze filming of a lesbian orgy, non to ze lap dances on Saturday nights, non to washing ze dirty clothes, but oui to preparing ze food and keeping ze 'ouse tidy.'

'Okay, I think we can agree to that,' said William. 'We'll be in for supper tonight, since we've already missed out on Sunday lunch.'

'Zare is one ozer zing. We are arranging a big discussion.'

'What about?'

'Repopulation.'

'Really? When?'

'In 'alf an 'our.'

'Who's going?' he asked.

'Everybody. You 'ad better get yourselves togezer, you all look stoned.'

'Including everyone at the hotel?'

'Non, I zink we can leave zem out of zis.'

He went to his room to take a shower and tried to make himself look presentable for the meeting. He was just coming downstairs when he saw Gina directing everyone into the dining hall. Taking his usual seat, he watched a small scuffle as William unsuccessfully tried to get Anna away from the head of the table.

'Okay then, this meeting is to let you all know what Mike and his conspirators have been up to recently. So Mike, if you'd like to explain exactly how far you've got with your experiments, I'm sure we'll all be amazed.'

'Umm, okay. As you are all probably aware by now, I've been able to enter a parallel world. I've called it the *Neverness*. Everything is in suspended animation...people, animals, even the spaceships! I've discovered that by attaching a special device to these individuals, and animals, it's possible to bring them back. In fact, all the new arrivals at the hotel were obtained this way. We haven't brought that many out yet, so it's too soon to draw any real conclusions, but it looks like they were all from a specific area. Look at this map... I've plotted where people were when they disappeared. It's my suspicion that everyone we find in future will have been inside this band running from the Pyrenees up to Lincolnshire, taking in London. Also, they all definitely disappeared on Friday the thirteenth of August when we were returning from holiday.'

'So, where has everybody else gone then?' asked Carmen. 'If you think that the *Neverness* only contains a proportion of Europe, what about the rest of the world?'

'We don't know.'

'Okay then, now that we're all up to speed we can get on to the real reason for the meeting,' said Anna. 'We need a debate about how we can go about repopulation.'

'Perhaps we should be more specific,' said Carmen, 'how we go about freeing everyone from this *Neverness* place.'

'The question is, do we want to?' said William.

'We cannot just leave zem, zey must come out,' said Xenia.

'It's not that easy. For one thing there's law and order. We've got our own survival to consider.'

'Yeah, we don't want to be freeing axe murderers or loonies,' said Mike.

'Or police, or government employees for that matter,' he added. 'They'd just start the elitist state thing all over again.'

'Hmm, you do have a point,' said Danii, 'but there must be a lot of good people in there.'

'Well, we've come up with a plan already,' said William.

'Have we?' said Mike.

'Yes, you know...bringing individuals out and interviewing them?'

'How would that work?' asked Carmen.

'Umm, well, we thought that if they were nice, roundy...er, I mean ordinary, ordinary unassuming people, then we could let them stay. What do you think about that then?'

'And the meek shall inherit the earth.'

'Quite.'

'No, you're going to have to release everybody, so it'll be back to normal,' insisted Anna.

'But it wouldn't be back to normal, would it?' argued William. 'We had a society that protected us then.'

'Anyway, there could be millions of people in there, it'll be impossible to get them all out,' added Mike.

'Oh really, why's that?' asked Anna disbelievingly.

'Well, for a start you have to attach a clip to each individual. Only then can he or she be recovered. Even if we could retrieve a hundred people a day, which we couldn't, we still wouldn't get them all out in our lifetime.'

'That problem's easily solved. We bring a hundred people out, make a hundred more of your kits and get everyone onto the job of retrieving.'

'Not possible. I need specialised components. I've only got a few spares. We'd have to manufacture some very complex chips. It would have to be done inside ultra-clean sealed labs as well. It's just not feasible, it would take decades.'

'There are other problems too,' he pointed out. 'Each person we recover will want us to find their friends and relatives. It'll be awful, we'll spend the rest of our lives being harangued about getting old Mrs Fudges out next because she's got a gammy foot, or Mary's uncle Nobby because he's good with roses. It'll be a nightmare. We could even end up with a situation where we release a woman, but can't find her husband for another ten years.'

'So?' snapped Anna.

'Well, she'll have aged, he won't have. He'll start chasing younger women.'

'He'd do that anyway,' said Danii.

'Taking it to extremes,' he continued, 'children could end up older than their parents.'

'Hmm, you're right, it's not that simple, is it?' she conceded.

'Also, there are always troublemakers in any group. There could be total anarchy.'

'I agree with Victor. We might even end up losing Poffington,' said

William. 'It's far too dangerous to go bringing people back willy-nilly. I think we should put this idea of yours on hold sis, until you've had time to think it through.'

'Suppose so,' said Anna sulkily.

'Just one thing before we finish,' said Stefan, 'I wonder if you'd mind looking out for some of our boyfriends? They're nice people, they won't give you any trouble. I'll nip upstairs and get their photos.'

'Ooo, I can think of a few others to look out for as well,' said Marco, 'we won't be a minute.'

Most of the pictures that Marco produced had been cut from glossy magazines. The girls also deluged them with photos and he was feeling more and more under pressure.

'Hang on, hang on!' he said. 'That's enough for the time being.'

'Yes, quite,' agreed William, scooping the cuttings into a carrier bag with his arm. 'We'll get all confused if you give us any more. We'll start searching the next time we do a mission. Come on Mike, Victor, we've got work to do.'

They entered the workshop and William dumped the bag on a bench.

'What are we going to do with all these?' said Mike, pulling out a handful.

'We'll have to get a sheet of ply and stick them on...a *Blokeboard*.'

'Are you mental Ogroid, or perhaps you're turning gay?' said William, throwing the bag into an old metal cabinet. 'There, that's where they belong. Now then, whose turn to roll one?'

'Another? We've only just recovered from the last lot,' said Mike. 'I think we should find the girls a bloke first, keep them sweet.'

A short time later, an interview was going exceptionally well with a spotty geek called Hector Gerbill.

'So, you're a computer buff then?'

'Yeah, I can do anything. It's what I do all day, every day. I've got my own web business.'

'Do you have any other interests, girls for instance?'

'Umm, no. Is that a problem?'

'Not at all. Not gay, are you?'

'No.'

'Well, I think you're just the sort of chap we're looking for. We can set you up with a flashy car and you can do what you want. There'll be a few bits of work from time to time of course.'

They proudly presented Hector to the girls and because he was such a goof, they saw no reason why Anna's idea of giving him one of the large attic rooms couldn't go ahead.

'Hmm, perhaps we should set up a special house just for blokes?' he suggested, as they traipsed back to the workshop.

'Yes, miles away from the hotel…and Poffington,' agreed William. 'Still, we can see to that some other time. Let's do a few more sorties.'

William soon returned with a middle-aged man. After taking a good long look, he thought there was something familiar about him. He grabbed William's arm and led him outside.

'What is the matter with you, Victor?'

'That's Erin Freewitt, isn't it?'

'Yes, he's my favourite author. He lives in a shack somewhere in Andorra.'

'He went to prison, didn't he? What do you want with a criminal?'

'He's no more a criminal than I am. Convicted on a technicality, that's all.'

'A technicality? If I remember rightly, he entered that big prize quiz show on television under his real name, Simon Dander, and went on to choose the novels of Erin Freewitt as his specialised subject!'

'So what? You're a thief too.'

'Look, you're forgetting that I'm entitled to it. It was me that got the certificate from Downing Street saying that I was in charge.'

'Oh yes, *this woman*, ha, ha, ha!'

'That was an unfortunate mistake. Sorry, he's going back.'

'Oh, all right. I expect he's too old for the girls anyway.'

For once he wasn't looking forward to his turn because it meant fishing for blokes. However, almost immediately he saw Sheil floating a little way ahead.

'I've got her, I've got her!'

'Who?'

'Sheil! Sheil the sop pinger!'

'Sop pinger? Oh, pop singer. I'm getting the hang of this now,' said William.

He sat in the module unable to take his eyes off her.

'Hello Sheil,' he said, giving her a little wave. 'Er, I can call you Sheil, can't I?'

'Yeah, course you can. What am I doing here then? I should be in make-up for the gig right now. Who are you?'

'Well, something really weird has happened, I'll explain…'

She listened carefully to the news, took it all in and even seemed quite cool about it.

'So you're the only ones left then?'

'No, no,' said William. 'There's a whole bunch of other girls. Some of them are models…and actresses, but they're away at the moment, and there are a few chaps as well…oh, and four people in Germany.'

'And some animals,' he added. 'William, why don't you nip over to the house and break the news? I'll take Sheil to the hotel while Mike checks the equipment.'

He showed her to a nice room above the restaurant, which Jasmine offered to clean while they had a drink in the bar. Ernest already seemed a bit merry, which was surprising because it had only just gone five o'clock, but he did agree to cook whatever she wanted, as long as it was steak.

'Would you like me to go and find you some new clothes?' he offered.

'Yeah, that would be great, obviously I haven't got anything with me.'

'Where were you staying before this happened?'

'In London. I've got an apartment in the West End. What part of the country are we in then?'

'Oxfordshire. I can show you around one day, if you want? Right, I'd better be off. I'll be back with some clothes soon.'

He sped into town and set about selecting something suitable before the light went. Returning to the car, he was surprised to bump into somebody he knew in the High Street.

'Hello Hector, have you settled in okay?'

'Yes thanks. I was just getting myself some things. It is okay, isn't it?'

'Sure, just help yourself.'

'I'll have to go home and collect my own stuff sometime.'

'So, where's home?'

'I've got a flat in Portsmouth...tiny. That attic room's twice the size. What have you got there?'

'Umm, a mini-skirt and a spaghetti strap vest thing. Not for me, you understand! We've just retrieved Sheil, the pop singer. I'll introduce you to her.'

'Excellent, I'm a real fan! Still, better get off, I've got loads more to get.'

'Yeah, I'm in a hurry too. See you around.'

Pleased with his selection, he paused outside her door and took a deep breath before knocking.

'Hello again. I've got your clothes.'

'Oh Victor, it's a bit chilly to only be wearing that.'

'Sorry, it's all I could find.'

'Oh, they'll do for now. If you could get me a jumper and some jeans, I'd be grateful.'

'Would you? We can go shopping tomorrow, if you like?'

'Yeah, I might just take you up on that, thanks. If you'll excuse me now I think I'll get changed. Thanks again, see you later.'

After she'd closed her door, he realised there was little point in hanging around and left before the models caught him. Going up the driveway, he saw a pair of headlights flash past the entrance, then the glow of brake lights. A vehicle reversed and hesitantly turned in. He pulled over and the car stopped alongside. It was the actresses.

'Hello,' he said, winding down his window.

'Oh, we thought we'd never find you again,' said Natasha, looking relieved. 'We've been driving around for ages.'

'How was your trip?'

'Creepy, everywhere was deserted, so we decided to come back.'

'Things have improved here. We've got a chef now, his name's Ernest. Just tell him when you're ready to eat…and there's a chambermaid called Jasmine. Oh, Sheil the pop singer is staying too, she's in room eight.'

'That's great! We'll go and say hello.'

'Yeah, see you soon, bye.'

He walked into the workshop thinking that things were really looking up.

'Where the hell have you been?' asked William.

'Oh, I had to get Sheil some clothes. So, were the girls annoyed?'

'Pulled a few faces. Gina seemed the most pleased. Said they'd call in and introduce themselves later.'

'The actresses are back, by the way. Bumped into them as I was leaving. I think they're intending to stay, the car was full of gear.'

'That was to be expected I suppose. At least they're polite and more self-sufficient than the models. Now then, where's that suit? There's time for another sortie before supper.'

William had been unusually quiet for the duration of his trip, but then suddenly broke through on the radio.

'I've bot the gastard!'

'Total gibberish,' said Mike, shaking his head. 'Sorry William, what was that?'

'I've bot the gastard, you'll see! Now get me out quick!'

A decrepit, miserable-looking man of about ninety appeared in the cage.

'Who the hell is that old fart?' he asked.

'It's Judge Addlematter! The bastard who ordered the estate to be taken from me. I've got him. Ha, brilliant!'

There was a loud snort and the judge woke up.

'Order! Order in court! Now, as far as I can see this is a cut and dried case. The marijuana plants have obviously been grown for sale and distribution, making you a drug trafficker! I therefore have no option other than to sentence you to life imprisonment! Next case!'

'Shut up fart face!' he shouted, as William looked on gleefully.

'You! You there!' said the judge, pointing him out. 'How dare you speak to me like that in court? Intolerable insolence! Take him down officers, two life sentences for you!'

'Are you stupid or something?' he replied. 'Don't you even realise this isn't a courtroom?'

'Good one Victor,' said William.

'So it's not,' said the judge, casting a quick eye at the bars of the cage. 'Ah, so I must be on a tour of a prison and you must be three inmates. Criminals that I've sent down most probably. I'll have a word with the chief warden on my way out, get your privileges taken away.'

'You're the one behind bars, dimwit!' said William, joining in.

There was a brief silence as the judge took a closer look at his surroundings.

'This is outrageous! I've been kidnapped! No matter, you'll be caught and I'll make sure that you all rot in jail for this. I demand to be set free. I order you to set me free at once! Be sensible, if you let me go now, I give you my word I won't jail you for longer than ten years each. In effect, I'll be letting you off.'

'Look fat face,' said William.

'Fart face,' he corrected.

'Yes, I mean fart face. If you don't shut up, I'll come in there and gag you.'

Within a minute, the judge sat tied to the chair, gagged.

'What are we going to do with him?' asked Mike, as the judge struggled with muffled objection.

'He'll stand trial for being an incompetent idiot. Hmm, Xenia was a law student, she can help. Oh, what a good day this has turned out to be! Now then, I'll start planning my case while you lock him up in a police cell.'

By the time they'd returned, supper was being served. William was very pleased with himself because he'd already set a date for the trial. Xenia was going to be prosecuting on William's behalf and Sazoa had offered to be court clerk.

It had seemed like an extraordinarily long day, but far from being tired he had an abundance of energy. He decided that tonight would be a good time to start acquiring some precious stones and maybe some more gold. First, he needed something to put it all in and decided to fetch an old wooden chest he'd seen in the workshop attic. Unfortunately, Carmen saw him as he was struggling across the hallway.

'Looks heavy,' she observed. 'You'll have a parrot on your shoulder next. Did you fill the hole in?'

'Ha, got away with it. What does she mean, a parrot on my shoulder? And what's this hole she's talking about?'

He manoeuvred the chest into a corner and then placed his stash of coins inside.

'Hmm, not so good. Looks like it's been raided. Right, London it is then, get a shit-load to fill it up.'

Not wanting to disturb Jappa from his sleep, he set off alone, arriving in the capital shortly before two in the morning. He cut the engine, turned off the headlights and rolled to a stop. According to his *A to Z*, the *Banque de Europas* sat at the top of the street on the right. He felt excited. This was the same bank that had been robbed in one of his favourite films, *Broke Bloke and Two Sticks of Dynamite*.

Taking the kit bag, he unwrapped a new packet of tights and pulled them over his head. He walked quietly towards the building, all the time ready to jump into a doorway if he was surprised. He stopped dead in his tracks…a huge pile of debris was scattered across the pavement. He could feel his heart thumping as he clutched the shotgun to his chest. Kicking a couple of bricks to the side, he gazed into the shattered entrance. A large shadow loomed in front of him.

'**Whhuuhhh!**' they exclaimed in unison.

In a moment of terror, the shotgun went off, hitting a vehicle that had been left slewed across the road.

'William?'

'Oh, it's you Victor! Oh, my poor little heart, you gave me such a fright. Damn you! My *Fido* has been peppered with shot. Look, one of the tyres is flat and there's liquid dripping from underneath.'

'Oh stop fussing, it's nothing,' he said, flashing his torch over the damage.

'You're changing that wheel, mark my words. What are you doing here anyway? Especially with those tights over your head. Pervert!'

'I am not a pervert.'

'It was you that stole Marco's tights, wasn't it?'

'No. Anyway, you're just as bad, you've got some hanging out of your pocket.'

'No, no, that's a knee support. Been playing me up again recently.'

'So, robbing this bank, are you?'

'Robbing it? I'm not robbing it. I was just passing and saw the doors open. Thought that I might as well…'

'What a load of rubbish, you were robbing it!'

'So what if I was?'

'What did you get?'

'Nothing.'

'Nothing?'

'No. I can't get in properly.'

He looked over at the demolished entrance.

'It looks like you've had a bit more success than you're admitting to.'

'Yes, but I still can't get in. The dynamite on the internal door won't go bang.'

'You've been using dynamite?'

'You can't expect me to bash my way in with a sledgehammer, can you? Not with my bad back…and knee.'

'Anyway, what do you mean, it wouldn't go bang?'

'I pressed the button, but nothing happened.'

'Great, a botched job.'

'Let's go home.'

'Go home? We can't just leave it.'

'Why not?'

'Because somebody might blow themselves to smithereens, that's why. Right, you hold the torch and I'll take a look. Now show me where it is.'

He tentatively followed William across the lobby to the staff entrance. At the bottom of the door were two sticks of dynamite.

'Oh look, the detonator's hanging out. I'll stick it back in,' offered William.

'Leave it alone idiot, I'll deal with it.'

After the explosion, they waited for the dust to settle.

'Come on then, we'll rob it together,' he said.

'Oh goody! I say this is exciting! Ooo, we can call ourselves *Smarglebolt and Ogfoot*.'

'Er…nah.'

They arrived home just as it was getting light. Ahead of him a thin mist hung over the lake looking tranquil and serene, but on checking his mirror, he could see that William was still angry. Unbeknown to him, the *Fido* had spluttered to a stop on the Westway and he'd got as far as High Wycombe before he'd realised it was missing. By the time he'd retraced his route, William was hopping mad. He'd soon discovered that the fuel tank had more holes than a colander, so to save himself from further abuse he'd pretended the vehicle had an electrical fault. He'd suggested that they dump it, but William had insisted on being towed back to Poffington.

There was a stony silence as he separated out the crates of gold and bags of loot into two piles. They used two padlocks on the workshop doors, each retaining a key so the stash couldn't be tampered with until they were both present. William went off to his room in a temper, so he collected the dogs from the Winter Garden for an early morning walk.

Later, he lay on his bed admiring the little house he'd built Jappa, which stood over in the far corner near the window beside his treasure chest. It was actually just a small wooden shed, but he'd divided it into two floors, put some stairs in and with a few bits of tiny furniture scattered around, it resembled a giant doll's house. He'd also been quite busy training Jappa, who could already make tea, operate a remote control and use a proper toilet. All in all, he was very pleased with his monkey.

Although he hadn't slept, he was fed up with fidgeting about and decided that he might as well get dressed. He splashed his face and looked despairingly in the mirror. Several clumps of hair were sticking up and wouldn't stay down when he tried to flatten them. In fact, it hadn't been right since he'd over-washed it after the incident with the tights.

Just before lunch he trotted downstairs and immediately spotted William standing with the cellar door open, peering down into the blackness. He wondered if he was still in a bad mood.

'**Boo!**'

'**Ahhhhh!** Oh, I hate it when people creep up like that.'

'What are you doing?'

'Shhh!'

They listened together.

'What is it?'

'Someone's in the cellar.'

'Are you sure?'

'Yes. Look, if that damn monkey's down there Victor, I don't know what I'm going to do.'

'Well, he's not. I've just come from my room, he's asleep in his bed.'

'In his bed?'

'Yeah, I made him one, it's inside his little house.'

'How extraordinary. Well, I don't think there's anybody down there after all, but I do need some better lights fixing up, see to it will you?'

'What for? The lights are perfectly all right. You're just a coward.'

'No I am not! Don't start winding me up, I'm not in the mood for it. I've hardly had a wink of sleep and it's making me feel irritable.'

They wandered through to the kitchen and found Danii busy rolling out pastry.

'Want a drink William?'

'Yes.'

'Yes, what?'

'Yes I do want a bloody drink…and hurry up, I'm parched.'

'What about you Danii?'

'No, I'm okay thanks, had one just before. William, what is the matter with you? Stop jigging about.'

'Fuck you and fuck your pie! I was only trying to help!'

'By getting in my way and shaking the counter?'

'Why are you so horrid? Nothing I ever do is right! You always have to pick on me. Pick, pick, pick!'

Danii raised her eyebrows as William stormed off. He sat at the kitchen table drinking his coffee, self-consciously trying to smooth his unruly hair. He thought he caught her staring at it, so decided to see if Marco would cut it for him straight away.

'Oh dear, what's happened to you then?'

'I slept on it funny, that's all.'

'You look like a guinea pig. It's swirling around all over the place. What a mess. Come on, let's get it washed and conditioned, then perhaps we can sort it out.'

An hour later Marco was still snipping bits off.

'Ah, there you are Victor, been looking for you everywhere,' said William, popping his head inside the door.

'Yeah, just having a trim so it's tidy for my birthday tomorrow.'

'I've just come from the hotel. Seems they've got a problem with the water again, you'd better get over there and see to it. They're creating merry hell.'

Parking by the front entrance, he reluctantly went inside. Indala was sitting on Pershia's lap in an armchair by the inglenook, and he sensed their aggression before they even spoke.

'Umm, what seems to be the problem?'

'This hotel is useless! The hot water's stopped now!' shouted Pershia. 'We were all soapy in the shower when it suddenly went cold. Can you imagine what that was like? Can you?'

'I'm trying…'

'It was agony rinsing off. My nipples are still hurting.'

'Yeah? Go on.'

'What do you mean, *go on*? Get it fixed!'

'Umm, the boiler's probably gone out. I'll check it over.'

'And be quick about it!'

He went down to the basement, opened the boiler room door and was horrified to see that it had flooded. A fountain of water gushed from the calcified lump on the wall. He went to break the news.

'It looks like you need a new boiler.'

'You mean *you* need a new boiler! So, how long will it take?'

'Can't really say at the moment.'

'You're hopeless. What are we meant to do in the meantime?'

'Er, you could heat some water up in a saucepan.'

'Oh, this is intolerable!'

'I'm sorry, but you'll have to wait until it's fixed. I'll get to work right away though.'

'Yes, you'd better!'

Returning to the basement, he set up a pond pump to deal with the flooding. The level was draining quite slowly, so he thought he might as well have a walk in the garden rather than stand there watching. As he sauntered around, he noticed how overgrown everything was. He glanced up at the windows and caught an unexpected glimpse of Jasmine's boobs as she pulled on a T-shirt.

'*Cor, wouldn't mind getting all soapy with her! I'll have to make a move soon.*

Must think of a chat-up line first though.'

By mid afternoon he'd managed to detach the old unit from the wall. It was in a terrible condition, in fact the only thing holding it together was the lime scale crust. He dragged it out to his van and set off to look for something similar. He had quite a problem finding one because it was a much bigger unit normally used for houses, but smaller than those designed for industrial purposes. By the time he'd located one it was too late to fit, as he had to get back for dinner, so he just dumped it by the basement steps.

'Here's the new one. I'll fit it tomorrow. Oh no wait, I can't tomorrow, it's my birthday. I'll do it on Wednesday then.'

'I don't care if it's your birthday or not,' said Pershia. 'I want this fixed, understand?'

'And what are we supposed to do about showers this evening?' added Indala.

'You could use my bathroom if you want.'

'Okay. Indala, get your things together.'

'Er, later would be better. I might have to clean up a bit first.'

'Well hard luck, we're coming now.'

'I came in my old van, you won't want to travel in that, will you? I'll go and fetch something more suitable.'

'We're filthy already so it won't make any difference.'

He was relieved that no one had seen them enter the house. They went up in the lift and he chivvied them along to his room. As he closed his door he kept an eye on the suitcase full of rubbish, hoping it wouldn't fall over again. The models were sure to be offended by the contents should they spill out and he resolved to make an effort to get rid of it soon.

'What is that awful smell?' asked Pershia, pulling a face.

'That'll be my monkey.'

'Is this the bathroom?' said Indala, trying the handle. 'It's locked!'

'Er, wait a sec,' he said, giving a little knock. 'Jappa? Jappa, daddy's home.'

The sound of the toilet flushing preceded the key turning. The door opened and Jappa jumped up into his arms.

'Oh, the smell!' said Indala, as she went in holding her nose. 'It's filthy! Urrgghh, there are streaks in the toilet!'

'They were there when I moved in,' he lied.

'Come on Pershia, there must be a cleaner bathroom somewhere in this place.'

He watched them disappear down the hallway, too embarrassed to follow. For a few minutes he contemplated cleaning the toilet in order to get them back, but in the end decided that it wasn't worth the effort.

'Hmm, I should have taken them to a guestroom,' he thought, slumping

onto the bed. *'Damn, why didn't I think of that at the time?'*

Half an hour later he was still sitting on his bed daydreaming about showers, when he heard shouting coming from the direction of the main staircase. Going to investigate, he realised that one of the voices was Gina's.

'You 'ave used my towels, it is disgusting! I will 'ave to burn zem!'

'Oh, yours were they? Yes, I thought they smelt of cheap scent.'

'I will 'ave to disinfect everyzing!'

'Use your perfume darling, it smells like it was designed for the job.'

'You are a toffee nosed beech, zat is all. Why do you not return to your sordid little 'otel and per'aps do us all a big favour and stay zare!'

'We were leaving anyway, you tart! Where's that chauffeur?'

Chapter 7

He was woken on the morning of his thirtieth birthday by a gentle push on the shoulder. Screwing up his face, all bleary eyed, he struggled to pull the figure into focus. It was Jappa, carrying a breakfast tray. He led there hoping that Gina would appear like last year. It didn't happen, so after drinking his monkey's tea, which was actually much better than Gina's, he got out of bed to see what the day would bring.

Throughout the morning he became increasingly put out because he hadn't been taken for another lap dance. By lunchtime, the likelihood of it happening was fading fast and he sat silently at the kitchen table listening to the others, feeling a bit sorry for himself.

'Mike, I've noticed that our frozen food is being depleted rather rapidly with all these newcomers. We haven't got a limitless supply. Once it's gone, that's it.'

'Hmm, good point Carmen.'

'Oh dear, how much is left?' asked William.

'If we carry on at this rate we'll probably run out of most meat and fish by the end of February.'

'Damn, should have got more when we had the chance. Now it's all rotted.'

'Well, we weren't to know, were we?' said Danii.

'Still, on the bright side, the vegetable garden is very productive and we're getting the surplus frozen,' continued Carmen. 'Our potato crop is really good too, so we're not going to starve. Having said that though, the day will come when all tinned and dried food will be out of date. We're going to have to become totally self-sufficient.'

'Shit, what will my dogs eat?' he thought.

'Wait a minute, I've got a brilliant idea!' said Mike. 'There are massive stocks of canned and packet foods in warehouses all over the country. All we have to do is send it into the *Neverness*. Then we can recover it when it's needed.'

'Not going to save our bacon though, is it?' said William glumly.

'We could easily retrieve some pigs.'

'Yes, but who'll do the deed?' asked Anna, looking around. 'See, none of us will kill for meat.'

'We'll just have to wait until one dies of old age then, won't we?'

'Urrgghh, that's disgusting William!' said Carmen. 'How would you know it wasn't diseased?'

'Perhaps we could run one over then, you know, like in an accident?'

'Right, I'll make a start on this new project tomorrow,' said Mike, ignoring William.

'I'll give you a hand,' offered Carmen. 'Hey, we can send in all kinds of things, like medicines and seeds.'

'Yeah you're right, everything will eventually perish. We'll have to organise crates of electrical components and other stuff like car tyres and rubber seals. The sooner we make a start the better, everything's been lying around for a year already.'

He wasn't really in the birthday mood and decided that he might as well fit the new boiler. It was actually much easier than he'd expected, and after firing it up, he even managed to sneak away without bumping into the models.

By early evening everyone had gathered in the sitting room, where a large pile of presents was waiting for him. One smallish box had been wrapped in brown paper and was signed, *from Serge*. It was very light and didn't rattle. He turned it over and noticed a corner was missing from the bottom. He ripped it open.

'It's empty.'

'Oui. Zare was a mouse inside…it escape.'

The girls all screamed and jumped up in panic, brushing down their legs whilst frantically looking around the floor.

'Great, thanks,' he said sarcastically.

'Dog merchant.'

Fortunately, some of his other presents were much better. As usual Mike had given him the best gift, a car-transporter full of classic cars, which he'd have great pleasure in adding to his collection.

His party was well under way by the time the hotel group arrived. Ernest already looked a bit wobbly, but still managed to stagger directly to the drinks table as if he'd been there before. The models just stood inside the doorway staring at the ceiling until Marco approached them with a bottle of champagne. Gina accosted Sheil and the actresses, while Jasmine looked around the room as if searching for someone. When she caught sight of him she came straight over, clutching a carrier bag.

'Happy Birthday Victor,' she said, giving him a peck on the cheek.

'Oh, thanks Jasmine. You needn't have got me anything,' he said, taking the bag.

'No, it's not a present, it's Pershia's hairdryer. She asked for a new one, but I thought you might be able to fix it.'

'Oh right. Yeah, I'll do it tomorrow, it's probably just the fuse. Can I get you a drink?'

'Ooo, yes please.'

Being jostled from all sides, they fought their way to the drinks table.

'What would you like?'

'A beer if you've got one.'

'Would you like a glass?'

'Nah, I don't mind, in the bottle will be okay.'

'Ah, there you are,' said Pershia, appearing at his side.

'Oh, hello.'

'Where's my new hairdryer?'

'Umm, need a bit more time. Shouldn't be a problem though.'

'It had better not be! And listen, we demand some different food. That chef only cooks steak.'

'I'll have a word with him… Oh look, there he is, I'll speak to him now.'

He smiled at Jasmine as he led her through the hordes towards Ernest, who was leaning against the wall swigging from a bottle.

'Victor, Victor,' said Nadesche, squeezing in, 'we want some music, but it is your party so we ask first. Is it okay?'

'Sure, go ahead.'

'Ooo, zank you. You are a kind boy,' she said kissing him on both cheeks, before vanishing into the crowd.

'Ah Ernest. The models are getting fed up with the choice of food. The quality's fine, it's just that they'd like something different.'

'Oh aye? Snotty nosed bitches, they are. I worked in a steak house, me. It's the only thing I can cook. Tell them if they want something else they can get it themselves.'

There was an ear-piercing screech of feedback before the music kicked in. He turned around to see Serge standing over a turntable deck shaking his head, headphones pressed to one ear. Xenia and the sisters skipped off to dance, dragging a few people with them. It was extremely loud, but at least he didn't feel so hemmed in.

'Can't you do macaroni cheese or something?'

'What? I can't hear no more, not with this bloody racket.'

'Can you cook macaroni cheese?' he shouted.

'Look pal, I do twenty-eight varieties of steak, me. They can like it or lump it. Now leave me alone, you're stopping me from drinking.'

He was feeling stressed, the models were ruining his party. He went upstairs to look at the hairdryer and took the opportunity to roll himself a joint. Wafting away the smoke, he prised the fuse from the plug. It was fine, so he concluded that the problem must be internal. He took a long drag, blew it out slowly and then pushed the window open to get some fresh air. After carefully unscrewing the outer casing, he flicked the clip with a screwdriver to release the motor brushes, only to see them shoot out into the darkness.

'Fuck!'

Jappa appeared at an upper window of his shed looking irritated and snatched the curtains closed.

'Sorry Jappa,' he whispered.

He stuffed all the bits back into the bag and quietly left the room. He went directly to the workshop and after only a few minutes found what he was looking for…a heat gun. It was designed for stripping paint, but in an emergency could easily double as a hairdryer, and this was an emergency. He had another joint while he decided if this was his best course of action and in the end concluded it was.

Rejoining the party, he constantly had to duck and dive to avoid the models.

'Ah, there you are Ogroid! Have you fixed my *LandFido* yet?'

'No, I haven't had time, I had to replace that boiler. Why don't you go to the showroom and get a new one?'

'Because there aren't any in the right colour. I only like the green ones, you know that.'

'Oh, I'll get one from Swindon for you, they're sure to have one there.'

Just then he unluckily made eye contact with Pershia. She pointed a finger and mouthed, *You, here, now!* As he shuffled towards her, Xenia intercepted him.

'Victor, come and dance.'

'Umm, later perhaps? I've just got to sort something out, trouble with the models again, you know,' he said, giving her a pathetic smile.

Xenia danced her way back to the sisters and he braced himself before facing Pershia.

'Umm, er, I've replaced that hairdryer, there's a new one in this bag.'

'Good. What about the food situation?'

'I've spoken to Ernest and I'm afraid he only cooks steak.'

'Look here!' she said, breaking from her clutch with Indala. 'We're sick to death with meat, we want something different, do you understand?'

'Yes, I do. Actually I'm considering employing another chef, just for variety. It might take a few days though.'

'So Victor,' said Gina stepping in, 'why are you wasting your time talking wiz zese 'orrible beeches?'

'Look, just do us all a favour darling and fuck off!' snapped Pershia. 'The hotel food has nothing to do with you.'

'Oui, you are right. I 'ave no interest in what you are eating. You can eat each ozer for all I care, but zen again, you probably are.'

'Listen you foreign cow, our sex life is a private matter!' shouted Indala.

'Stupid bimbos, I 'ate you.'

He quickly guided Gina away to the drinks table. Sazoa then pushed into him, giggling as William chased after her with a manic look on his face.

'Zis 'ouse is becoming more disgusting each day.'

'Gina, I'm sorry about the models. I'll try and keep them away from the house in future.'

'Why do you 'ave interest in such people?'

'Well, er…'

'Ah oui, do not bozer to explain. What 'az 'appened Victor? We used to 'ave such fun togezer.'

'What are you two up to?' slurred Mike as he staggered past, clinging on to Carmen.

'We've had a bit too much to drink,' she said with a wry smile. 'I'm taking him up to bed.'

'Oh right, goodnight then.'

'Oui, do not do anyzing zat we would not do.'

'What's that then?' he asked.

'Come, we 'ave anozer drink. We will see.'

He was having more and more fun with Gina as the party progressed. In fact it was just like old times and he felt certain he'd score. By three in the morning practically everyone had retired, so he thought he might as well try his luck.

'Do you want to go up to my room?'

'Oui, why not? You go and I will join you in a few minutes. I 'ave a little surprise. Do not fall asleep.'

'Not a chance!'

He bounded up the stairs two at a time and raced along to his room. He stood inside the door looking around at the mess, then quickly kicked all the dirty clothes into a corner. The lighting was far too bright, so he improvised something more subdued. Little snoring noises were coming from inside Jappa's shed, indicating that he was asleep and unlikely to be a nuisance.

'This is it! I wonder what outfit she'll be wearing this year?' he thought, tearing off his clothes and jumping into bed.

He lay there waiting for a few moments and then noticed that the pants covering the lamp had started to give off a strange odour. He reached over and knocked them onto the floor.

'Ah, much better. I'll be able to see everything as well now.'

He waited and waited, but still she didn't come. Eventually he went along to her room, tapped on the door and tried the handle. It was locked and the house was in darkness. She must have forgotten and gone to sleep. Upset and dejected, he returned to his room and slumped on the bed.

In the morning he awoke alone, feeling really disappointed.

'Why the hell didn't she turn up? Must have been just teasing me. Probably ended up with Xenia again. Perhaps she really is a lesbo. But then again, if she is, she'd be a bit more tolerant of the models. Whatever the reason, it doesn't

explain why she led me on like that. Cruel…especially on my birthday.'

He swallowed a couple of pills with a mouthful of water from the tap and ventured downstairs. Crossing the hallway he heard a strange noise coming from the cellar door.

'Hello?'

'Victor? Victor, is zat you?' came the muffled reply.

'**Gina?** What are you doing in there?'

'It is zat idiot William. I 'ave come down 'ere last night to bring us some champagne and 'e 'az locked ze door and gone to bed. I am so cold, 'urry, get ze key.'

'Oh, that dickhead! I'll smash his fucking face in!'

He finally found William pacing up and down outside the library door wearing a black gown and wig.

'Ah, there you are Ogroid. I could have done with your help half an hour ago. Wrenched my back setting up the courtroom. It's almost ten, the trial's due to start shortly.'

'You fucking idiot, Smargle!'

'What?'

'You are a complete moron! Gina's locked in the cellar, isn't she? Been down there all night!'

'Oh dear. I wonder how that happened?'

William rushed to the cellar door and fumbled with the lock. Gina stood there looking dishevelled and cold.

'Idiot! Merde!'

'What were you doing in there anyway?'

'I wanted champagne, is zat a problem?'

'Stealing, were you?'

'You are such a dickhead William. Didn't it occur to you to check it was empty before you locked up?'

'There shouldn't be anyone down there, full stop. Anyway, why are you so annoyed? Gina's the one who's suffered.'

'Oui. Out of my way. I am going to 'ave a shower and go to bed.'

'Do you want me to help you?' he asked hopefully.

'Non. Ze moment 'az passed.'

He watched her cross the hallway wondering if he'd ever get another chance. William locked the door, then gave it a final push to satisfy himself it was secure.

'So, where is he then?'

'Who?'

'Addlematter of course, who do you think?'

'He's still locked up, isn't he? You never said I had to collect him. Anyway, I thought you were going to hold the trial at the police station?'

'No, I've got it all set up in the library. Damn, now there'll be an

114

adjournment before I've even started. Go and get him then.'

'Go and get him yourself.'

'I can't, can I? I don't know where you've put him.'

'What? Who's been feeding him then?'

'I thought you and Muffton were taking care of that?'

'We thought you were doing it!'

'Oh dear, he'll have starved to death.'

'No, it's only three days. Nobody in history has starved to death in such a short space of time.'

'Did you leave him any water?'

'Umm...'

'Well that's just brilliant, isn't it? He'll be dead and I'll have been cheated from my revenge. Come on, we'd better go and see what state he's in.'

After the short drive into the city, they entered the spookily silent police station and went down to the cells.

'Water...ugghh...water.'

'Get him out and give him a drink, Victor. Then get that stupid cloak and wig off and put him in this orange boiler suit...and chain his ankles.'

Shortly before eleven he took his place in the library, where everyone had assembled waiting for the trial to begin.

'All rise for Judge Smargle,' called Sazoa.

William strode in from a side door, looking very severe.

'Be seated. Bring the prisoner in!'

There was a lot of bumping and bashing from behind the doors before Mike pushed Addlematter into the room, strapped in a wheelchair.

'That's pathetic. Feigning illness won't make me feel sorry for you,' snarled William.

'He's too weak to walk,' explained Mike, positioning the wheelchair in the dock.

'Cecil Addlematter, you are on trial today for the hideous crime of making wrong judgements. How do you plead, guilty or not guilty?'

'You can't try me, I'm the judge here. Arrest that impostor at once!'

'Silence in court! How do you plead, guilty or not guilty?'

'Not guilty of course you blithering idiot! Now let me go. I've been starved for days by these kidnappers. When I instruct the newspapers to write this story, the public will probably have a vote to bring back hanging. You'll be...'

'Be quiet you wizened old fool!'

'You can't speak to me like that!'

'I think I just did. Right Addlematter, you've had your chance, I'm putting a gagging order on you. Victor!'

After a minor scuffle, the job was done.

'Now then, who is acting in your defence?' resumed William.

'Ummugghh, ummmuuugghh!'

'Nobody, good. Who's prosecuting on my behalf?'

'I am your 'onour.'

'Thank you Xenia. Please proceed.'

'You are ze judge zat 'az ruled in favour of ze case two years ago between ze state and William Smargle, oui?'

'Ummugghh.'

'Zat is all, zank you.'

'Cecil Addlematter, you are a grotty little man and the ugliest I have ever seen in my courtroom. You are a twisted, corrupt, evil person and I have great pleasure in convicting you for making wrong judgements. I have taken into consideration some of your other cases and can only conclude that you're insane and should therefore be institutionalised. Given that there are no loony bins to put you in, I have no option other than to give you a life sentence, *suspended* for infinity. Take him down!'

William strode ahead with his gown flapping in the wind as he and Mike pushed Addlematter across the lawn.

'Hey, perhaps we should put a traffic cone on his head so he'll be readily identifiable in future.'

'Ooo, good idea Mike, I like it,' said William, rubbing his hands together. 'There are a couple knocking about by the stables, go and get one. In fact, any other rejects could get the same treatment, couldn't they? Ooo, this is getting better and better! Later, go and get a load of cones from the council depot, I'll probably need them. Oh, and keep an eye out for that Wilberforce ginger freak while you're driving around. I want to take him to court as well.'

'What for?'

'For being a taxman of course!'

Mike came running back with a cone and jammed it on Addlematter's head.

'Good riddance then Addlebrain, hopefully never see you again,' William said gleefully, as the judge disappeared. 'Well, that's that idiot gone. Let's go and have a celebratory drink.'

'Not for me thanks,' said Mike. 'Carmen and I are going to collect some packing boxes, we want to make a start on the supplies. See you later.'

'Just you and me then Victor, let's get sloshed.'

By the time he'd got up the following morning the house was a hive of activity. While most of the others were running relays to various warehouses, the sisters were in the ballroom sorting and labelling the stock. His job was to wheel the packed boxes to the workshop, where Mike was sending them into the *Neverness* by the pallet load.

The operation was going well until William appeared, wanting to hold an emergency meeting.

'We're a bit busy, can't it wait?' said Mike, just as another batch was swallowed by a green flash.

'Don't worry about that, I've called a halt to the proceedings, told everyone that all the noise was giving me a headache. They've all gone to the kitchen for lunch. Anyway, I think we've done enough work for today. Now then, it's obvious to me that we haven't got a hope in hell of scoring with these celebrity retrievals...'

'Celibacy retrievals, more like,' he quipped.

'Quite. So perhaps we should revert to my original idea of getting some prostitutes.'

'I think we should give it a bit longer before we resort to that.'

'Hmm, actually that Jasmine is quite a looker. Not the brightest, but still plenty up top, if you get my drift.'

'Hands off Smargle, I recovered her.'

'Well hard luck Ogroid. I haven't seen you make any moves on her yet, so I've decided to have a crack myself.'

'You don't stand a chance.'

'Yes I do. In fact I'm planning on chatting her up soon. If that doesn't work I've got a few other ideas up my sleeve. Anyway, I want to go into the *Neverness* right now, so get that pallet of crap out of my way.'

'Okay, but no prostitutes,' insisted Mike.

A little while later they heard a crackle on the radio and William's voice called out.

'I've got one. Ginally I've fot one!'

'Got one what?' asked Mike.

'You'll see, now bring me back!'

He could see Mike hesitate before flicking the switch.

'I've got a surgeon!' exclaimed William, hardly able to contain his excitement. 'Look, operating cloak, facemask...and he's still holding his scalpel!'

'Yeah, but what do we want with one of those?'

'In case of medical emergencies, stupid. Oh, this is good news! ... Hello there old chap, are you all right?'

'Umm, I feel a bit tired, a bit woozy,' said the man. 'What am I doing here? I was in surgery just before...'

'Yes,' said William interrupting him. 'I'm afraid something strange has happened. The end of the world came, but we've survived.'

'What? What are you talking about? Just a few minutes ago I was removing an in-growing claw from a hamster's foot. How did I get here?'

'A hamster, did you say?'

'Yes, I'm a veterinary surgeon. Lionel Swivvers of Henley-on-Thames, pleased to meet you.'

117

'Oh no, this can't be happening. A veterinary surgeon, are you sure? Sorry, what was your name again?'

'Lionel. Lionel Swivvers.'

'Yes of course, Lionel. Right, umm, just wait here a moment, I need to have a word with my colleagues in private.'

They stood outside the workshop wondering what William was up to.

'We'll have to send him back, he's not a real surgeon.'

'Why? He seems like a decent sort,' he said. 'Anyway, we could do with a vet, he'll be useful with all the animals we're collecting. Hey, do you think the girls will like him?'

'Er…not necessarily,' said Mike.

'He's ancient, practically bald. I think we should keep him. At least we've got another bloke for them. Let's offer him a position.'

'Oh, do what you want,' said William irritably. 'I'm going in again. Thought I caught sight of father's catamaran. Most weird, just like that dream I had.'

'You can't go bringing catamarans into the workshop. If you do find him, you'll have to manhandle him off the deck before attaching the clip.'

'Look Muffton, I can't be manhandling father off the deck of his own boat! It'll be much easier if I just fix the clip to the rigging.'

'We'll have to set up on the lawn then.'

'Why? It's perfectly all right where it is.'

'No it's not. That boat would have been moving when it disappeared, wouldn't it?'

'So?'

'Well, it'll still be moving when it reappears. It'll go straight through the wall and probably won't stop. There could be untold damage.'

'Oh, move it if you must, but I'm not manhandling him, understand?'

'Okay, you brief Lionel and take him to meet the girls. Victor, can you give me a hand to shift the kit?'

William returned saying the girls were delighted with the new arrival and that they'd given him a spare room in the attic next to Hector.

'Right, the kit's all connected up,' said Mike.

'Hmm, looks satisfactory. Now listen, I'm not coming out until I've got him.'

'There's only enough air for three hours, you'll have to come out then, ready or not.'

At first they kept in constant communication, asking William what he could see and if he'd spotted his father yet. They were told to shut up and mind their own business, so they decided to leave him to his own fate and kicked a football around instead. Another hour went by before they heard anything.

'**Got him! Ha ha!** *Right, just clixing the fip!*'

118

'Is that a boating term?' he asked Mike.

'Nah, I think he means fixing the clip…stand by.'

A huge catamaran appeared from nowhere and as anticipated, skidded across the lawn with a terrible racket, cutting deep furrows as it went. Luckily, the clip slipped off the rigging, saving the equipment from being dragged to the ground. The catamaran finally came to a halt some fifty metres away.

'Well done Muffton! I say, this kit is brilliant!' shouted William, as they raced after the boat. 'I always knew you'd come up with something useful in the end.'

'William?'

'**Father! Father!** Oh, this is splendid! Are you all right father? We thought you were dead.'

'Dead? Why would I be dead? What's the catamaran doing here?'

'You've been missing for years, the Bermuda Triangle claimed you!'

'What on earth are you talking about William? I've been held captive by pirates, you silly boy.'

'What?'

'Yes, they took me to a small island somewhere off the coast of Venezuela and stole all my booty. I finally managed to escape when they accidentally set fire to their own camp. Swam out to the cat and I was away. I made good progress across the Atlantic and was just nearing the French coast…now I'm suddenly on my lawn!'

'Something weird has happened father. Everyone's disappeared and there were these spaceships…oh, there's such a lot to explain, I don't know where to begin. Umm, you remember Mike, Mike Muffton? Well, I commissioned him to build this device, which allowed me to enter another parallel. When everyone disappeared, that's where they went!'

'It's called the *Neverness*,' said Mike

'Yes, I went in there and rescued you father!'

'How extraordinary. Excellent William, and well done that chap Muffin.'

'Muffton,' said Mike.

'Actually father, while you were missing I found out about your double life.'

'Ah…'

'Yes, and about Gina being our half-sister. Why did you keep all that a secret?'

'Had to old chap. If word got out that I was posing as all these different people, it would have ruined everything. The money I've saved in taxes is astronomical.'

'So, you *are* a tax evader then?'

'And smuggler,' said Claude, looking pleased with himself.

'So, you did get fifty million for that wooded hill?'

'Yes, good price, wasn't it? Pays to have friends in high places.'

'Do you know what Anna and I have been through? We've had the indignity of having to go to court I don't know how many times...we were about to lose everything... Poffington, *Gypsy Girl*, the lot!'

'Oh no, terrible old chap.'

'But now that everyone's disappeared, it's still ours! I've even been all over the country destroying the paperwork and computer files they had against us. Oh, and I dealt with the judge who tried to ruin us.'

'Well done William! But what about Château Montmaran?'

'I've been there. It's pretty much as you left it, so Gina says. I even brought that special wine from the cellar to Poffington. In fact, I've been going around getting everything you sold at auction to all those collectors. The cellar's brimming! Did you really work for the French Secret Service?'

'No, of course I didn't. Did you just say that you've been collecting up all that wine I sold at auction?'

'Yes, didn't I do well? I'm planning another trip soon to...'

'Oh William, you are a stupid boy. All the wine I sold was fake. I bottled it myself at the château. Didn't you find that secret room in the cellar with the printing press and boxes of labels?'

'No? All fake? Damn, you mean I've been traipsing around all this time collecting up crates of useless plonk?'

'I suppose that makes you a plonker then.'

'Pardon Victor?'

'Only joking.'

'You didn't happen to visit Ledehoogs Castle, home of *E. Gold Shoe*, did you?' continued Claude.

'Yes, why?'

'I am *E. Gold Shoe*!'

'You mean I've blown the doors off my own father's castle?'

'Oh, William!'

'*E. Gold Shoe* though?'

'Made it up on the spot at an auction one day when giving my details. It's an anagram of Ledehoogs. Clever, wasn't it?'

'But if *E. Gold Shoe* is you, why were you so disappointed when *he* outbid you for that fantastic collection the day I accompanied you to that special sale?'

'Because it was my wine already! I had Nanny Muttlecroft on the phone in the foyer making bids every time I gave her the nod. Ended up pushing the other buyers a bit too far. They stopped bidding and I got landed. Still, can't win them all, can you?'

'Oh yes, I forgot Nanny Muttlecroft was with us. Hang on, a few minutes ago you said *all these different people*! Don't tell me there are more?'

'Yes. I'm Claude Smargle, Jean Le Garms, Count van Gristlevook, Henry de Winterberry, Tom Mustings...that one was used to gain access to places when I was posing as a tradesman, you understand. Er, Lord Fontings of Dukesbury, Annabelle Yidd, Sir Vivian Cleaver...'

'Annabelle Yidd? My God, I kissed her at a party once!'

'Yes, I remember that, unfortunately.'

'Urrgghh, what have I done?' said William, wiping his lips. 'It was tongues and everything!'

'Only on your part.'

'Why didn't you say something?'

'Couldn't old chap. I was too close to the prize.'

'I don't think I want to hear any more.'

'I do!'

'Shut up Ogroid! Haven't you got work to do? Prize? What prize?'

'The wine. If I'd revealed myself to you at that particular moment, I'd have given the game away. Our host, Colonel Humpfusty, had an extremely valuable stash I wanted to get my hands on. Anyway, you were very persistent. Began to wish I'd never got you to go in my place.'

'That's why you sent me along, was it? So you didn't have a headache after all?'

'No.'

'You've been posing as a woman to get your hands on valuable wines? Damn, wish I'd thought of that.'

'No harm in it, is there? Not if it gets you what you want. So William, tell me a bit about yourself, got a little woman yet?'

'Er, yes. Yes I have, actually.'

'Just a girlfriend or something more serious?'

'Oh, much more serious than that. I've got a fiancée!'

'Well done old chap. What's her name?'

'Yes William, what's her name?' he asked.

'Danii. Why don't you buzz off, Ogroid?'

'Danny? That's a chap's name, isn't it? Not on the turn, are you?'

'No, no father, gracious no! It's spelt differently for a girl. You should see her, she's beautiful.'

'Well, I think I'll leave you to tell your father all about your *fiancée*. Umm, it's nice to meet you, er...'

'Just call me Jean Claude, it'll be less confusing.'

'Okay, Jean Claude, see you later.'

'Oh Victor, get Anna and Gina, will you? Don't tell them why though, I want it to be a surprise.'

'I'll get Danii as well, it'll be quite a surprise for her too.'

'No, I'll speak to her myself later, now stop meddling and go away. Ooo, tell me about the pirates father, it all sounds so exciting!'

After sending Anna and Gina outside, he thought he'd give the Smargles some time to themselves and disappeared to his room. The smell hit him as he walked in; a certain odour had been building up, which wasn't entirely pleasant. He threw the windows open and started to do a bit of tidying.

'I can't believe Jean Claude is Sir Vivian Cleaver…what a tit! And dressing up as a woman to get wine! No wonder William's weird. Urrgghh, kissing his own father…with tongues…and he enjoyed it! Urrgghh!'

After a great deal of effort the room still looked as though it had been burgled, so he gave up and decided to teach Jappa a few new tricks instead. Eventually he went downstairs to see what was happening.

'Oh, what a day!' said William, gleefully rubbing his hands together. 'I can't believe my luck. I've found father, and listen to this Ogroid, I've been to the hotel and got a date lined up with Jasmine in my room tonight. Ha!'

'Yeah, and you've got a fiancée.'

'Damn, what did I have to go and say that for? He's always wanted me married off. Didn't want to disappoint him.'

'What about Danii?'

'I'll find an opportunity to explain it to her, you'll see. Now then, I'm picking Jasmine up at nine, so I mustn't forget to defrost the caviar and put some champers on ice.'

'Won't you be spending the evening with your father?'

'No. He likes to be alone after about eight, so I doubt if he'll get in my way. Hmm, don't want to bump into Danii when I'm with Jasmine. Don't suppose you could do me a favour and keep her occupied?'

'No, it's your problem, you deal with it.'

'Oh Ogroid, you're so horrid. Call yourself a friend? Anyway, your days are numbered now that father's home. By the end of the week you'll be back in that squalid damp shit-hole you rent. There'll be mould on the walls and it'll smell even worse than it did before.'

He'd been lying there for about twenty minutes and was having a good fidget while he still had the chance. He was surprised at how dirty it was under William's bed and thought some of the boxes looked rather suspect. Just then he heard the door open, so he held his breath and listened.

'Now then Jasmine, this is my room. You can put your handbag on *the bed* if you want.'

'No, I'll hang on to it thanks. Big, isn't it?'

'Oh, does it show?'

'What?'

'Oh, the room, ha! Yes, it's the biggest one in the house as a matter of fact. Feel free to have a walk around. If you're not back in half an hour I'll send a search party for you. Ha!'

'Nah, I'll have a sit down though.'

'Would you like a drink?'

'Yeah, thanks.'

'Good. Let's start with some champers then. Ooo, I'll put some music on, shall I? How about Ravel's *Bolero*?'

'Whatever.'

He couldn't believe that William was trying to seduce her with caviar and culture; when it came to girls, he really didn't have a clue.

'Urrgghh, what's this then?'

'Caviar.'

'It's horrible, it's frogspawn and it makes me feel sick. I'm more of a fish fingers girl, me.'

'Really? How interesting... What about jokes then, do you like them?'

'When they're funny, yeah. Why, you got some, have you?'

'Umm, I can't think of one just now, er...oh yes, how about a silly rhyme instead?'

'Go on then.'

'Right here goes... *Mary had a bicycle, she rode it on the grass, every time the wheel went round the spokes went up her arse!* Ha, ha, ha, haha! Oh dear, ha, haha, ha! Or what about this one? *Mary had a bicycle, she rode it back to front...*'

'What's that over there?'

'What? Oh that. It's just some modern art I created from chicken wire. It's actually a goldfish in a bowl.'

'Blimey! Clever bloke, aren't you?'

'Yes, I am. I've painted a number of masterpieces too. I even had an exhibition in the city recently. Perhaps you heard about it? No? Oh well. Anyway, I sold everything on the opening night, these are still waiting to be delivered. Now then, this first one... I remember that I was feeling particularly melancholic that day...'

The proceedings were so boring that he actually fell asleep, only waking again when the door banged shut and Jasmine let out a drunken shriek. The whole event had been excruciating, but at least he'd managed to pick up a couple of useful facts. For one thing he'd learnt that Jasmine couldn't drive. This would provide him with a perfect premise to strike up a conversation with her.

The following day everybody resumed the task of collecting supplies and by the time William had developed another headache, more than thirty pallets had been sent into the *Neverness*.

'Right Victor, take these provisions to the hotel while Mike and I clear up a bit, or rather Mike clears up while I point things out.'

'Why do I have to go?'

'You know I can't lift things with my bad back. Anyway, my head's thumping.'

'Oh, all right. By the way, how did you get on with Jasmine last night?'

'Excellent, thank you.'

'Did you, umm…?'

'How crude you can be, Ogroid. Yes, I snogged her if you must know. Now get on with your chores.'

As soon as he entered the hotel Pershia pounced on him.

'Ah, there you are! These clothes are for dry cleaning, see to it.'

'Umm, I thought you didn't wear anything twice. Can't you just get some new stuff?'

'How dare you argue with me! These are favourites, we always have our favourites cleaned!'

He unloaded the supplies from the van and took them into the kitchen. Ernest was nowhere to be seen, so he just left it all stacked on a prep table. Just then Jasmine walked in.

'Hello there, how's things?' he asked.

'Good thanks.'

'Umm, I've noticed that there's another car outside.'

'Yeah, it belongs to Ernest.'

'Haven't you got one for yourself yet?'

'No point, can't drive, can I?'

'Really? You must let me teach you, it's easy, you'll soon get the hang of it. You'll be able to go shopping and things. What about it then?'

'Yeah okay. My cousin was going to teach me, but we never got out of the driveway.'

'Oh?'

'Yeah, spent hours in that car we did. It was weeks before my mum pointed out that it didn't even have any wheels. Propped up on bricks it was. He could be a real devil at times.'

'Er…okay…'

'Ooo, I'm really excited now! I'll need an hour though. I'd like to freshen up and paint my nails.'

Delighted with his success, he went to the laundry room with the bag of clothes.

'Right then, what's dry cleaning? Oh yeah, it's washing with a solvent instead of suds. I'll get something from the van.'

He returned with a litre of thinners and stared at the washing machine.

'Hmm, if I put it in there it'll mix with water and that'll be no good. I'd better use the tumble dryer. It'll evaporate out of the vent.'

He tipped the whole container into the washing bag and gave it a good shake. He then held his breath while he emptied the contents into the drum. Satisfied it was spread around evenly, he closed the door and hit the switch. He was just about to leave when a big explosion blew the door off, shooting out a fireball, which skimmed his legs as it went past. It hit the opposite wall with a terrifying flash, spreading flames all around the room. He hopped up and down in a panic, trying to stamp it out with a sort of dance. He was quite pleased with some of his footwork and thought it might be useful the next time they had a party. As he frantically trampled the remains of the models' clothes around the floor, he noticed that his shoes were ablaze. He staggered to the sink, splashed water over his feet, then opened the window to let the smoke out. Thinking that he'd got off quite lightly, he left the charred rags smouldering and sneaked off home to change.

He returned to the hotel with a sporty little number for Jasmine's first lesson. In reality it was totally unsuitable, but it was the only vehicle he'd got that was fitted with racing harnesses. This would make it much safer just in case she was hopeless, but that was by no means the real reason he'd chosen it. He was delighted when he saw her walking towards the car wearing a mini-skirt and thin, low-cut, clingy top. He was certain she wasn't wearing a bra.

'Okay, first things first, let's get you belted in.'

'Ooo, these seat belts are all funny, how do you get them on?'

'Here, let me help you. First get this part over your head,' he said, almost salivating at her perfect breasts as he fiddled unnecessarily with the straps. 'Then pull that other end up between your...er, yeah, that's right. Hmm, jeans might have been more comfortable.'

'I like a short skirt, especially for sitting in cars.'

'Yes, me too...er, I don't mean that I wear a skirt when I'm driving, or any other time in fact. It's just that I know what you mean. Right...umm, I'll let the straps out a bit so you'll be more comfortable.'

After a considerable amount of wriggling and fidgeting about, he sat back in his seat and wound the window down.

'Phew! Getting a bit warm in here, isn't it?'

'Can you smell burning?'

'No.'

He gave her a brief rundown about the controls and how to pull away. Lurching off with wheels spinning, he instantly felt unsafe. He gripped his seat with both hands as they crashed into one thing after another. Even before the end of the first ten minutes, all the airbags had gone off and he wasted a lot of time trying to deflate them before they could continue. He experienced a multitude of emotions, from sheer terror to great delight. The highlight was when he suggested that she try reversing to save the front end from further battering. Watching as she twisted around in the seat, the harness pulled her top awry and her boob popped out. He wanted to reach out and play with it, but was stopped from doing so because they'd just smashed into something.

'Ooo, now I've hit that parked car. Were you looking?'

'No! No, I wasn't, honest!'

'Ooo, I'm all dishevelled,' she said, covering herself up.

'Umm, actually Jasmine, I think we need to work on reversing. Let's try it again, shall we?'

In the end the hour went all too quickly and they stuttered up the driveway to the house, stalling outside the workshop.

'Why are we here then?'

'I'm afraid the car won't make it to the hotel, look at all that steam coming from under the bonnet.'

'Sorry, not very good, was I? Do I have to pay for the damage?'

'No, of course not.'

'Oh good. Ooo, that was real fun that was.'

'Do you want to come up to my room for a drink?'

'Ooo, I don't know, I've had rather a lot already. Oh, all right then. Cheeky, aren't you?'

He couldn't get her upstairs quickly enough. As soon as they burst through the door, Jappa scampered into his house and looked out at them from a window. It was just then he became aware that the piles of magazines he'd been meaning to get rid of had become partially uncovered. Right there in big type the word *Gay* flashed like a neon sign before his eyes. There was no doubt she'd seen it. He nonchalantly adjusted the sheet to cover it back up, but only succeeded in exposing a large erect penis on another pile.

'Oh,' she said, raising her eyebrows.

'They were here when I moved in! The room was full of them. They're mostly gone now though, I take a few to burn every time I go out.'

He thought he'd probably got away with it and left her looking around while he slipped into the bathroom to prepare. Trousers around his ankles, he flopped onto the toilet and reached for his new aftershave.

'Ouch, ouch! Shit, it's in my eyes! Aaaggghhh, now it's burning down there. God, it's on fire!'

With his eyes watering profusely, he staggered to the basin clutching his privates. He splashed his face with water, then tended to the other problem. Pulling up his trousers, he shuffled into the bedroom and felt around for the bottle of Russian sparkling wine that William had given him during a moment of generosity.

'Er, Jasmine... I've got something in my eyes, I can't see you.'

'I'm ready, sitting in bed. Hope that's all right?'

'Yeah!'

He hurriedly untwisted the safety wire and was just about to wrap his hand around the cork when it went off like a cannon. A fountain of wine hit the ceiling some ten feet above their heads. A good proportion went into the light fitting and the rest rained down over the bedclothes. His eye was throbbing after taking the full force, but he still managed to tip the dregs into her glass before passing out.

'Victor? Victor?'

'Urrgghh, what happened?'

'You must have fainted, are you okay?'

'Fine...my eye's throbbing a bit though.'

He regretted that he didn't get to see her naked, but quite frankly it didn't matter because he'd finally got a shag.

'That was quick!' she said.

'Let's do it again!'

'Ooo, is that the time?'

'No, that wooden clock stopped ages ago.'

'I've got to go, I'm supposed to be hoovering the restaurant. We could meet up tonight though.'

'Okay, I'll pick you up at umm...'

'Half ten?'

'Yes, half ten it is then. Come on, I'll get you home.'

Later that evening, he felt very smug as he took his seat in the dining hall.

'Right, I've just taken father's supper tray up, he looked quite pleased,' said William, joining them. 'What's with the red eyes then Victor?'

'I had an accident.'

'Really? Must have been a funny accident for you to keep smiling like that, or perhaps you're just going mad?'

'Actually it was something Jappa did. Made me laugh, that's all.'

'What was it?' asked Danii.

'I don't want to hear about it right now,' said William, 'I've just started eating. It's only going to be something distasteful.'

'It's not actually, but I won't say anyway.'

'You're in a dream world Ogroid. Probably taking too many drugs.'

'Oh no, supposing it was just another fantasy while I was unconscious? No, keep calm, it was real, it was real!'

He helped clear the dinner things away, excused himself from the group and sneaked off to the hotel. To his surprise, Jasmine was already waiting at the gate.

Chapter 8

He lay in his warm bed slipping in and out of sleep, reliving the previous night's escapades, satisfied that nothing had been in his imagination.

'I'm thirsty, got a kettle up here, have you?'

'Urrgghh, sorry…what?' he said, finally opening his eyes.

'I'll make it, you don't have to get up. Here, you was really funny in the night.'

'Was I?'

'Yeah. Do you know what you did?'

'Er, no?'

'You farted on my legs and said, *that'll keep you warm*. Cute it was.'

'Are you sure you didn't dream that?'

'Nah, course I didn't. It smelt horrible and I had to open the window. That monkey of yours has been staring at me.'

'Call him Jappa. He's ever so friendly…and intelligent.'

He sat up and looked over to the little house. A pair of beady eyes peered out at them.

'I think he must be a bit shy. Normally he'd be swinging from the light fittings by now.'

'Small, isn't he?'

'William said you went to his room the other day.'

'Yeah. Strange one he is.'

'Did he kiss you?'

'No way! Let a bloke like that snog me? Anyway, I don't think he wanted to. All he went on about was paintings and wine. Bored I was, couldn't wait to get home. Do you want to meet me at lunchtime?'

'What, you want to carry on seeing me?'

'I know, let's do it in my room.'

'No, that would be a mistake. If the models know I'm there, they'll disturb us. They'll have us doing all kinds of jobs. No, it'll be better if I pick you up like before. Is one o'clock okay?'

'That'll be fine. Those models don't eat lunch, well not the usual sort anyway.'

'Oh, you know then?'

'Yeah. Really noisy they are sometimes. Makes you wonder what they get up to.'

'I've never really thought about it,' he lied.

He sneaked Jasmine back to the hotel, then went to the workshop. Mike was already busy making fine adjustments to the kit. It wasn't long before William called in, seemingly unaware of two large pulsating spots either side of his chin.

'Ah Victor, I want a word with you.'

'Morning skewer face.'

'What are you talking about?'

'Those spots, it looks like someone's pushed a skewer through your jaw.'

'Rubbish, they're hardly noticeable at all. I probably caught them from that damn monkey of yours.'

'Don't worry, they'll be gone in a week or two.'

'A week or two? Oh, what a bother.'

'Have you been to bed with your *fiancée* yet?'

'Shut up!'

'You must have at least spoken to her?'

'Well I haven't...and don't you dare go interfering. You are a menace Ogroid. Now you've reminded me about it and it'll ruin my day.'

'By the way, I've scored.'

'I don't need any more drugs, I'm in enough trouble as it is.'

'No, I've done it.'

'What?'

'*It*. You know, *it*.'

'Really? Who with?'

'Not telling.'

'You're making it up, you haven't done it at all.'

'Jasmine.'

'Really? What was it like? Did you do it doggie style?'

'Not telling.'

'Liar, liar, pants on fire! Well, if it's true I want a crack. You're going to have to put in a good word for me.'

'No way! Besides, she told me that she didn't kiss you...and wouldn't in a thousand years!'

'Liar, she never said that. I nearly kissed her. A couple more drinks and I would have. Just didn't feel it was the right moment, that's all. Okay then Ogroid, I'll give you shit-loads of gold if you set it up for me.'

'No.'

'Look, I've got some very special gold bars. They're embossed with a mermaid logo. You like mermaids, don't you?'

'Forget it.'

'Right then, you've asked for this. If I catch you with her in your room, or any girl for that matter, you're finished, understand? Finished!'

He wasn't unduly worried about getting her upstairs at lunchtime, because there were endless corners to hide in if they were surprised. The route he most favoured was across the lawn to the ballroom, enter by one of the French windows, sneak into the hallway, up in the lift and then they would be practically home and dry.

Jasmine thought it was a real giggle and made rather a lot of noise. He was glad that they hadn't been rumbled and closed his door with a sigh of relief. He watched her pull off her T-shirt and gawped at her beautiful breasts as they wobbled freely in front of him.

'I'm just going to take a shower before we start,' she said, heading for the bathroom.

'Okay, I'll get the drinks ready,' he replied, already aware of the throbbing sensation in his groin.

He joyfully skipped across to his refreshments table and selected a couple of flashy glasses. One had a nasty smear, so he picked up some old pants and polished it clean.

'There, that'll do.'

Just then, there was a rap on the door.

'Shit, I bet that's William. I'll have to get rid of him.'

He was rather taken aback to discover it was Danii. She was in a swimsuit, her wet hair dripping onto a towel hung loosely around her shoulders.

'Oh, it's you!'

'Yes. Er, I can tell you're pleased to see me.'

He nonchalantly let the pants dangle in front of the protrusion.

'Just clearing up a bit.'

'Can I come in then? That's if I'm not interrupting anything.'

'Phuurrr, no, not at all.'

'It's just that I don't want William to see me. I'm sure he's following me, but I think I managed to give him the slip by taking the lift. I want to ask you a favour.'

'Yeah?' he said, casting a worried look over his shoulder at the bathroom door.

'Are you sure I'm not stopping you from doing something?'

'No, of course not, go on.'

'Well...'

She was cut off by another knock on the door, which to his horror started to open. He reacted with a lightning movement, jamming his foot against the bottom.

'Victor? Victor, are you in there?'

'It's him! I'll hide...see what he wants,' she whispered, heading for the bathroom.

He desperately lurched out and grabbed her arm, keeping his foot in place as William repeatedly tried to push his way in.

'Not in there, the wardrobe, the wardrobe.'

'Victor, what are you up to?' called William.

'Nothing, just a sec!' he called, waiting for Danii to disappear.

'Come on, come on!'

'Ah, William,' he said, finally letting him in. 'Look, I'm a bit busy at the moment, can't it wait?'

'You don't even know what I'm here for yet, it might be something beneficial to you.'

'Well, is it?'

'No. I've remembered what I wanted to say to you earlier, before you side-tracked me with those sickening lies about shagging Jasmine.'

'Shhh, somebody might hear.'

'Don't worry, this place is built like a fortress. The inner walls are fifteen inches thick. I could shout as loud as I wanted, nobody would hear.'

'Well don't, I've got a headache.'

'What's that smell?'

'My monkey.'

'No, it smells more like perfume, quite strong.'

'It's just something I spray as an air freshener.'

'Well, it doesn't work. I'd get a different fragrance if I were you. Anybody would think you were on the turn with that pong lingering around. How on earth can you live in such a mess anyway?'

'Look, what do you want?'

'I want to inform you...'

They were distracted by a loud chatter from Jappa as he jumped up and clung to the bathroom door handle, trying to pull it open. He was praying that Jasmine wouldn't come out.

'Jappa, get down!'

'If he leaves claw marks on that door Ogroid, you'll be replacing it, understand?'

The monkey dropped onto the carpet and began a frantic search, then held up a piece of wire like a prize before trying to pick the lock.

'Jappa! Jappa, down!'

Unable to get the door open, Jappa scampered to the window, where he restlessly walked back and forth.

'And that windowsill will be wrecked. I knew it was a mistake to allow you to keep pets.'

'Whatever. Look William, I haven't got time for this.'

'What in God's name is it doing now?'

Jappa had pulled a dead plant from its flowerpot, dumped it on the windowsill and was using the empty container as a toilet.

'Disgusting, utterly disgusting! No wonder that plant's dead. Oh, this room is a disgrace, can't even find anywhere to sit down... Oh my God, he's wiping his arse on the curtains! I want a new pair fitted before the day's out, do you hear?'

Just then the key turned in the bathroom lock.

'**Aaaggghhh, aaaggghhh, aaaggghhh!** Oh, terrible, I need the toilet too! Must have been something we ate. Out of my way, quick!'

He dived in and thrust his hand over Jasmine's mouth, locking the door behind him.

'Shhh, William's out there,' he whispered. 'He'll be jealous if he knows you're here.'

'Why, does he fancy you then?'

'No, you.'

'Here, that monkey's been rattling the door handle. Scared to come out, I was.'

'Shhh, please keep your voice down, he'll throw me out. Look, I'll pretend to have a...umm, go to the toilet. When I go back out stay hidden and keep the door locked until the coast is clear.'

'Ooo, this is so naughty, it's getting me all worked up.'

'Excellent.'

He nipped out of the bathroom thinking he was getting away with it, but was horrified when he saw William with the wardrobe door open, going through his clothes.

'Get out of there! What do you think you're doing?'

'Just looking at your pathetic tie collection. What kept you? I'm dying for a pee.'

'No, you can't use my toilet!'

'Why not?'

'Because I wouldn't recommend it. My window's jammed, I've been meaning to fix it.'

'Oh, what a nuisance. Now I'll have to go all the way back to my room. Don't go away, I won't be long.'

He waited until William had gone, then went straight to the wardrobe.

'God, that was close. I can't believe he didn't see you,' he said, peering through the tightly packed hangers.

'I know, what a fiasco. I nearly started giggling. What was he saying about Jasmine? It was all muffled, I couldn't hear properly.'

'Umm, just some porno film he's got, *Shagging Jasmine* or something. You know what a pervert he is. Picked it up in Amsterdam.'

'On a similar subject, why are you hiding all these gay magazines in your wardrobe?'

'They were here when I moved in! I just haven't got around to throwing them out yet. In fact, I think I'll throw them out of the window right now...then I'll burn them. I'm definitely not gay, you know.'

'Are you all right? I mean, do you need anything for your stomach?'

'No, I feel much better now. Umm, on second thoughts I might visit the bathroom again. Why don't I come and see you later?'

'Yes, if you like. Well, I'll leave you to it then.'

He breathed a sigh of relief as the last bundle of magazines fluttered into the vegetable garden. He couldn't understand how he'd got away with it, but then remembered that William could return at any second, so he hurried along the hallway to head him off.

'Oh, it's you,' said William, opening the door.

'Yeah, what do you want?'

'What do you mean? You just knocked on my door.'

'No, before. You came along to my room.'

'Oh yes, so I did. Right, it appears we've got a new priority for the *Neverness*. We've got to find Gina's mother. Father wants her back. He wants to go and live in the château with her, just like it used to be. Gina's been badgering me all morning about it too. Now then, here are some photographs. Her name's Ingrid, study her face well. There'll be a nice reward for the person who succeeds.'

'Okay, I'll tell Mike, we can make a start this afternoon. I've got one or two things to attend to first.'

He stood watching the bonfire until every last magazine had been consumed, glad to finally be rid of them. It was on his mind that he ought to go and see Danii. He sniffed his sleeve and thought it was a bit smoky. For a moment he considered getting changed, but quickly dismissed the idea and made his way up to her room.

'Hi Victor, why don't you come in?'

'Er, yeah, thanks.'

He was pleased to actually be invited inside. It was tidy and smelt really pleasant. There was a comfy looking sofa at the end of her bed with a neat pile of freshly ironed clothes.

'Sit down if you want.'

'Thanks. So, what did you want to see me about?'

'It's William, he's acting peculiar.'

'Well, that's because he is peculiar.'

'He had his face pressed up against one of the windows while I was having a swim. He's been stalking me all day.'

'Why don't you just ask him what's up?'

'I did. He ran away.'

'He's probably feeling embarrassed.'

'Embarrassed? Why?'

'He told his father you were his fiancée.'

'Oh, he didn't?'

'Yeah, he's probably trying to pluck up courage to ask you to play along.'

'He is such an idiot. Why did he say that?'

'He felt under pressure to say he had somebody.'

'Ah, I see. Where is he?'

'Probably with his father.'

'Right, I'll soon sort this out... Can you smell burning?'

'No.'

During dinner he noticed that William seemed quite bad tempered. He suspected it might be about Danii and deliberately took his time eating. He helped with the clearing up, and while William's back was turned, escaped to the workshop with Mike. A minute later there was a loud crash as the door was kicked open.

'Ha, there you are! You can't hide from me.'

'What's wrong?'

'You told Danii about the fiancée thing, didn't you?'

'Might have.'

'Well, that's brilliant, isn't it? Thank you very much. Dropped me right in it.'

'Look, I had to say something, she thought you were stalking her.'

'I was trying to tell her, and would have if you hadn't interfered.'

'So, what happened then?'

'Embarrassing, most embarrassing.'

'What did she say?' asked Mike.

'She just came out with it, right in front of father. *Sorry, but there has been a misunderstanding, William and I are not engaged.* Then she walked out. Left me looking like a real chump.'

'What did you tell your father after she'd gone?'

'Oh, just that she was a drug addict and had trouble remembering things. Said I couldn't stand it any more and was going to break it off once and for all. Told him I had my eye on another girl. He seemed quite pleased.'

'So, you got out of that then?'

'Looks like it, no thanks to you. Okay, let's get on with the task of finding Ingrid, shall we?'

He'd been paddling around for some time and decided to send a progress report.

'Still no good, not a sign of her anywhere. Wait a sec...shit, I don't believe it!'

'What? What is it Victor?'

'Junty Bunipers.'

'Who? Bunty Junipers?'

'Yes.'

'Bring her back! Bring her back!' ordered William.

'No way, she's mental.'

134

'Bring her back! Bring her back at once, I say!'

'No, sorry, she's gone. I'm coming out now.'

He removed the helmet and climbed out of the module. William stood in front of him with his arms folded.

'Damn you Victor, why didn't you get her for me?'

'What do you want her for? She's crackers, said so yourself many times.'

'She's fun, not like you lot.'

'Not like any lot.'

'Oh, shut up. You're just jealous because she wouldn't do favours for you on that holiday.'

'I spent the whole time trying to fight her off... Ah, that's why you want her, is it? Pervert!'

'At least she'll be up for it. Now get out of my way, I'm going to find her.'

'It's not your turn, it's mine. You're always pushing in,' said Mike assertively.

'Ooo, you two are so spoilt. Spoilt, that's what you are. And I am not a pervert! Anyway, I bet if I looked closely enough into your backgrounds there'd be more than one or two skeletons lurking in your closets.'

Jasmine flashed through his mind. He couldn't believe he'd forgotten about her.

'Er, actually I've got to go now, my stomach's playing up again.'

When he walked into his room, Jasmine and Jappa were sitting on the bed playing Scrabble. Jappa was winning. She wasn't at all cross about being left for so long and had even cleaned the bathroom.

A couple of days later he loaded some boxes of supplies into his van and set off for the hotel. He was feeling very upbeat and almost missed the driveway entrance as he daydreamed about Jasmine. Skidding to a halt on the gravel, he was dismayed when he saw Pershia standing in the doorway with her hands on her hips, snarling at him.

'There you are, you little worm. I want to know where the new chef has got to?'

'It's a bit difficult finding the right people these days.'

'You're useless! It's days since we complained and still nothing's been done. That chef is hopeless. He's pissed the whole time and he's a real slob. Have you seen the state of his fingernails? Get rid of him, or else!'

'And another thing,' added Indala, appearing behind her, 'where's our dry cleaning?'

'Ah yes. It seems that the deliveryman has gone missing. We've been trying to trace him, but haven't had any luck so far.'

'If that fire in the laundry turns out to be anything to do with our clothes, there's going to be big trouble, do you understand?'

'Oh, you heard about that, did you? Umm, look I've just got to drop these boxes off, then I'll go and find you another chef, okay?'

'You've got until this evening. Then you're finished!'

He drove home in a bit of a daze. Ideas were rushing through his head about exactly how they might kill him.

'Hmm, perhaps they'll suffocate me to death with their naked breasts… Death by Boobs? Nah, too small… Maybe they'll lock me in their room and shag me to death? Nah, face it Victor, they're going to castrate you.'

He wasted no time in calling an emergency meeting.

'If we don't get another cook, we're done for.'

'Why don't we just drug them and send them back?' said William.

'We can't do that, as horrible as they are.'

'No balls, that's your trouble, Victor.'

'That's exactly what I'm afraid of.'

'Let's keep it simple,' said Mike, reasoning it out. 'In the short term we just have to find another chef. Given time, if we're lucky, they might leave of their own accord.'

'I agree. Come on, the sooner we start, the better chance I have of not being finished.'

'What?'

'I'll explain later.'

In his panic to find someone suitable, he almost retrieved a mortuary technician and then a laboratory worker. Just as he was on the verge of giving up, he spotted an Indian chef. The tall hat perched on top of his turban looked a bit odd, but he decided they should do an interview anyway.

'Hello there. I'm Victor, that's Mike and this is William.'

'A very good evening to you sirs. Please be taking a seat and I am getting you a menu. You are very lucky gentlemen indeed. You have chosen the finest curry house in Kettering.'

'Er, I'm afraid you're not in the restaurant any more.'

'Oh no, I have been demoted. I have been put in a cage to be taken back to India. I am very sorry for whatever it is I am doing that is offending you sir. I am in eternal shame.'

'No, look, you don't understand. I'm here to offer you a new job.'

'Oh bless my soul, a new job. Thank you most kindly sir. I am naturally accepting your kind offer and I assure you of your utmost satisfaction.'

'Excellent! What's your name?'

'Sanjeev, Sanjeev Sandhu. I am most pleased to be meeting you, sir.'

'We're pleased to meet you too, Sanjeev. Right then, come with us and we'll show you the hotel.'

'That is most excellent sir. I am thanking you from the bottom of my heart. I am coming to England only last year after escaping from my wicked master. To be away from that nasty man who is treating me worse than a dog, is a benefit in itself. I have since been working in my cousin's restaurant for my food and lodging.'

'Well, you're in safe hands now, Sanjeev.'

'Please may I be asking you, will you kindly be letting me have a blanket if I am to be sleeping in another outbuilding, sir?'

'No, you'll have your own bedroom, with heating, lights, hot water and all the food you can eat…and I'll pay you fifty thousand a year, tax-free. You'll get quite a bit of time off as well, how's that sound?'

'Most excellent. I am forever in your debt, kind sir.'

'Please stop calling me sir, it's just Victor.'

'Yes sir, kind Victor.'

William went to break the news to the girls while he and Mike took Sanjeev to the hotel. It was getting dangerously close to the deadline and he was praying that the models liked Indian food. Incredibly, they seemed pleased and immediately gave their orders for dinner. Sanjeev was delighted with his room and was keen to start work. Leaving him to get settled in his new kitchen, they drove off feeling relieved.

'Why are we going this way?' asked Mike.

'Got to call in at the bank. I said I'd pay a month in advance. Umm, fifty thousand…er, that's just under a grand a week. Call it five thousand a month, with bonuses.'

'What's he going to do with it, money's useless?'

'It shows good faith, that's all. We'll give him whatever he wants…cars, jewellery, anything. We can go to the *Recteller*, I've already blown the doors off.'

'Really?'

Entering the bank, Mike stopped and shone his torch around the lobby.

'Urrgghh! Be careful Victor, it looks as though some stray animal's been in here. Look, it's crapped all over those smashed photos.'

'Yeah, let's get the dosh and go.'

137

Chapter 9

Since Sanjeev's arrival, the situation with the models had stabilised and he felt that a great weight had been lifted from his shoulders. He bounded downstairs full of energy and trotted towards the kitchen for breakfast. Passing the surgery, he thought he spotted something out of the corner of his eye. He stepped back two paces and saw Danii staring into William's mouth with a torch.

'Actually, your tongue does look a bit yellow,' he heard her say.

'What's up with you then?' he asked.

'I'm dying, can't you see that? I've probably got some dreaded monkey fever. My head's rotting off and I've got a terrible sore throat.'

'Come on, we'd better take your temperature,' said Danii, moving over to a cabinet filled with instruments.

He watched her pull a thermometer from a long wooden case.

'Clear off Ogroid, you don't have to see this,' said William, loosening his trousers.

'What are you doing?' she exclaimed, looking horrified.

'Nanny Muttlecroft always did it this way.'

'With this thermometer?'

'Yes, that very one. It's an antique, so be careful inserting it.'

'Urrgghh! Oh well, at least nobody else has used it. Come to think of it, I can't remember anyone ever feeling ill.'

'Umm, I saw Stefan put it in Marco's mouth just last week,' he said.

'Well, there's a surprise. Come on, we'll pop it under your tongue.'

'Wash it first.'

'I was going to make coffee, do either of you want one?' he offered.

'Yes...and put a shot of brandy in, it'll do my fever good.'

Danii came into the kitchen just as he was stirring the drinks.

'He's normal, believe it or not.'

'That'll be the day.'

'Lionel turned up and I was ushered out. What are they up to?'

'No idea. William's been trying to befriend him just recently. I'll see what I can find out.'

William and Lionel were sitting on the desk together when he opened the door.

'Here's your coffee.'

'Don't want it. Lionel's brought me this nice bottle of wine to try.'

'It's only ten o'clock. How can you drink at this hour?'

'It'll numb my throat. Now clear off!'

He pulled the door up with a loud bang, but purposely kept hold of the handle, letting it slip open a crack. He peered through and listened.

'Lionel, I want to ask a favour.'

'What's that then?'

'It's a slightly delicate matter.'

'Come on man, don't beat about the bush.'

'Actually, that's exactly what I want to do. I was wondering if you could perform a sex change? You know, off with all the tackle.'

'Hmm, interesting idea. I used to specialise in castrations.'

'Oh, that is a bit of luck! Not just the gonads though, the whole lot's got to go, sausage included.'

'Okay, I'll do it, but it'll only be cosmetic. There will be no possibility of children.'

'Don't care about that, as long as it looks authentic.'

'Okay, I'll give it a bash.'

'Brilliant! When?'

'Well, I'm not doing anything today as it happens,' said Lionel, taking William's glass.

'Today? That's even more brilliant!'

Lionel disappeared from view for a moment, then reappeared with a refill.

'Drink up then.'

'Happy days, happy days indeed! Bottoms up!'

Until now, they'd had no luck in finding Ingrid. However, he was still hopeful because she'd been in La Rochelle when everyone disappeared, and had therefore been within the area Mike had indicated on the map.

'Mike, I've been thinking. What if the spaceships were each responsible for a portion of the planet's surface?'

'Go on.'

'Well, they could have been working together, you know, like a fleet of fishing boats. I was wondering if Serge could be right about aliens taking everyone for food?'

'That's a horrible idea.'

'Yeah, but perhaps something went wrong. One of the ships could have malfunctioned.'

'Oh right…and somehow the catch ended up in the *Neverness* instead of being taken?'

'Yeah.'

'But it doesn't explain why we were spared, does it?'

'Maybe they leave enough life for it to be able to recover.'

'Hmm, it's a good theory, but we'll never know for sure. Okay, I'm ready to start. Where's William?'

139

'Getting his testicles done.'

'What?'

'I'll explain later.'

It was like searching for a needle in a haystack. Trying to recognise people when they were upside down was particularly difficult. Just yesterday, he'd sat considering a woman for several minutes before he paddled around to the same orientation and discovered it was the cross-dressing MP for Totnes.

After lunch he went to the surgery and stood next to the sick bed. Lionel put his hand on William's shoulder and shook him gently.

'Willamina… Willamina…'

'Oh, what time is it?' said William, fidgeting slightly as he let out a long yawn.

'A complete success, old chap.'

'Er, what? What was a success?'

'The lopping.'

'Oh that. You've done it already? Gosh, you are efficient Lionel, well done. Oh dear, I am feeling sleepy, must have been all that wine. Help me sit up, will you?'

'What are you doing? Lie still for a bit.'

'No, no, I've got to see her.'

'All in good time, just lie down and rest.'

'Yes, do as Lionel says, get some rest.'

'Rest? What on earth for? And what are you doing here Ogroid, haven't you got work to do?'

'Now then, you'll be up and about in a few days,' said Lionel. 'Take it easy, have another sleep.'

'What are you talking about? Wait a minute, I've just remembered something! You can't have done the operation because I was about to tell you who wanted it done when…well, that's strange, I can't remember.'

'Er, did you say you were *about* to tell me who wanted it done?'

'Yes. Sazoa. She's going to be delighted to… Hang on, you said that you'd already done it, didn't you?'

He watched Lionel stare pointedly at the support frame that covered William's midriff.

'Oh my God William, what has Lionel done to you?' he gasped.

'**Aaaggghhh! Aaaggghhh! Aaaggghhh!**'

In the ensuing panic, he slipped out of the surgery. He decided to hide in the billiard room knowing that William would come after him. As he set up the balls, he could hear doors slamming in the hallway and then heavy footsteps approach.

'Oh, very funny, very funny indeed. You'll pay for this Ogroid!'

'You're up and about then?' he said, playing a rather fine shot into a pocket at the far end of the table.

'I could wring your neck!'

'Well, there's gratitude for you. You'd be a girl right now if it wasn't for me. Do you know how close he was to cutting your nads off?'

'Yes, okay, okay, no need to go on about it. It's making my toes curl just to stand here,' said William, watching the pink ball plop into the netting.

'A bit of a *close shave* in the end, wasn't it?'

'Have you been looking? What did you see? Ooo, that Swivvers has had it! I'm going to get Mike to send him back. He's totally incompetent. Fancy drugging people like that with no consultation.'

'He's not used to consulting his patients, is he? He's a vet.'

'He's a menace! Anyway, I'm most annoyed at him going along with your mindless prank. It's enough to scar a person for life.'

'Ah, there you are William,' said Carmen, appearing with Danii. 'Do you know what day it is?'

'Kill Victor day?'

'No, it's Hallowe'en. Let's have a spooky party.'

'No, no, I can't allow that.'

'What's the matter, afraid the ghost of Poffington Hall will get you?' he taunted. 'You just don't have the balls, do you?'

'Has this place really got a ghost?' asked Carmen.

'Yeah, apparently it lives in the wine cellar.'

'No it does not,' said William insistently. 'Actually, it lives in your bedroom Victor, and I wouldn't be surprised if it gets you!'

In the morning he felt a bit guilty about tormenting William and thought he'd better find out if he was all right. He found him just inside the library, stuffing things into a large cardboard box.

'Good morning William.'

'Yes, it is actually. I feel quite optimistic today for some reason. I've even decided to forgive you for that stupid prank.'

'Oh good. What are you up to then?'

'Father wants me to get his sailing trophies cleaned. I was going to ask Jasmine to do it. I'll pay her of course…hmm, maybe invite her to my room again. Hello, what's this one for?'

William screwed up his face and blew a thick layer of dust from the large silver plate; most of it stayed put, so he wiped it on his sleeve and squinted to read the etching.

'What the… Annabelle Yidd, Wimbledon Champion, 2018?'

'Your father won Wimbledon *as a woman*?'

'Yes, I told you he was good, didn't I? Oh look, there's a photo stuck to the back, he's holding up the trophy! By the look of it he was wearing some false boobs…probably the ones I lent you for *The Pimps and Tarts Ball*. Hmm, almost attractive.'

'Is that why you snogged him?'

'Shut up, Ogroid! You're going to have to return those boobs. Thinking about it, you should have given them back before now. Pervert!'

'Oh, morning Jean Claude,' he said, noticing a portly figure appear in the doorway.

'Morning Muffin.'

'Still no sign of Ingrid, I'm afraid.'

'Never mind, keep trying.'

'Father, why didn't you tell me you'd won Wimbledon as Annabelle Yidd?'

'Well it wasn't something I could openly brag about, was it?'

'Who did you beat?'

'Some Russian fellow... Yes, they were all at it in those days. His stubble used to start showing towards the end of some of the longer matches. Now, what was his name? Oh yes, Tatiana Lobbova.'

'I was telling Victor about the time I was a ball boy.'

'Oh that. Didn't really work out, did it? Your uniform was a bit tight for a start. But you know, we might have got away with it if you hadn't interrupted that rally.'

'The ball came right at me!'

'You ran on court William. Admit it, it was a disaster!'

'Anyway, what do you mean, *might have got away with it*?'

'You were an impostor.'

'What? You mean I wasn't specially selected after all?'

'No. Got you in via the back door. Suppose it was my own fault. Should have given you some ball boy practice before we went.'

For the next week they concentrated their efforts on finding Ingrid and didn't even recover a single other person. Their time wasn't wasted however, because at the end of each trip they grabbed an animal or bird that could be released into the wild.

He and Mike were sitting in the workshop playing cards while William took his turn. He watched a couple of sparrows fluttering around the rafters as Mike dealt the next hand. He'd brought them out earlier that morning, and although they were now free to fly off, they hadn't yet found their bearings. Just then an excited voice came over the loudspeaker.

'*Oh, I say!*'

'What is it William?'

'*Damn, if I could only get these other things out of the way.*'

'What's up, what's going on in there?'

'*Nothing's going on. I've bound a feauty. Wait a sec, yes, yes...that's better.*'

'What, have you found Ingrid?'

'*No. This one's for me. Stand by... Oh no, the damn clip has sprung out of my*

142

hand! Bugger, she's getting away.'

'I'm bringing you out!' shouted Mike.

'*No!'* complained William.

Mike ignored him and flicked the switch.

'Oh, you damn fool Muffton. What did you go and do that for?'

'Umm, William?' he said tentatively.

'What?'

'Did you mean to bring that back?'

'Bring what back? What are you talking about Ogroid?'

'That...behind you.'

'**Aaaggghhh,'** shrieked William, as a long hairy arm reached through the bars and gripped his shoulder. '**Help! Help!'**

'Wait a sec...that's Binky, isn't it Mike?'

'Oh yeah! Don't panic, it's okay, it's only Binky.'

'Binky? Binky who?'

'The famous circus gorilla. He's very placid, been on television and everything. He can even play the bagpipes.'

'Really?' said William, sounding surprised.

'He's quite affectionate too, if I remember correctly.'

'Oh my God! Get it off me, get it off!'

'Okay, try standing up...then move slowly away from the cage.'

'Oh dear, now it's got me by the shoulders. Help!'

'You'd better sit back down. I'll go and find some tinned fruit, it might distract him.'

Several empty cans littered the floor, but at least William was more relaxed at being in the gorilla's grasp.

'Hmm, he doesn't seem to be that fond of the pear halves, Victor. Open another tin of pineapple rings, he really likes those.'

'He's had three cans already, are you sure?'

'Look, those wretched dogs of yours eat tin after tin of meat, I've seen them. You're not going to begrudge my pet a nice morsel, are you?'

'Oh, he's your pet now, is he?'

'Yes, I think I might keep him. He seems to like me. He's much better than that hairy midget that follows you around.'

'He doesn't follow me around, I take him along.'

'Well you'd better get used to Binky, because he'll be coming along with me from now on.'

'What, even in the aeroplane?'

'Why not?'

'He might grab the controls.'

'Hmm, we'll see. I haven't completely made my mind up about that yet. Anyway, I want you to build him a hutch in my room like that one you've got, but bigger. He's going to come in useful, I can tell. He'll be excellent for accompanying me to the cellar, to carry bottles and things. Look, he loves me, can't you see that?'

'That's what I'd be afraid of.'

He spent the rest of the evening erecting a sizeable garden shed in William's bedroom. As soon as he'd finished fitting the door, Binky elbowed him aside and slumped down in a corner. William added the final touch by pushing an enormous litter tray inside, then stood back in admiration.

The next morning he was on his way to the kitchen when he again saw William in the surgery, this time holding a wet rag to his face.

'What's up with you now?'

'It's my damn nose. It's getting worse, hurts like hell.'

'Let's see.'

William removed the rag to reveal a large pulsating bulge.

'Ouch, ouch, don't poke it! Get away! Carmen's dealing with it for me. It's an in-growing hair.'

'On your nose? Perhaps you're turning into a gorilla?'

'Don't be stupid! One of the nostril hairs has started to grow outwards. She says there's a dark spot in the middle.'

'I'm ready now,' said Carmen. 'Come over here, will you?'

'Can I watch?'

'If you want,' she said.

'No, go away, I don't want you watching.'

'Why, worried that you're going to show yourself up by being a baby?'

'No, of course not. All right then, but there will be no distracting her during the operation, understand?'

Carmen sat William at the table where she'd laid out a small tray containing a scalpel and a few other instruments. She adjusted the light and began to pick away at the surface.

'Ah, there it is. Hmm, it's really bristly,' she said, trying to coax it out.

'Ouch, ouch!'

'It's no good, I'm going to have to try the tweezers...'

'Ouch!'

'What on earth is it? It's like a thorn. These tweezers keep slipping off, I need something with more grip.'

'Try the pliers on my gadget-knife,' he offered.

She got hold of the protrusion and gave it a quick tug.

'Aaaggghhh!'

'What's this?' she said, holding the extracted item under the lamp. 'It looks like the tip of a fishing hook...look Victor, you can see the barb... Victor?'

As he dived out of the surgery, he caught sight of Marco and Stefan peering from the salon door, obviously wanting to know what all the noise was about. He skidded, caught his balance and made off down the hallway with William in pursuit.

'I'll catch up with you Ogroid, you can't hide for long! I'll get Binky to beat you up!'

He decided to keep out of the way and spent some time at the hotel catching up on a few maintenance jobs. He went back for the evening meal, knowing that William would have cooled off, and took his place at the dining table with the others. Carmen had completely bandaged William's head again. He suspected that she had deliberately made it look silly and once or twice saw her exchange an amused smile with Danii. After they'd finished eating, William tinkled his glass with a spoon to get everyone's attention.

'Right, because of my nose trauma, I'd like a few days to convalesce. Does anyone have a suggestion of where we could go to get away from Victor?'

'We could go to *EcoWorld*,' said Carmen. 'The weather looks like it's going to be grotty, it wouldn't matter there.'

'Excellent idea. We'll leave in the morning. Anna, make a note of who wants to come and organise the supplies. Victor is banned of course. I've got to take my pain killers now and see to Binky.'

'Who's Binky?' asked Danii.

'Oh, quite forgot to mention it. I've got myself a nice pet from the *Neverness*.'

'What is it, a cat or something?'

'Umm, no, he's a gorilla actually.'

'A gorilla? You can't be serious?' said Carmen, looking horrified.

'He's perfectly safe. He's a circus gorilla, really soft and gentle. I'll bring him down if you want.'

'You keep him in your *room*?'

'Yes, Victor's got that monkey in his.'

Everyone was so amazed that they agreed to meet the gorilla there and then.

'Hmm, he does seem to be quite docile,' said Danii.

'Look at 'im, 'e is standing just like you William,' said Gina.

'Well, they do say that pets tend to copy their owners. Now then, Binky will be coming with us, if nobody has any objections?'

'I don't mind,' said Danii, 'but I think it would be best if you took him in a separate car.'

In the morning he watched William set off with Binky, leading the convoy of five vehicles bound for *EcoWorld*. He was surprised to see Sheil and the actresses join them, following in the black saloon.

'Hey, I could spend some time with Jasmine while they're all away!'

He dashed up to his room to get ready. After ripping off his clothes, he stuck the plug in the bath and turned the taps on full. Then he filled the basin with warm water ready for a shave. Within a minute, he was splashing away the suds, looking at himself in the mirror.

'Hmm, think I'll skip the bath, I look quite clean now.'

He went around the room picking up clothes at random, giving them a good sniff to see if they were wearable. He then made his choice from the few items that didn't smell.

'Green corduroys, blue shirt, flying jacket…not bad, not bad at all.'

Arriving at the hotel, he drove around to the side door and entered the kitchen. A nice tray of samosas sat on a table, so he took a couple and sneaked upstairs to Jasmine's room.

'Oh hello Victor, haven't seen you around much.'

'Yeah, sorry. We've been busy looking for William's stepmother. Listen, everyone's gone for a short holiday. I was wondering if you'd like to spend a few days with me at Poffington? I can drive you back when you've got work to do.'

'Ooo, that's a good idea. I'll just get some shoes on.'

By the time the *EcoWorld* group returned, William was in high spirits and had forgotten about being angry with him. However, he still had to fend off awkward questions as to why he looked so tired.

They quickly resumed their old routine of searching for Ingrid. It wasn't possible for William to participate because he claimed that the bandages would make breathing difficult inside the helmet. After lunch he wasn't surprised when William made an excuse and disappeared into the cellar. He half-heartedly got suited up for the third time that day, thinking that this whole *Neverness* thing had become quite a chore. As the minutes ticked by, he aimlessly paddled around in the green-tinted twilight.

'Huddy blell, I think I can see her! I'm making my way over.'

'Are you sure?' asked Mike.

'Yes, it's definitely her…she's right in front of me!'

'Excellent, get the clip fixed.'

'Ready, bring me back!'

Ingrid seemed quite shocked to suddenly be inside a cage.

'Don't panic,' said Mike. 'Everything's okay.'

'Am I dead? Is zis 'eaven?'

'No, you're alive. Claude is alive too, he's here.'

'Who is zis Claude?'

'I mean Jean. Gina's here as well.'

'Jean? Jean is alive, 'ow is zis possible? Ooo merci, I knew zat 'e was not dead. I tell zem so. Gina is 'ere also? Where am I? And where are zey?'

'Quick Victor, go and get them. I'll explain everything while you're gone.'

146

He set off across the lawn feeling relieved that they finally had some good news for Jean Claude, but didn't get far because William was walking towards him.

'I see the bandages are off then?'

'Yes, Carmen's just removed them. Said they could have come off a couple of days ago, but she forgot.'

'We've got a surprise for you.'

'A surprise for me? Excellent! What is it?'

'It wouldn't be a surprise if I told you, would it?'

He made William close his eyes, then pushed him inside the workshop.

'Oh, this is exciting! Can I open them now?'

'Go on then.'

An insane grin spread across William's face.

'Brilliant, you've got me a prostitute! Ha, I'm going to get a shag! A bit old though, isn't she?'

'Shut up idiot,' he hissed. 'That's Ingrid!'

'Oh dear, so it is. A completely different hair-do from the photos. Well, it's a good job she doesn't know who I am. I'm off then...shame about the shag though.'

'William, get back here!'

'Brilliant Victor, now she knows my name. Ooo, perhaps she doesn't speak English?'

'I am afraid zat I do,' said Ingrid sternly.

'Bugger.'

'Well, I'll fetch Jean Claude and Gina. See you in a bit.'

He ran to the house, shocked at how tactless William had been. Gina and Anna were with their father in the sitting room, so he told them the good news and they all dashed back together.

'Ingrid my darling, you're safe!'

'Jean! I cannot believe it, you are alive!'

'Maman, maman! I am zinking I 'ad lost you!'

The fussing seemed endless and he just stood quietly, wondering what it was like to have a family. Nobody had ever cared for him in that way and he was quite absorbed by it all. William then suggested that they go to the house for drinks. As they set off there was a lot of shouting in French. The group then stopped in the centre of the lawn while Jean Claude introduced William and Anna to Ingrid. There was an awkward silence before the arguing started again, this time much more heated.

'I know,' said William, trying to smooth things over, 'let's have a curry in honour of my beautiful new stepmother! Victor, go and get Sanjeev.'

He drove slowly to the hotel thinking about how complex Jean Claude had turned out to be. William didn't seem to know his father at all and he wondered how many more surprises were still to come. Pulling up outside, he peered through the lounge window and saw that there was nobody about. He stepped into the hallway, but nearly jumped out of his skin when Indala came bursting through, squealing loudly as Sanjeev chased after her with outstretched arms.

'Please to be kissing you young missy, please to be kissing you!'

'Serves her right,' he thought, as he watched her escape up the stairs. 'Hi Sanjeev. How's it going?'

'Very well thank you kind sir. I am having more fun than I ever thought possible.'

'Do you think you could do a curry tonight?'

'Certainly sir. Are you wanting a takeaway or restaurant service?'

'We'd like to eat in the dining hall at home. Umm, how many of us are there now?'

'I can do a meal for any amount you are requiring kind sir. Yesterday I am going with my new friend Ernest to some of my countrymen's restaurants to borrow their provisions.'

'Well, could you do enough food for about twenty?'

'Not a problem, I am only too pleased to be of service.'

'I'll pay you extra of course. Is there anything you'd like?'

'In India I had my own bicycle. It had a big box on the rear and was difficult to peddle when it was loaded with my master's supplies. I would like such a machine, but without the box. It would only bring back bad memories.'

'I'll get you the best bicycle I can find. You'll have it tonight. It'll have lights and everything. Come on, I'll help you load the van. You can cook at Poffington.'

He and Mike had been promoted from their usual seats in the middle of the dining table to ones nearer the top. This gave him a good vantage point to follow the conversation between the extended Smargle-Le Garms family. Ingrid pretended to be outraged when she discovered the truth about Jean Claude's multitude of identities, but the wry smile across her face showed that this wasn't the first time he'd surprised her.

'I really do not know what to say, except per'aps it is just as well zat everyone is gone, ozerwise you my darling would be in prison.'

'No, no, that's not fair. They'd never have caught me.'

'Maybe not, but I would 'ave found you out eventually. Zink yourself lucky Mister Jean Claude.'

'Ooo, by the way father, Gina and I have a score to settle. Can you please tell her that you're English, not French.'

'Non. Papa, tell 'im you are French, not English.'

'Ah, you're both wrong, I'm Australian actually.'

'So,' said Ingrid, 'I zink we must drink a toast to my saviour…'

He blushed a little as they all reached for their glasses.

'I would just like to say zat wizout zis person I would not be sitting 'ere as 'appy as I 'ave ever been in my life. Let us drink to Mike and 'iz special *SAR*.'

He raised his glass along with everyone else, but felt sorry for himself, thinking that he deserved some recognition too.

'If I could just add a few points here,' said William standing up. 'Most landlords wouldn't hear of tenants setting up laboratories in their roof. I however, in the absence of my father, saw the potential of this clever device and encouraged its development from start to finish. So, if you'd all like to raise your glasses once again, we'll drink a toast to *Visionary Landlords*!'

'Well done William!' shouted Jean Claude.

'Oh, Mike is such a nice boy Gina. I zink 'e is very 'andsome and clever. You could do a lot worse for yourself, non?'

'It was me who saved you actually, Ingrid,' he muttered, as they all talked over the top of him.

'It all seems like a dream. I am so 'appy. I cannot wait to get back to our old life at Montmaran.'

'Yes, listen everybody…another announcement! Father and Ingrid have decided to go and live at the château and they're kindly throwing their doors open to anyone who'd like to join them. So, who's interested?'

He watched tentatively as hands began to rise.

'*Serge, excellent! Nikki, Nadesche…*'

There was a quick exchange between Nikki and Xenia in French, which resulted in Xenia shaking her head.

'*Excellent! Oh, Anna. Well I won't miss her… Oh no, not Gina?*'

For a fleeting moment he considered putting his own hand up, but quickly rationalised that there was more to keep him here.

'I 'ope zat you are coming to live wiz us also, Mike?' said Ingrid, with a warm smile.

'Umm, nah. My equipment's here. It's all set up and…'

'Well, I 'ope zat you will visit us often. I will make you especially welcome. After all, I owe you so much.'

'Yes, of course I'll visit.'

'Do not make me wait too long, will you?'

He could tell that Mike looked a bit uncomfortable and wondered exactly what she meant.

'Victor!' shouted Nadesche above the torrent of chatter. 'Nikki and I would like to take Drac wiz us. Do you agree?'

'Oh, I don't know about that.'

'Actually, I think it would be a good idea,' said Carmen. 'He's been a bit frisky of late, we don't want any incidents, interbreeding and all that.'

'Er, no, I suppose not. Umm okay, you can take him.'

'Also ze 'orses, zey must come,' said Gina.

'As you and Anna are the only ones riding, that was a foregone conclusion,' said William. 'Okay, that's all settled then. Everyone who's going, have your things packed by a week on Wednesday. I suppose you intend bringing that hairy midget along, Victor?'

'What do you mean? I'm not going.'

'Yes you are, you've got to set everything up.'

When the meal was over he was still feeling put out. He was also unsettled about the prospect of losing Drac and Gina, and decided to cheer himself up by asking William for his reward while the others were busy clearing the table.

'Reward? What reward?'

'For finding Ingrid.'

'Oh that. Just go into the cupboard under the stairs and take a crate of wine.'

'I don't want fake wine. You said *a nice reward*, so I want something *nice*.'

'Oh, you are a menace. Now I'll have to think of something.'

'What about that mermaid gold you mentioned?'

'Oh yes! No, I'm saving that.'

'Victor, I'm sorry about Ingrid,' said Mike, coming over to join them.

'What do you mean?'

'Giving me all the praise. I've just reminded her that it was you who found her. I think she'll give you a kiss for it later.'

'Are you mad? She'll never kiss him in a million years! Now listen both of you, I've thought of a little job that needs seeing to before we take father to Montmaran.'

'What's that then?' he asked.

'I want you to get the lights working in the old Channel tunnel. The ramp on *Cressida* is still broken, don't forget.'

'Lights? We'd have to get the ventilation system working too, there probably won't be enough oxygen down there.'

'Yeah, it hasn't been used in years,' added Mike. 'It must be dodgy. I mean, there had to be a reason why they closed it.'

'It might even be flooded.'

'What's the matter, scared?' goaded William. 'Better be careful, there's probably something lurking down there! Right, the sooner you get it done, the sooner you can start getting this list of supplies together.'

'Ah, Mike, zare you are,' said Ingrid, appearing in the doorway. 'Come wiz me, I would like to 'ave a little chat wiz you.'

Wanting a bit of time on his own, he sat in the workshop attic reflecting on how things at Poffington would change after several of the group had moved out. In the end he decided it was going to be okay, his day-to-day life would be relatively unaffected and it would be easier having less people under one roof. He turned his attention to the immediate problem of sorting out the Channel tunnel and started to make a list of equipment they would need to get it operational. He heard the door bang and Mike came running up the stairs.

'So, what did Ingrid want then?'

'Nothing.'

'Nothing?'

'Oh, I'm not proud of this, but she's really coming on to me. Keeps saying how clever and handsome I am.'

'Is that all?'

'No. She wants me to make the trip to France so I can help her set up a secret love pad. She said I mustn't tell anyone about it…ever.'

'Really? Well, you could do worse.'

'She's old enough to be my mother!'

'Yeah, but she's looked after herself. She could easily pass for late thirties.'

'You do it then. You set up this *love pad.*'

'Victor? Mike? Are you up there?' called William.

'Yeah, but don't bother joining us unless you've got my reward.'

The rafters shook with William's weight as he climbed the stairs.

'Here you are then, catch.'

A small pouch landed at his feet. He picked it up and loosened the drawstring.

'They're Kruger Rands. Where did they come from?'

'None of your business.'

'Have you got more?'

'Yes, quite a lot actually.'

'How many?'

'Not telling.'

'I've got a shit-load of real diamonds. As big as conkers they are. It's well hidden, and only me and Jappa know where it is. It's all alarmed and everything.'

'Actually, I've got so much gold that I can't even keep it in the house. The floor would collapse,' bragged William.

'What, yours would fit in the house? Mine wouldn't fit into five Poffingtons!'

'Shut up Ogroid! I'm going to get ten times what you've got, so there! Right, you'd better go and take a look in the mirror. I'm getting Hector to do a group photo in half an hour while we're all still together. I can't have you in it looking like that.'

Chapter 10

Turning the truck into the driveway, he saw the welcoming lights of Poffington and breathed a sigh of relief. They were home. It had been an unusual trip, but at least everything had gone smoothly and a great deal had been accomplished in only a few days. William had cried noisily at having to leave his father, but had made a dramatic recovery once they'd reached Calais and loaded up with booze.

Jappa scampered up a drainpipe and disappeared over the roof, so he picked up their luggage and followed William and Binky inside. They were taken aback when a tanned male model walked across the hallway, oblivious of their presence.

'Who the hell is that?' he said.

'Muffton's done the dirty on us. He's got a hunk for the girls.'

'Wait a minute. No, it can't be… Hector, is that you?'

'Oh hello, didn't know you two were back.'

'What's going on?' snapped William. 'What's with the haircut and the snazzy clothes?'

'The girls talked me into it. Gave me a makeover. What do you think?'

'Well really, I didn't think such transformations were possible! There's hope for you yet, Ogroid.'

'I'm just on my way to see Danii,' said Hector, making for the stairs. 'By the way, something weird has happened. Do you remember that group photo I took before you left for France?'

'Yes,' said William in a bored tone.

'Well, I made a print and it seems there's one person we can't account for.'

'They were probably in the toilet or something.'

'No, I mean an *extra* person. They're standing behind *you*!'

'What rubbish! You'd better go and get it, I'll soon sort it out.'

William had a good look at the photo and then fetched his magnifying glass to examine it under the desk lamp.

'Look William, whoever it is has got a hand on your shoulder.'

'Shut up Ogroid! That's not a hand, it's just a shadow.'

'But you can see clothes and everything.'

'That idiot Gerbill has been up to no good on his computer, that's all.'

'It could be the ghost of Poffington Hall.'

'Shut up, shut up, shut up!'

He went to look for Mike and caught up with him in the observatory.

'Hey Victor, you're home!'

'Yeah, it was a really long haul, I'm exhausted.'

'How was the tunnel?'

'Fine. No leaks. William was a complete coward. He held Binky's hand and kept his eyes closed all the way through.'

'Typical. So we wasted our time getting those lights working. Did you get the *Antimatter Particle Reactor* going okay?'

'Yeah, took a couple of days, but the château's fully powered up now. I got the radio kit sorted too.'

'Carmen told me you'd called... I've been locked away in the lab. What happened with Ingrid then, did you...?'

'No!'

'Shit, it's me she's after, isn't it?'

'Actually no. You won't believe this, but she wants us to release her lover from the *Neverness*.'

'Her lover? But she's only just got Jean Claude back.'

'I know, but don't forget he was missing for a long time. Anyway, I haven't finished yet, there's a really weird coincidence. Remember when William and I went to Monte Carlo?'

'Yes.'

'Well, it only turns out that her lover is François Malinguerer! The very same person whose house we searched for wine.'

'Bloody hell!'

'Yeah, she's probably got as many secrets as Jean Claude.'

'But there's no guarantee we'll find him, is there? I mean, it depends on where he was when everybody went missing.'

'He was on holiday in La Rochelle with his wife. Ingrid was meeting up with him secretly.'

'Really?'

'Yeah, disgraceful, isn't it?'

'So, he probably will be in the *Neverness* then. What did William have to say about all this?'

'I haven't told him.'

'Why not?'

'Because he hates Malinguerer, he'd probably kill him. Anyway, things are complicated enough.'

'Did she give you a photo then?'

'Yes. Here, you keep it.'

He'd had a restless night and still felt tired from the journey, so decided to laze around in his room. He'd been playing Jappa at chess and had lost quite badly. Jappa wanted the best of three, but he couldn't bear the humiliation and pretended to be busy. He picked up the instruction book for his 3D unit and ignored the persistent tugging on his sleeve.

'Stop it Jappa, daddy's trying to read. Hello, what's this then? *Your Ultimate Chip Accessory Card is taped to the underside of the box lid. Insert the card into slot B for a truly ultimate experience. Keep it safe, it is unique to your unit and no replacement will be available.* Fuck, I threw the packaging away. Where will it be? ... Serge!'

He rushed downstairs and tried to raise Montmaran on the radio. There was no reply, so he searched for William and found him examining the mermaid statue in the sitting room.

'Hi, seen any ghosts recently?'

'Bugger off, Ogroid!'

There was an awkward silence as William dragged his fingernail between the scales on the mermaid's lower half and then sprinkled the flaky white substance onto the floor.

'Filthy! I'll have to scrape out this whole area now. What on earth is this stuff? Better just taste it, see if it's acid or alkaline.'

'Don't do that!' he said, knocking William's hand away. 'It might be poisonous.'

'Whatever it is, it's left a tidemark. I'll have to get my polish. Anyway, what do you want? You know I hate it when you hang around like this.'

'Do you know where Serge dumped our rubbish?'

'Yes, I do as a matter of fact. I told him to tip it into the *Ark* pit. Why?'

'I threw something out by accident.'

'Excellent, serves you right! It'll be full of disgusting things by now, all mouldy and festering...and there's something living down there. I hope it bites you! I'm getting sick of your jokes and all these stupid references to ghosts. Childish, that's what you are, childish. You might as well know I'm on the verge of throwing you out on your heels, along with that other good-for-nothing, Muffton.'

'We were considering moving out anyway. There's a nice pad not far from the hotel. We might do it up. Of course it'll mean you'll be excluded from entering the *Neverness* again, but that's your problem, isn't it?'

Taking Wolfie, Zeta and Jappa, he went up to the *Ark* to see if he could spot the packaging. William was right, it was a horrible mess and stank to high heaven. There was plenty of rubbish floating on the stagnant pool of water, but regrettably no sign of what he was looking for. He'd have to return later with some suitable equipment. In fact, a fire engine would do nicely.

He hung around in the woods with his dogs while the water was pumped from the pit. Then, safely clothed in an NCB suit and facemask, he climbed down the ladder, gripping each rung carefully through the fingers of his heavy-duty gardening gloves. He began wading around in the soggy debris, nearly jumping out of his skin when one of William's discarded dolls popped up at him after he'd trodden on her legs. It made him lose his balance and he cracked his shin on something solid. It was the metal wheel he'd spotted last year. He kicked away a couple of black sacks and exposed a small raised hatch, similar to the type found on a submarine. He felt a rush of excitement and tried to force it open, but it had rusted and wouldn't budge. Fetching a crowbar from the fire engine, he levered until it would turn by hand. He looked in amazement at a deep shaft that disappeared into the blackness below.

'Bloody hell, what's this? Hmm, there's a ladder. That means there's definitely something down there.'

Finally he plucked up enough courage to descend. At the bottom he cautiously began to feel his way around the wall until his fingers touched a switch. He was stunned when a neon light flickered on above his head.

'Shit, where's the power coming from?'

He stood silently looking around the metal-clad walls of a small circular antechamber. There was a single doorway, but no obvious way through, except for a small slot to one side.

'It's the *Ark*! I've bloody well found it! That slot must be for the key, the card key from Downing Street!'

He scurried to the surface and raced back to the fire engine. He lifted the dogs into the cab and pushed Jappa off the steering wheel. It was tempting to have the siren going, but he remembered how stupid William had looked in the ambulance and thought better of it. Arriving home in record time, he ran through to the sitting room shouting excitedly.

'William! William!'

'What do you want now? And look at the state you're in. You should take those filthy overalls off before coming into the house, I've told you before.'

'What did you do with the credit card key from Downing Street?'

'I probably let go of it when I fell. Why?'

'I think I've found the entrance to the *Ark*!'

'What? What are you talking about?'

'The entrance to the *Ark*! There was a hatch underneath all the rubbish. It leads into a bunker and there's a door with a slot for the key you lost!'

'You're making it up.'

'No I'm not. And there's something else.'

'What?'

'There was a light switch. I turned it on!'

'And?'

'No, that's it! I turned it on, there's power!'

'If this is one of your jokes Victor, I'll get Binky to sit on your face.'

'It's true, come and see for yourself. I'm going to find Mike, meet us outside.'

155

William became quite excited about getting a ride in a fire engine and demanded that he take over the driving.

'The girls will really fancy me when I get all togged up in the uniform. In fact, I might organise a fire drill at the hotel, see if I can interest Jasmine. What do you think, Victor?'

'Not a hope...and stop fiddling with those switches.'

As they entered the compound, there was a clunking noise above their heads. He noticed the cradle had begun to extend out over the cab roof and was ripping through the trees as it ascended. Finally they became so entangled in the branches, they had to abandon the engine and walk.

'There it is!' he said, pointing down at the open hatch.

'Oh I say, this is exciting! I was only joking about throwing you out, you know. Ooo, I've just had a horrible thought. Supposing there are military personnel down there? They'll shoot us for looting and we'll die. You'd better fetch some of those machine-guns you've got stashed in the workshop attic.'

'Have you been snooping in my crates?'

'No. One of the lids was dislodged.'

'Have you taken anything?'

'No. One was missing already.'

'How do you know how many there were supposed to be?'

'Oh shut up Ogroid! You can be so tiresome at times. Just go and get the weapons while Mike starts looking for the key.'

'I'm not going anywhere. You get them if you're so worried.'

He followed Mike down the ladder and they systematically began shifting everything into a heap. It was an unpleasant task and he felt irritated that William was nowhere to be seen.

After an hour of fruitless searching, he came across the pen set he'd given Serge last Christmas and was annoyed that it had just been thrown away. Next, he found the chip for his 3D unit. It was still sealed in a small cellophane bag and he zipped it into his pocket. By now he was feeling really sick from the stench. Some of the black sacks had burst and nasty things oozed out over his feet. Fed up, he climbed out of the pit to look for William and found him trying on a fireman's uniform.

'See, I really look the part, don't you think?'

'If you don't get your lardy arse into gear right now, I'm going to hurt you.'

'All right, all right. God, you can be so horrid sometimes.'

Within a minute William was in the pit, but was of no help whatsoever and just walked around, hands in pockets, surreptitiously trying to flatten all the dolls that had become uncovered.

He was on the verge of giving up, when he noticed William snatch something small from a murky puddle.

'Here it is! Here it is! Hmm, still looks in good condition too.'

'Give it to me.'

'No, I found it.'

'You don't deserve to have found it, you weren't even looking properly! Now hand it over.'

'Oh Ogroid, you are such a bully.'

'Look, I'm in charge of the *Ark*. I discovered it!'

'Hard luck then. I'm not afraid of you. I've got Binky don't forget.'

They climbed down into the antechamber and he watched tentatively as William fed the card into the slot. A series of lights flashed on around the edge of the door before it slid open, revealing a small, mirrored room. Two buttons were mounted on a chrome plate; one had an arrow pointing up, the other pointing down.

'It's a lift.'

'Go and investigate Victor. I'll stay here with Mike in case something goes wrong, then we can rescue you. Oh, and if anyone's down there, just act normal, then get back here quick.'

'Why don't you go?'

'Because you're better at this sort of thing than me, isn't he Mike? Come on then, get on with it, we haven't got all day.'

The lift descended for longer than he would have liked. When it stopped, he hesitated and listened. There was silence. He stuck his head out, but quickly pulled it in again when the door started to close. Automatically, he was transported back up.

'Ooo, you're such a chicken,' said William nastily.

'It wasn't my fault, I didn't have a chance to get out.'

'Well, go down again and don't return until you've got something to report.'

This time he stepped out into a well-lit metal structure; it was just like standing on the bottom of a giant gas bottle. It reminded him of a film set. In fact, it was almost identical to the grand finale location for *The Spy with the Golden Pie*. The central floor area was covered with computer consoles and a huge video screen had been built into the wall. Metal walkways zigzagged up the side, leading to many different levels. He went up to the first floor and looked through some swing doors at a long corridor that disappeared into the distance. Walking around the catwalk to the opposite side, he peered through other doors with similar vast corridors. He wasn't sure how long he'd been down there and thought it was best to rejoin the others.

'Did you see anyone?' asked Mike.

'No.'

'How big is it?' asked William.

'Massive...unbelievable. It's definitely not a public shelter though, it looks very high tech, probably military.'

'Right, we'll all go down together now that we know it's safe. Oh, I can hardly wait to tell father about this.'

They agreed to meet by the lift in an hour so they could each explore on their own. William immediately ran up the walkway and disappeared from view. Mike was busy examining the computers, so he looked around wondering where to go first. A large metal door just a few metres from the lift caught his attention. Pressing a green button, it effortlessly slid open. He entered a large warehouse, lined on both sides with huge storage tanks that stretched ahead as far as he could see.

'Water…water…diesel… Hello, where does that door lead to then?' he said, going to investigate. 'Shit, a huge workshop! It's more like a factory. Looks like they've got every piece of equipment imaginable. Bloody cheek, they've sorted themselves out good and proper, and sod everyone else!'

He looked at his watch and saw that he still had forty-five minutes left. Retracing his steps towards the lift, he noticed a huge floor to ceiling plaque. It looked as if it was made of stainless steel and had a large star embossed in the centre.

'Why bother with such a boring picture?' he thought, running his fingers down the edge. *'Hang on, it looks like a secret door. Hmm, no slot for a key card…no control pad or anything. How are you meant to get in?'*

Leaving it for another time, he systematically went through each of the doors that led off the ground floor. They all seemed to be communal facilities or warehouses. He then went up to the first and second levels to continue exploring. When the hour was up he reluctantly went back to the lift, but had already decided to return tomorrow.

They had spent so long underground that it was dark when they got to the surface. He took charge of the fire engine, reversed it out until they were clear of the trees and then retracted the hydraulic arm. Back at the house, William rushed directly for the radio.

'Montmaran, are you receiving me? Montmaran? Bugger, it's just a hiss.'

'Oui Montmaran 'ere.'

'Oh Gina! I need to speak to father urgently, is he there?'

'Non. Zis morning 'e 'az gone on a trip. I ask 'im to call when 'e returns.'

'Tell him I've found the *Ark*! It was there all the time! I'll explain everything when we come over before Christmas.'

'Zare 'az been an accident wiz Serge.'

'Is he still alive?'

'Oui, but it 'az taken us nearly all day to untangle 'im.'

He lunged forward and snatched the microphone from William.

'Was it the washing line?'

'Oui, 'ow do you know zis?'

'Umm, just guessing. What was he doing with it?'

'Oh, 'e is using it to dry leaves from 'iz plants. Zen it get 'im.'

'Got to go now, thanks Gina. Speak to you again soon.'

'What's all that about?' asked William.

'Nothing,' he replied, feeling smug that his trap had worked.

'Ah, there you are,' said Danii, wandering into the hallway with Carmen. 'We've been searching for you boys everywhere.'

'We've found something!' he said.

'Really? Well, by the smell of you, you'd better get rid of it again quickly. We've got a problem, the tennis net's broken.'

'Well, I've got some bigger news,' said William. 'I've found the *Ark*!'

'I found it, you liar!'

'Where?' asked Carmen.

'There was a secret hatch…'

'Yes, it was there all the time!' William butted in.

'Are there any people down there?' asked Danii.

'No, it's empty.'

'So, what's it like, how big is it?'

'Huge, it's got everything.'

'Did you find any storerooms?'

'Yes, there's enough food to feed an army. There's a deep freeze warehouse too. Meat and fish forever!'

'It's all powered by *APR*,' said Mike.

'We also found a pub, cinema, sports hall, gym and swimming pool,' he added. 'It's all been set up for the elite by the looks of it. There are loads of luxury suites with military titles on the doors…and huge dorms for soldiers.'

'I found a health centre and operating theatre!' said William excitedly. 'I'll give you a tour first thing in the morning.'

He was late getting up, but was just in time to see William leading Danii, Carmen and Xenia across the hallway, weighed down with stores from the *Ark*.

'Ah, there you are Ogroid. Take this for me, it's heavy,' said William, handing him a carrier bag containing a few packs of smoked salmon.

'Victor, I can't believe the *Ark* has been there all this time and we didn't know about it,' said Carmen.

'Oui, all zat food!' exclaimed Xenia. 'We 'ave no worries for ze future now.'

'Yeah, it's not just food though,' he said, 'there's fuel, medical supplies, everything we could ever need. Here, let me help get this lot to the kitchen.'

'Wait a minute Ogroid, I want a word with you. Now then, I've realised it's going to be a bit of a pain for the girls traipsing all the way to the *Ark* and then having to scale those ladders with bags of food.'

'We don't have any choice, do we?'

'I've had a think about it and come up with a brilliant idea. I want a tunnel digging from the maintenance cellar across to the *Ark*. It'll make all the difference during inclement weather when we need a piece of fish for supper or something.'

'A tunnel? You can't be serious? It's got to be nearly a mile, it'll take months.'

'Don't exaggerate. If you dig a bit each day you'll soon have it done. Anyway, I'm sure there's some equipment you can acquire to make it easy for yourselves. Look, I've got to go now. Meet me by the basement door in half an hour and I'll show you where I want it to begin.'

'What are you doing then?'

'If you must know, I said I'd take Binky for a stroll around the lake.'

'Can't we make it this afternoon? I was just about to nip over and see Jasmine.'

'No, she'll have to wait, my tunnel is much more important. Now stop arguing and go and find Muffton.'

By the time William and Binky had returned from their walk, they'd already been waiting for twenty minutes.

'If I'd known you were going to be late, I'd have gone to the hotel.'

'Oh, you're so touchy!' said William, as they went down the steps. 'We had to stop to pull a thorn from Binky's foot. Right, while we're here Victor, take a look in the pump room and check that it's all working properly.'

'I thought you were the expert. Why do I have to do it?'

'Because I'm looking after Binky.'

'Oh, okay.'

'Well get on with it, what are you waiting for?'

'The door's stuck,' he said, tugging at the handle with both hands.

'Stand back, Binky can deal with this.'

'No, it's okay, I've got it.'

He continued pulling, but it wouldn't budge, so he put his foot on the wall to get better leverage. Suddenly it burst open, hitting William on the arm.

'**Ouch!** You idiot Ogroid! Now you've cracked my fucking elbow!'

Binky carried William to the surgery while he went to get help.

'Nothing broken, you'll live,' said Carmen.

'That's as maybe, but it's going to make it awkward for flying, isn't it?'

'Good job we're not going anywhere then,' he said.

'We are actually. Before we left France father gave me a lead for some rather nice wines. It's near Hamburg, so we can call in on that dipstick

Hans while we're at it.'

'The radio link to Montmaran is working well. Why don't you take some kit for them too?' suggested Carmen.

'Oh, I don't know about that.'

'We ought to be able to contact him, and him us for that matter, just in case of emergencies. You could take a few chickens and cockerels with you too. Now that we've got all that food, we can afford to give some away.'

'What, chickens for the Germans? That's not fair, I haven't had an egg for ages.'

'That's because we've been incubating them,' said Carmen, adjusting the knot on William's sling.

'So, when are we going then?' he asked.

'Tomorrow, elbow permitting.'

He thought it would be nice if Jasmine could get away from the hotel for a bit and drove over to ask if she'd like to go with them. The models were prowling around the lounge area, so he went to the back garden and threw a stone at her window. He was sorry to discover that she had a fear of flying, but was pleased that she still wanted to meet up when he returned.

Going down for breakfast the next morning, he found William arm wrestling Binky at the kitchen table.

'I see your elbow's all better then?'

'What are you talking about? Oh, that. Yes, I soaked it in embrocation last night. Seems to have done it the world of good. Right, I'll just drop Binky off at Danii's room, then we can leave.'

'Are you serious? She's not going to want a gorilla in her bedroom!'

'Don't interfere Ogroid, I'm sure she won't mind.'

After securing everything into the rear of the plane, he strapped himself in and prepared for take-off.

'Keep an eye on those chickens, Victor. If they lay any eggs, fry them up.'

'Fry them up? We're the ones who'll get fried. You can't cook eggs on an aeroplane.'

'Commercial flights do it all the time. Well, used to do it all the time.'

'In a microwave.'

'Well we don't have a microwave, do we? Now get that pan and stove at the ready, and keep that monkey under control.'

The Germans seemed genuinely pleased to see them. They were delighted with the chickens and Jürgen immediately set about converting an old shed into a coop. Hans was keen on the idea of the radio kit and helped him erect the antenna, just to one side of the house. As they entered the kitchen to test it, William was stuffing his face with cake, looking on excitedly as Hilka cut another large slice.

'I vill put ze plug into ze vall for ze power, ja?'

'Goody, is it finished? I want to call Montmaran, then I must check up on Binky.'

'No, you'll have to wait a bit, eat your cake... Poffington, can you hear me? Poffington, come in.'

'Poofington here. Stefan speaking, how can I help you?'

'It's Victor, I'm testing the radio. Is Mike there?'

'Afraid not.'

'What about Hector then?'

'Ooo, Roger that.'

'Can I speak to him?'

'He's not here love.'

'Oh, bye then.'

'Roger and out.'

After the evening meal, Hans lit a fire in the sitting room and they sat around the blaze with a bottle of schnapps. Hans was in a rocking chair on one side of the hearth smoking a large pipe, while Helga sat on the other side with her wickerwork. Jürgen stayed in a corner playing tunes on his accordion with Jappa watching attentively.

'Oh ja Herr Villiam, I am forgetting, I have a present for you,' said Hans, rummaging in a cupboard. 'Ja, here it is. You are liking?'

'Ooo, a tray of driving gloves! Most kind of you Hans. Look at that Victor, a few bob's worth there.'

'Hmm, very nice. Leather, wool...oh, and wicker.'

'Vee are seeing more animals in ze fields zese days,' announced Helga.

'Yeah, what sort?'

'Rabbits und birds. Ja, vee have also seen an Adler.'

'A snake?'

'Nein, nein. Adler. You know, an eagle. Vee have been trying to make friends vis it. Vee are putting some meat on ze gatepost, but it is not coming to eat. Not yet anyvays. Vell, I zink it is time for sleeping.'

'You take the bed, William, I'll be all right on the sofa.'

The weather was cold and damp as they set off for Hamburg. William seemed quite pleased with himself after having a soft-boiled egg with soldiers for breakfast, or maybe it was more to do with the cache of wine he was about to secure before flying home.

'Have you thought any more about that tunnel, Victor?'

'No,' he said, removing the wicker helmet from Jappa's head.

'Well, I'm telling you I want it done!'

'It's too much effort. Mike said we'd have to use a giant mole. Think of the mess it'll make of your lawn.'

'I don't care about that, just do it. I'll give you a reward if it's done by

162

the New Year.'

'The New Year? You have to be kidding?'

'No, we might have another bad winter. We'll need to access that food, won't we?'

'Hmm, the guy at Lollington who robbed the bank might have left his mole on site somewhere. I'll find out about it when we get back.'

On arriving home, he and Mike immediately set off for the Science Park. He'd had quite a hectic day and found it hard to believe that he'd been in Germany only that morning. Luckily, they found the mole in the compound behind the lab block. It was already on a trailer, so all they had to do was hook it up and tow it to Poffington.

After they'd finished he went to his room and relaxed in a steaming hot bath, then dressed in some clean clothes. As he drove to the hotel, he marvelled at how much his life had changed since his days at the boatyard when he'd lived in that grotty house in Dellfield. Feeling very upbeat, he walked into the bar to meet Jasmine and was pleased to see that Sheil and the actresses were also there.

'Victor,' said Sheil, 'Jasmine tells me you've got a monkey.'

'Yes, that's right,' he said, helping himself to a drink.

'So, were you in a circus before all this happened then?'

'God no! I'm a mechanic. No, never been to a circus in my life.'

Suddenly there was a loud scream from the hallway.

'Help! Quick, help!' cried Indala.

'What on earth's the matter?' asked Nicole.

'A mouse! We heard a mouse scurry across the ceiling!'

'Oh, is that all? Anyone would think the hotel was on fire,' he said.

'Where's Pershia?' asked Natasha.

'Under the bedclothes. Come quick!'

'Okay I'll see to it,' he said, getting up. 'Nothing to get fussed about.'

Taking a torch from his van, he followed Indala upstairs. He couldn't believe how untidy the models' room was, there were shoes and clothes strewn everywhere. The bed looked like a rat's nest with a quivering hump at one end, which he assumed was Pershia.

'Umm, I'll have to find a way up,' he said, looking at the ceiling. 'There must be a hatch on the landing.'

Going back along the hallway, he spotted an opening above a recess and dragged a small chest underneath. Hauling himself up, he shone his torch around the loft space. A large chimneystack rose in front of him, tapering up to the roof, obscuring the void over the models' room. He balanced on the ceiling joists and carefully made his way forward, all the time scanning for mice. As he got closer he heard something. A chill travelled down his spine as he became aware of a heavy breathing sound. He froze to the spot. Whatever this thing was, it was big. For a second he considered running, but the thought of something leaping on his back made him change his mind. His heart thumped as the torch beam swept across the rafters. Then in the shadows something moved. Suddenly the loft was flooded in light and he blinked, unable to believe his eyes.

'William?'

'Yes, what do you want?'

'What are you doing up here?'

'I could ask you the same.'

'The models sent me, they heard a mouse. What are you doing above their room?'

'Oh, above their room am I? I never realised. This is my sanctuary. Been coming here for weeks. Look, I've even got an inflatable armchair, coffee table, standard lamp…'

'Pervert. You've been spying on them, haven't you?'

'No! This area of the loft just seemed to be the most cosy, that's all.'

'What are all these cans between the rafters?' he asked, picking one up. 'You've been drilling spy holes!'

'No I have not! That mouse probably chewed them. I only put the cans there to cut out the draught.'

'Yeah, right,' he said, bending down to peer through one. 'Bloody hell, you can see directly into their shower!'

'Really?'

'So, how have you been getting up here?' he asked, as he checked another hole.

'There are some stairs at the back of the cleaning cupboard on the landing.'

'Hello, what's this cable for then?'

'Leave that alone!'

'Well I never, a video camera!' he said, dangling it from its cord.

'No it's not!'

'Liar!'

William lunged forward to grab it, but lost his balance and fell through the ceiling. He now had a good view of the models' bed and William had landed right on top of it. Pershia was screaming and flailed around under the sheets as William lay face down between her legs, pretending to be unconscious.

The next two days were spent making preparations for the tunnel and they were now ready to begin. He stood on the lawn, staring down at the giant mole that they'd just lowered into the ground.

'Right, direction and angle of descent are set up on the computer,' said Mike, scrambling up to join him.

'Excellent.'

'Well, I'm pleased to see you're finally doing something,' said William, turning up in a hard hat with the words *Site Manager* written across the front.

'What are you talking about?' he objected. 'We spent the whole of yesterday digging this hole! Anyway, where have you been, painting your hat I suppose?'

'How snide. Look, are you sure this is in the right place? The tunnel is supposed to start near the boiler room. If my wine cellar gets damaged I'll have a nervous breakdown.'

'Stop fretting, it's all under control. The wine cellar's right at the other end. Can't you visualise it at all?'

'Not really, no.'

'You didn't seem to have any trouble finding the models' bedroom when you were in the loft!'

'I wondered how long it would be before you threw that in my face. Ooo, you can be so nasty! Well, I just hope this mole is pointing in the right direction. The last thing I want is to be connected to the hotel because of your incompetence.'

'Look, we've checked the alignment three times, it's fine!' said Mike emphatically. 'Now get out of the way, I'm just about to start it up.'

Mike threw the lever and with a heavy thump the mole began to disappear, a few inches at a time.

'It's jarring a bit, isn't it?' said William, looking worried. 'Oh dear, look at the state of my lawn, it'll never be the same again. It'll have lumps and bumps everywhere, won't help my croquet game one bit.'

'I did warn you,' he said.

'Oh well, I'm too busy to worry about that today. Now then, because you're such good workers, I'm inviting you to another exhibition.'

'Not again?'

'Yes, my work is much more developed and if I must say so myself, quite excellent. It's at the same gallery as before and the doors will be open from two, until...well, as late as anyone wants to stay. It's called *Abstract, Subtract, Distract!*'

'Why?'

'*Abstract* speaks for itself. *Subtract*, because I'm hoping you'll take something away from it, plebs though you are.'

'What about *Distract*?'

'Ooo, is that the time? Better get going. I expect to see you both there later.'

'Nah, I think we'll give it a miss. We've got to look after the mole,' said Mike.

'If you fail to turn up Muffton, I'll get Binky to trash your lab. You're both coming and that's final! Anyway, that thing looks like it can be left running by itself, it seems to be going nowhere fast.'

'We won't be able to stay long.'

'Just be there, that's all I ask. By the way, have either of you seen that idiot Swivvers recently?'

'Yeah, I saw him yesterday, he was going up to the attic with a pile of books.'

'Hmm, pity. I was hoping he'd left. Still, might as well invite him along, he might buy something.'

They left the mole pounding away and set off for a storage yard near Swindon to collect some semicircular tunnel sections. A load would only complete about fifty metres, so they decided to make a trip each day until they had enough. When they returned with the first batch, they set up a special machine to trail behind the mole. Once the first sections had been laid, it actually felt quite spacious and not at all claustrophobic. By early evening good progress had been made and the operation seemed to be running smoothly.

'Better nip along to this exhibition then, otherwise we'll be in trouble,' he said.

'Can't we just say we had a bit of bother with the mole or something?'

'It's not worth it Mike, think of all the moaning.'

Pulling up outside the gallery, they were surprised by the big party atmosphere that spilled out onto the street. As they approached the doors, Xenia and Sazoa came struggling through, carrying a painting each.

'Ah, it is Victor and Mike,' laughed Xenia. 'You 'ad better be quick, zare are not many left.'

'Really?' he asked, watching them head for their car. 'Drunk, the only explanation.'

'Either that or he's spiked the punch with horse tranquilliser.'

Inside, he looked around the walls at the mass of dazzling canvases, the majority of which already displayed a sold sticker. The pictures were excellent, not at all what he'd expected.

'Oh good, it's the construction workers. Glad you could make it. Come on, grab a beer and I'll show you my masterpieces.'

'Shit, you've really come a long way. I like that one…and that. Abstract seems to be your strong point.'

'Thank you Victor. I'll show you what's still for sale. That one there for instance will cost you a mere gold bar.'

'Hmm, quite good. What's it called?'

'*Pyjama Scuffle*, interested?'

'Might be. What's that big red splodge…blood?'

'Ha, no, no. Blood, ha ha ha! Actually, perhaps we can work something out because I need a favour. Umm, I'm a bit busy at the mo, looking after my clients. Why don't you pop along to my room in the morning?'

'William!' called Danii, as she came over with Carmen. 'Hi Victor, Mike. How's the tunnel going?'

'Yeah, good thanks,' said Mike. 'So, you two bought anything?'

'We have actually, they're much better than last time,' said Carmen. 'William, we were wondering if you were going to show us your penis tonight?'

'Pardon?'

'Your big willy.'

'What here, now? What for?'

'I mean *Willy of the South*!'

'Oh that! Umm, the truth is I had to abandon it. I was having a lot of trouble getting it to stay up, then one day I found it all floppy, drooped over the benches. Had to dispose of it.'

'Oh, that's such a pity. Did you have a sacrificial bonfire?'

'He stuck it down a well,' he said.

'A well? How big was it then?'

'Ooo, three metres, four maybe,' boasted William, 'and the girth...'

'Let's leave it there shall we, it's enough just imagining the scene.'

When he got up the next morning he remembered the painting and decided to collect it right away. As he approached William's room he could hear brass band music booming from inside. He knocked several times but there was no reply, so he pushed the door open. William was sitting on the bed sifting through a pile of paintings. Some were being carefully placed inside a portfolio, while others were thrown onto the floor.

'William! ... William!'

The music was so loud that William still didn't know he was there. Then he saw something quite startling. Binky, dressed in an artist's smock, was merrily painting away at an easel that had been set up by the window. He thought that Binky actually looked a bit like William, apart from the abundance of hair.

'William!'

'What? Oh, it's you.'

'Interesting.'

'Binky! Binky! Get away from daddy's easel!'

'So Binky's the artist then, is he?'

'Don't be stupid.'

'Yes he is. I'd know that style anywhere.'

'So what?'

'That's exploitation.'

'Nonsense. He's just earning his keep. Don't tell the others though, will you?'

'I could be persuaded.'

'Okay, I'll give you twenty gold bars.'

'Fifty, all mermaid variety and *Pyjama Scuffle*.'

'Forty, with the painting.'

'Done. So, what was it you wanted to see me about?'

'I've got to go on a trip for a few days and I want you to take care of Binky for me.'

'I'm a bit busy with this tunnel, why don't you get Danii to baby-sit for you?'

'She's not that keen.'

'I'll do it for an extra ten bars.'

'Oh okay. Come over here and sign these papers, then we can go through the list.'

'Papers, what for?'

'To say that you won't snoop around in my room while I'm away.'

'Where are you going anyway?'

'None of your business. Now then, sign here…here…and here… Right, this is Binky's feeding manual, and this is a list of *do's* and *don'ts*.'

'I won't need that, I'm used to handling primates.'

'Take it and read it. You're lucky, believe me, I had to learn the hard way.'

Later, he was checking on progress from an observatory window with his binoculars. The thick rubber air hose was gradually unwinding from the cable drum as the device crept ever deeper towards the *Ark*.

'Hey, William's down there…he's loading up the *Fido*. He must be about to leave.'

'Where's he going?' asked Mike, taking a look.

'He wouldn't say. Perhaps he's Christmas shopping.'

'Hang on, did somebody just duck into the back?'

'Nah, that was just a large bag, wasn't it?'

'Hey, talking of Christmas, what are you getting him?'

'Oh yes, I meant to tell you. I found this trick watch. It really looks the part. Works fine most days, then starts to go backwards or forwards at random. It's got an intelligent chip inside. Eventually, at an inopportune moment, it'll self-destruct…springs and innards everywhere. I can't wait to see his face.'

That evening before dinner, he decided to take a look at the manual William had given him. It consisted of over twenty pages, but was quick to read because some of it had been printed in large bold type.

'What's that you've got there?' asked Danii.

'Binky's feeding manual. Listen to this, point number forty-seven. *He particularly likes those dried banana bits in the crunchy cereal. It is time-consuming opening all the packets and picking them out, but it is preferable to letting him do it himself.*'

168

'Urrgghh, that gorilla's been mauling the cereal?'

'It gets worse, point number forty-eight. *If you should enter the bedroom and find him wearing my pyjamas, DO NOT try to get them off him! I repeat, DO NOT try to get them off him!*'

'The mind boggles. Where's he gone anyway?'

'No idea, he told me to mind my own business.'

'Carmen said she saw Lionel follow him out of the driveway.'

'Really? Oh well, I'd better go and feed Binky, I'll see you later.'

William had been away for a couple of days now, allowing them to progress with the work more quickly without his constant interference. The mole was proving to be so reliable that they were able to leave it running unattended, day and night. After returning from one of their Swindon trips, he called in at the hotel with a variety of supplies.

'Before you go sneaking off,' said Pershia, accosting him, 'we need a manicure, pedicure and total waxing, so get that Samoza here pronto!'

'You mean Sazoa. Okay, no problem. Just give me half an hour and I'll send her over.'

'You might as well tell Stefan to come too, we could do with a massage.'

He drove home and headed straight for the salon. He could see the neon sign flashing outside, so he knew they were open for business. Unexpectedly, William was just coming out and blocked his path by leaning against the doorframe.

'Oh, you're back!' he said.

'Yes, not that it's any of your business.'

There was a small altercation as he tried to push past, but he still couldn't get inside.

'I need to see Sazoa. Is she in there?'

'No!' said William sharply.

'Well, where is she then?'

'Ill, bad tummy.'

'But the models want the full works, what are we going to do?'

'Ooo, perhaps I could fill in for her?'

'I don't think that's a good idea, not if you value your manhood. So, is Sazoa in her room? I'll just ask if she feels well enough to go to the hotel.'

'She's not well enough.'

'She can answer for herself, can't she?'

'Oh, you're such a nuisance Ogroid. Go away!'

'Okay, I'm going up to speak to her.'

'She's not there. Look, if you must know, we were coming back from Christmas shopping in London when she fell ill. Lionel offered to take her to his old surgery in Henley to recover. There, satisfied now?'

'But we're so close, why didn't you bring her home?'

'Because…because he had some special pills that would snip it in the bud…er, I mean nip it in the bud. It just so happens that a dog was brought in with a similar complaint just before everybody went missing. He got the tablets flown in from Japan, special offer.'

'Have you lost your mind? Lionel's a vet! Anyway, we've got every medicine we could ever need in the *Ark*. Now get out of my way, I've got to ask Stefan and Marco to see to the models.'

'Just a minute Ogroid, I've got a bone to pick with you. I thought I paid you to look after Binky?'

'I did.'

'He's painted a mural on my bedroom ceiling!'

'I know, good isn't it?'

A week later, a loud clanging noise indicated that the mole had hit the thick metal outer structure of the *Ark*. Using cutting gear, they set about breaking through to the other side. A small slab of hot steel fell to their feet and a billowing cloud of steam filled the tunnel as they doused the hole with water. When it had cooled enough he risked putting his head through. He immediately saw that Mike had done a superb job of setting the alignment and it had come out just above the uppermost level as predicted. Looking up, he could see the heavy steel girders curving up to the centre of the dome. Twelve storeys below, the computer consoles looked like specks and it made him appreciate the true size of the structure. They continued cutting until the hole was the size of a doorway and then welded a supplementary staircase into position. It was now possible to get down to the twelfth level and by taking one of the internal lifts, the food stores could easily be reached.

They then turned their attention to the other end of the tunnel, breaking through the wall into the basement. Once they'd fitted the last sections and refilled the hole in the lawn, they were eager to give William an inspection tour.

'Hmm, quite impressive, but I'll need a big metal door across this gaping hole into the *Ark*. Makes me feel vulnerable and exposed with it like this. And lights, we must have lights fitted all the way along. See to it, will you? Otherwise well done. Now then, let's go and get a drink, shall we?'

'Yeah, let's get back, I'm starving,' said Mike.

'Hmm, quite a steep climb this, isn't it?' said William, getting out of breath. 'Still, I suppose the girls' legs will soon get used to it.' *

After a couple of days, the finishing touches had been completed. William proudly brandished a pair of scissors as he stood in front of the ribbon stretched across the new tunnel entrance.

'Right, your attention please everyone! It's thanks to the foresight of visionaries such as myself that projects such as these are undertaken. I now have great pleasure in declaring this tunnel open!'

There was huge applause as the ribbon fell to the ground. They all scurried along, trying to keep up with William as he strode purposefully ahead. It took ten minutes to reach the end where a bottle of champagne had been set up in an elaborate arrangement of tied ribbon.

'Behind this door lies a multitude of useful additions to my estate. In fact, it is so avant-garde in concept that I could have designed it myself. So, without further ado I take great pleasure in naming the *Ark*...the *Ark*!'

William hurled the champagne towards the door, but it just bounced off with a hollow *clang*. After lurching around trying to catch the bottle, William steadied himself before once again getting everyone's attention.

'I have great pleasure in naming the *Ark*, the *Ark*!'

Clang!

'Damn it! Ooo, pass me that lump hammer Victor, that'll do the trick.'

'Why don't you let me do it?'

'Stop interfering and give it to me... Right... Oh, my goggles, where are my goggles?'

'You're wearing them!'

'Oh, so I am. Silly me. Now where was I? Oh yes, I have great pleasure in naming the *Ark*, the *Ark*!'

Clang! ... *Clang, clang, clang!*

'Bugger! A bit tough, but I'm sure it'll go...'

Clang! ... *Clang, clang, clang, clang, clang, clang, clang...clang!*

'Ooo, gone a bit dizzy,' said William, holding his chest. 'What's that?'

'What?'

'That...behind you.'

'It's a sledgehammer.'

'Good, pass it here... Okay, stand back. I have great pleasure in naming the *Ark*, the *Ark*!'

Clang!

William missed the bottle by quite some distance, hitting the door handle instead, which snapped off and rolled across the floor.

'Okay, I need a volunteer. Umm, Mike, drive to the *Ark* and open it from the other side.'

He was glad to be home after all the hanging around and went straight to the kitchen. Hector was already there, making himself a drink. Mike had been left fixing the door while some of the others were raiding the *Ark's* food supplies.

'Hey, I've just thought of something.'

'Yeah?' said Hector.

'At the beginning of all this, I found a laptop at Downing Street.'

'Did it have any useful info?'

'Well, sort of. It flashed *Emergency* on the screen and said that an apocalyptic situation was implied, then it issued me with a certificate.'

'What did it say?'

'That I was in charge of the United Kingdom. I don't want to be in charge you understand, but there's an error and it's been bugging me. It says *this woman* instead of *this man*. And another thing, it took my photo unawares. It didn't really do me justice.'

'Ah, right, you want me to take a look at the laptop and see if it'll issue another one?'

'Please, with a better photo.'

'No problem, I'll see what I can do. Don't worry, we'll get you looking your best, I'm pretty good with a camera.'

'Great, thanks. It's just that William really took the piss when he saw it. I'd like to have a good copy on my wall as a keepsake.'

'I'll get it done in time for Christmas. Have you got everyone's presents yet?'

'No. I've been thinking about getting William a flight simulator.'

'That's a good idea. Actually, I know where the best one in existence is, *Boffin Bilge Pilots School*. Read all about it in *TechBits* magazine.'

'Oh, do you read that too?'

'Yeah, I love gadgets and technology.'

'If you want, I can have a chat with Mike and we'll send you into the *Neverness*, then you can see the spaceships.'

'That would be great!'

'Okay, I'll take him this drink and ask him right now. Then perhaps we can go to *Boffin Bilge*?'

By early evening they were home with the huge flight simulator. They had just manoeuvred it into the barn and covered it with a tarp when William pulled up in his *Fido*.

'What's going on in there?'

'Nothing.'

'What's that then?'

'A new supplementary cesspit.'

'Excellent! See that it's fitted before Christmas, will you?'

'Hector's just about to take a look at the spaceships.'

'Yeah, I can't wait, it sounds fantastic!'

'Drats, I wanted to go in myself,' said William, looking put out. 'Are you sure you want to do this Hector? It's not for the faint-hearted you know.'

'I'll be fine. I used to do pot-holing, so I'm not easily freaked.'

Hector had been in the *Neverness* for over an hour and still showed no signs of wanting to come out. William got fed up waiting for his turn and went off in a sulk.

This is brilliant! I'm close to one of the spaceships. There's a sharrow naft. I think it would be possible to climb up if I could get out of this seat.'

'Don't try it Hector!' Mike shouted. 'If you disconnect yourself from the *SDD* you'll get suspended.'

'Okay, maybe another time?'

'Hey Mike, if he could get inside one of those spaceships, we'd know what we were dealing with.'

'Good point. It should be fairly straightforward to rig the *SDD* to a roll of cable and attach that to the suit. I'll get working on it tomorrow.'

That night he lay on his bed wondering how anyone could get pleasure from crawling around between slabs of rock, deep underground. Hector had told them that he'd once become so jammed that even after fully breathing out, he could hardly move. The thought of it was making him feel panicky, so he jumped up and looked around for something to do. He then remembered that he hadn't tried the 3D unit since he'd inserted the special accessory chip. Grabbing an *e-disc* at random, he climbed inside the pod and looked at the title.

'Hmm, *Gargan, Troublemaker Extraordinaire*...could be different.'

An icy wind licked his face as he stared across some snowy fields. Then the voice-over started:

'Gargan was a troublemaker even from his early schooldays...'

Just then a snowball smacked into the side of his head and he felt the sting biting his skin in the intense cold. He looked over to where it had come from, only to see the giant hulk of a fat bullyboy charging directly at him. Suddenly, he was being strangled with his face pushed hard into the snow. Coughing and spluttering, he fumbled for the off switch.

'Jesus, that is so realistic! Hmm, now then, *Siren City... Siren City*, where did I put it?'

Chapter 11

'Victor, a little job for you,' said William, coming into the workshop. 'I've just been at the hotel and the models want these clothes repaired. Even with staff to look after them, they still manage to be a bloody nuisance.'

'What, they're speaking to you again now?'

'Yes, I said I had a heart attack while catching that rat for them. Told Pershia I had no memory of what happened…and she believed me!'

'Jasmine's good at sewing, why don't you ask her to do it?'

'She's cut her finger.'

'Again?'

'Yes, quite badly this time. Lionel had to put three stitches in it.'

'Oh, he's back is he?'

'Yes, came home last night. Sazoa seems to be on the mend.'

'That's good. Anyway, why was Jasmine helping in the kitchen, I thought we had chefs for that?'

'No, she was sharpening the blades on the motor mower. You really should have seen to those overgrown lawns yourself, Victor. I know it's all dead now, but she's been trying to mulch it up.'

'Why?'

'The models complained that it was unsightly. So then, this blouse needs a button. Apparently there's a spare on the hem.'

'What's a hem?'

'The folded bit at the bottom, don't you know anything? Anyway, what's the matter with your face?'

'What do you mean?'

'You're all red around the mouth.'

'Oh, it's my new aftershave, I must be allergic to it. What's that other thing you're holding?'

'A frock, it needs a new zip.'

'Is there a spare on the hem of that too?'

'Er, I don't know, I forgot to ask. Just do your best. You'd better get that oil off your hands before you start. Oh yes, the elbows have gone on my jumper. It's a favourite, could you stick some patches on for me while you're at it?'

'Take it off then, I'll see what I can do.'

It had been a trying morning. His finger was throbbing from being continually stabbed and he'd become quite bad tempered when the bloodstains wouldn't come out of the blouse. He'd tried spitting on it and scrubbing with a scouring pad from the kitchen, but the material had developed a nasty surface. He hoped it would look better once it had been washed. Just as he was finishing there was a knock on the door.

'Victor, is it ready yet? They insisted it was done before lunch.'

'Yeah, come in.'

'Goody. Where's my jumper?'

'Here, catch.'

William put it on and stood with his arms down by his sides, looking perplexed.

'My arms, I can't bend my arms!'

'The glue set a bit hard.'

'Glue? You're meant to sew them on!'

'You said stick them on, so that's what I did.'

'It's ruined. I can't walk around like this. The only thing it's good for now is Riverdancing. Oh well, show me the other stuff then.'

'There,' he said, holding up the blouse, 'what do you think?'

'Oh dear, that button looks like a blackhead on a stalk.'

'I read up how to do it in an old housewives manual. You're meant to whip the thread around the button for strength.'

'Hmm, okay. Give me that other item... Phuurrr, this zip's a bit chunky for such a delicate frock, isn't it? It's the wrong colour...and it's been stapled on.'

'It's on the back, so she won't even see it.'

'Where did you get it?'

'An old sleeping bag I found in the cupboard. The ring-pull toggle is a great improvement on that original fiddly thing.'

'I don't think they'll like it, you'll have to take it back.'

'Okay. I want to see if Jasmine's all right anyway. Hmm, I'd better get her a present. New underwear perhaps...or some more body cream? The other one's all used up...it was a huge bottle too!'

'Pervert! You'll make sure it's all properly folded if you know what's good for you. Look Victor, you're going to have to come up with a way of getting rid of those models. I've tried my best. Taken them to London, offered them tickets for a world cruise...even asked if they fancied living in Germany.'

'That was a good idea, what did they say?'

'Nothing. They just laughed...hysterically.'

'A world cruise?'

'Yes. Well, I saw the *Colossus* moored in Southampton. Thought if I got them aboard I could just point it towards America and jump ship. But do you know how far down it is to the water? Sickening, sickening, even from the lower decks. Still, it could be worse I suppose. At least they're not living under my roof.'

Jasmine's hand was heavily bandaged, so he thought there was little point in hanging around. He left the garments draped over the banister at the foot of the stairs and made his escape. Once home, he set about making himself a snack. Vigorously stirring his tea, it sloshed over the counter and the mug now sat in a puddle with a large bubble forming underneath. He took a bite from his sandwich and picked up the drink in his other hand. Tea dripped across the floor, looking quite messy. He slipped off a shoe and smeared it dry with his sock, then raised a leg to drag the bottom of the mug across his knee.

'What are you doing, Victor?' asked Xenia, coming into the kitchen.

'Oh, just spilt my drink.'

'For a moment I am zinking you are dancing.'

'Xenia, do you know why Serge always calls me a dog merchant? I mean, is it some sort of special French insult or something?'

'Dog merchant? Non, I cannot say zat means anyzing. Apart from a person who is selling dogs per'aps?'

'Hmm, I did give Drac away I suppose, but I certainly didn't sell him, so technically that wouldn't make me a dog merchant, would it? In any case, he was calling me a dog merchant long before that.'

'If it is bozering you I will ask 'im ze next time 'e comes 'ere, or maybe when I am going to France.'

'Would you? Thanks Xenia. Then perhaps you can translate my reply back to him.'

'Victor, have you got a bit of time to spare?' asked Hector, appearing in the doorway.

'Yeah, sure. I'm not busy at the moment.'

'Come on then, I'll do your photo.'

It was the first time he'd been to Hector's room. It looked like a stylish bachelor pad and was quite neat and organised. A couple of Binky's pictures hung on the walls and some expensive-looking oriental rugs were scattered over the wooden floor. A large area was taken up with computer equipment and a professional backdrop with lighting had been set up in front of one of the windows.

At first he felt a bit foolish posing and was aware that his face looked stiff and unnatural, but the final result was excellent. Hector had caught him when he was laughing and he thought it was the best picture he'd ever seen of himself.

'That's brilliant. You've got a real talent there.'

'I almost did photography professionally, but decided on a career in computing instead.'

'So, how's the work with the laptop coming along?'

'See that big computer? It's been crunching the secret access code since last night. As soon as it's done, I'll be in and you'll have your certificate.'

'Thanks Hector. Look, if there's anything I can do for you, just ask. Car trouble, help with the girls…'

'Thanks, but the girls have been throwing themselves at me since my makeover.'

'So I've noticed.'

'It's not all good, I've had to watch my back with the Swedes.'

'Actually, I've been thinking about getting my hair cut like yours, did Marco do it?'

'No, it was Danii. We all got a bit drunk one night and she got the scissors out.'

'Where did you get the clothes then?'

'Oh, umm, Cheltenham…some exclusive menswear shop. What was it called? I know, *Glamboys*, just off the main street.'

'Sounds a bit gay.'

'Yeah, that's what I thought, but the stuff's really good.'

'Well, I'll be off now, see you later.'

He raced back to his room to collect Jappa and they immediately left for Cheltenham. He was there in record time and spent the rest of the afternoon bagging up clothes until it was too dark to see.

After dinner, he bid everyone an early goodnight and locked his door so that he could try everything on. The *PepperBlue* range seemed to suit him best and this was confirmed when Jappa chattered loudly and danced up and down on the spot. He was a bit annoyed that he didn't look as cool as Hector, but put that down to his hair. He realised he'd have to wait until it grew before he could do anything about that, but resolved to ask for Danii's help sometime in the New Year.

The next day most of the household were out shopping, as Christmas was fast approaching. He and William were due to fly to the château the following morning, taking presents with them, but right now he was feeling fidgety.

'Hmm, what about that plaque in the Ark? I'm sure there's something behind it. Perhaps I should see if I can break through? It can't be any more difficult than a bank vault.'

Jappa launched himself from the landing and clung onto a chandelier, while he took the more conventional route down the stairs. Mike was perched halfway up a stepladder holding onto a bunch of balloons, patiently waiting for William to finalise the trip arrangements with his father.

'Yes, yes…the same to you. Oh father, don't forget to ask Serge to pick us up at the airfield… Yes, about midday… Okay, okay father, will do. Thanks, see you soon then, bye! … Mike come down here, father wants a word with you.'

'Me? What about?'

'Wine. Ah, morning Ogroid. Glad to see you could finally be bothered to get up.'

'I've been up hours!'

'Now then, where did I put that cellar key? Ah, left it in the library.'

'Yeah, yeah…yep, no problem. Bye then,' said Mike, hanging up. 'Jean Claude wants me to take a portable *SAR* kit to Montmaran. Something to do with storing wine. You'll have to do it for me Victor, I'm a bit busy at the moment.'

'It's okay, you're in the clear with Ingrid.'

'I know, it's just that I really am busy.'

'Is this about avoiding Anna?'

'No, I couldn't care less about her. I'm developing that idea about being able to leave the *TransPooP* device. I've started building a totally new kit, a *Neverness Chariot*.'

'A what?'

'It's a two-seater with onboard controls, so we could go in unattended if we wanted. It'll have mechanical arms and be self-propelled. Hector will be able to climb up one of those shafts like he suggested and get a look inside a spaceship.'

'What about being able to breathe?'

'Scuba tanks.'

'Brilliant! When will it be finished?'

'Very soon, but I'm having a problem with the aurora output.'

'What's that?'

'Basically the chariot envelops itself in a spherical beam. The trouble is it needs a *Beam Restrictor Device* to stop it spreading beyond the footprint of the chariot, *BRD* for short. Think of it as a gravity field, keeping it all compact. Without the *BRD* it would spread uncontrolled.'

'It sounds a bit dangerous. Oh, before I forget, are we going to try and find this Malinguerer character, or not? I can probably fob Ingrid off this time, but we'll have to make a decision at some stage.'

'Hmm, if we do get him, it's not going to be easy sneaking him to France.'

'I agree, we'd have to consider telling William about it.'

'Tell me about what?' said William, coming back into the hallway.

'Oh, umm…that I'm going to do the *SAR* operation for your father, Mike's too busy.'

'So, it looks like just you and me as usual.'

'And Jappa.'

'You're not intending to bring that monkey again?'

'Of course, I'm not leaving him here.'

'Okay, it can come, but it'll have to stay in France.'

'Why?'

'Quarantine, idiot. It'll have rabies and bite everyone. We'll all die.'

'You've never said that before.'

'I've only just thought of it.'

'You talk such rubbish William, that monkey is clean and healthy. The biggest scare we've had so far was when he bit Serge. How Jappa didn't catch anything then, I'll never know.'

'Nevertheless, I don't want it coming. It'll interfere with the controls. Probably get under the pedals like that damn cat, we'll crash and be killed.'

'Look, if Jappa doesn't come, then I'm not coming either. You can go by yourself. I don't care either way, so what's it to be?'

'Oh, okay then, but see Lionel about getting him vaccinated. Actually, I might bring Binky along as well.'

After some coffee he headed down the tunnel to the *Ark* with Jappa on his shoulder. Going directly to the plaque, he stared at the shiny metal plate wondering how it opened. He was just considering going to look for some cutting gear, when Jappa jumped up onto the framework.

'Jappa, Jappa, come down, good boy.'

Suddenly there was a heavy *clunk* and the plaque slowly began to open. Jappa panicked and scampered into his arms.

'Clever boy, you've triggered a secret button.'

He went down a long staircase and through a metal door at the bottom that led into a short corridor. Through another door was a staircase leading up. It all seemed a bit pointless, but he followed it anyway. He opened a sealed hatch and found himself inside a small, but luxurious room. Comfortable leather seats were set out in rows, rather like first class on a transatlantic flight. There was a large screen on the wall in front of the seating and he realised it must be some kind of private cinema. He felt disappointed, expecting it to have been something much better.

Returning to the house, he stepped into the hallway and was shocked to bump into a life-size inflatable Father Christmas. He pushed it to one side and trod carefully between the boxes of decorations littering the floor.

'Ah, there you are you lazy good-for-nothing,' said William. 'Come on, don't just stand there looking gormless, you're supposed to be helping me get ready for the trip.'

'I've just found a secret cinema.'

'So what?'

'Well, there's already a cinema in the main *Ark*, what do they need another for? It doesn't make any sense.'

'Where is it?' asked Mike, untangling a string of lights.

'Behind a hidden door. There's a really weird arrangement of staircases and corridors. It's well concealed.'

'Ooo, it could be a private cinema, if you get my drift,' said William, suddenly becoming interested. 'We ought to see what films they've got. Hmm, it'll have to wait until we get back from Montmaran though.'

After the evening meal William stood up to make an announcement.

'Listen everybody, Victor and I are leaving for the château tomorrow morning, so if you have presents or cards to send, leave them in the hallway.'

'Stefan and I have got good news for everyone,' said Marco.

'What, are you going to live in Sweden?'

'No, silly. We've been working on something for Christmas with Indala and Pershia. We're organising a fashion show!'

'Yes,' enthused Stefan. 'We've been all over the country to the best fashion houses. We've got a fantastic collection together.'

'My favourite is the *Pink Stallion* label.'

'I prefer *Bo Brindle* myself. Anyway, I'll be modelling the menswear with Hector. Exciting, isn't it?'

He escaped all the talk about clothes and went to his room to pack. Sitting on the bed, he took the small bottle of failed aftershave mix from his bedside cabinet and risked a tiny sniff.

'Urrgghh! Oh, that is terrible!' he exclaimed, quickly replacing the stopper.

He put the bottle into a small box and wrapped it in glittery paper.

'Umm, *To Serge from Victor*…there, that'll do nicely.'

As they drove to the airfield he started looking forward to spending some time with Gina. He was slightly concerned however, that William had decided to bring Binky on the trip. The windows of the *Fido* were already steamed up and there was a strong odour of tinned pineapple.

'Right Victor,' said William, pulling up. 'Go and remove the joystick from your side of the plane.'

'Why?'

'Because Binky will be taking your seat from now on.'

'No way! I'm not giving up my seat to your gorilla.'

'You'll have to. If we leave him in the back he'll unwrap all the presents.'

He spent the flight strapped into a fold-down seat behind the cockpit with Jappa on his lap. He could hear William continually talking to Binky, pointing out places of interest along their route. Eventually, Jappa struggled free and scampered off to explore.

'Victor, we're nearly there. Prepare for landing.'

'What do you mean?'

'I mean get your damn monkey under control. I can't see properly with its tail dangling in my face!'

While they circled around, he could see Serge waiting as arranged. After touchdown, William cut the engines and they drifted to a halt beside the van. A biting cold wind whistled around the fuselage as Serge helped him transfer the load. Only when they'd finished did William and Binky climb out of the plane to join them for the short drive to the château.

'Hello father!' said William, running up the steps to shake his hand.

'Glad you made it, my boy! Ah, Muffin, good to see you.'

'No, I'm Victor. Mike stayed behind.'

'Oh, who's this other chap then?' said Jean Claude, shaking Binky's hand.

'Do you want to take a look at the mobile *SAR* generator before I bring the presents in?' he asked.

'Yes, why not?'

He slid the side-door open and pushed some of the parcel sacks out of the way.

'A bit small, isn't it? Are you sure it's up to the job?'

'Yeah, Mike said this kit could handle something the size of a caravan.'

'Who's Mike?'

'The person who invented it.'

'I thought that was you?'

'No, Mike Muffton invented it.'

'Mike Muffton? Hmm, quite similar to your name Muffin. We'll have to be careful we don't get you two muddled up.'

He unloaded the van and then went to the kitchen in search of some coffee. William, Anna and Jean Claude were sitting at the table sharing a bottle of wine, while Binky rummaged through a box of cereal.

'Hello Victor.'

'Oh, hello Anna. Carmen and Danii said to say hi.'

'Right Muffin, I've got a map here that shows the vineyard I want you to visit. Some of the barrels are at the pinnacle of perfection. These papers detail exactly what has to be sent for storage. Put simply, every barrel and vat marked with a big yellow cross, save it.'

'Yeah okay, we can make a start tomorrow.'

'No Victor, you'll be going alone. Father and I are much too busy. You've got the lists and map, that's all you need.'

'What, you expect me to do all this by myself?'

'Of course not. You'll have that hairy thing with you.'

'I'm not going with Serge.'

'I'm talking about your monkey, idiot!'

'Oh right. But it's miles from here,' he said, looking at the map.

'What's the matter, scared?'

'No.'

181

'Good, that's settled then.'

'So, you are all boozing,' said Gina, joining them.

'Hi, nice to see you,' he said, kissing her on both cheeks.

'Oui, you too.'

'Hello Gina,' said William. 'Getting on okay? Good. So father, tell me everything you know about the *Ark*.'

'Well, I knew it was some sort of secret bunker, what else could it have been? But I knew nothing more than that.'

'Typical, isn't it? They take our taxes and use them to ensure their own survival. Crooked, that's what they are, crooked.'

'Well, enough about that. So, what have you been up to recently, William?'

'Actually, I'm working on a new wine salvaging plan of my own.'

'Got something up your sleeve, have you?'

'Yes, as you know I've got the sales register from the auction house. I've decided to only go after wine that you didn't sell.'

'That would be recommended.'

'There's a fantastic collection that I pieced together from almost five years of sales records. It belongs to a chap called François Malinguerer.'

'Ha, François Malinguerer. Yes, know him well.'

'I've been to his house!' said William competitively.

'I was best man at his wedding. Beautiful little wife, quite a bit younger than him actually. Had the reception at his house as a matter of fact. Lots of collectors there, all snooping around to see what he'd got.'

'I couldn't find anything, just a letter from a Swiss bank. It confirmed the availability of a chilled safety deposit box at their Geneva branch. Went there too, but it was empty, damn him.'

'Can't say I'm surprised. Very distrustful is François. Thinks the whole world is out to steal his wife… I mean wine.'

'Where do you think he's hidden it then?'

'No idea, old chap, could be anywhere.'

Gina raised her eyebrows to him and let out a little sigh.

'Come wiz me Victor. I show you what we 'ave done 'ere. I am getting bored wiz all zis talk of wine.'

'Yeah, me too. Actually, I'd like to see Drac, where is he?'

They went outside to the stable block where Nikki and Nadesche were mucking out a stall. He could see his dog running around the paddock where the horses were grazing. He whistled, and Drac immediately came bounding over, jumping up and snapping at his face with excitement.

Gina had suggested that they ride the horses around the grounds and he now wished he hadn't agreed to it. He'd slightly pulled his groin getting up and the bouncing around was making his eyes water. He didn't know whether to laugh or cry. In fact, he'd never been on a horse before and couldn't think why he'd told her he could ride. Drac was going mad, barking and constantly trying to round him up, making his horse skittish.

'Serge and ze sisters 'ave done a lot of ze gardening.'

'Really?'

'You do not look zat comfortable, are you okay?'

'Yeah,' he replied.

Suddenly, his horse reared up on its hind legs and jumped a fence. He felt himself falling, but tried to cling on, ending up hanging from the horse's neck, staring into its mouth. He couldn't help noticing how brown its teeth were. It cantered quite a long way with him gripping on for dear life, finally stopping for a drink at the water trough, where he was able to let go and fall to the ground. Gina led the horses back to the stables, while he hobbled along behind.

'So, we go for somezing to eat now.'

'That would be great, I'm starving.'

'It is 'urting, non?'

'I'll be all right.'

'Maman!' called Gina, spotting her mother head for the house with a handful of eggs.

Ingrid waved and waited for them by the kitchen door.

'Bonsai.'

'Bonjour Victor.'

'Yeah, I mean Bonjour.'

'I am sorry zat Mike did not make it zis time. You will send 'im my warmest wishes and tell 'im 'e must visit soon.'

'I will,' he said with a furtive shake of the head, letting her know they hadn't had any luck with the secret mission.

In the kitchen, the Smargles were still sitting at the table droning on about wine.

'Maman, Papa, Victor says zat zey 'ave a fashion show at Poffington for Christmas. Would you like to go?'

'Non, I do not zink so. It all sounds too tiring for me.'

'Your mother's right for once Gina, I think it would be best if we just have a quiet time here.'

'I think I'll stay too,' said Anna.

'I zink I go. I will ask ze sisters too,' said Gina.

That night, he was just getting ready for bed when there was a knock on his door.

'Yes, I bet that's Gina! With some massage oil for my groin, most probably.'

Despite his stiffness, he bounded over and opened it eagerly.

'Oh, Jean Claude.'

'Ah Muffin, I've a favour to ask.'

'What's that?'

'It's a secret. Don't tell anyone…not even William.'

'Not even Ingrid?'

'Especially not Ingrid.'

'Oh, right.'

'Now then, this is a photo of someone I want you to look out for in that *Neverness* place.'

'She's pretty, who is it?'

'My mistress. Wife of a friend. Her name's Cecile Malinguerer. I want you to see if you can find her and bring her to France. I'm setting up a special place where we can be alone together. You understand, don't you?'

'Yeah, perfectly.'

He felt relieved at this strange twist. With both Jean Claude and Ingrid having their little secrets, William would be unable to pass judgement and he couldn't be blamed for his part in it.

It was almost time to leave and he'd been sent to ask Serge for a lift to the airfield. He was still frustrated that he'd spent the last two days sorting out Jean Claude's vats, which meant he'd had no time with Gina. The wine trip had been a complete pain and he'd only arrived back late last night. He'd had terrible trouble trying to follow the map, because it bore no resemblance to the road system and on numerous occasions he'd got hopelessly lost. The vineyard was also just as confusing and he'd traipsed around the complex maze of tunnels for hours, looking for a way out.

He found Serge dozing in an armchair beside the bed, holding on to a smouldering bong. He was disgusted to see a mouse crawl out of his hair, cross his forehead and disappear into the other side. He guessed that it was probably the same mouse he should have had for his birthday. For a moment he considered trying to coax it out because technically it was his, but the matted felt clumps were just too disgusting, so he left it where it was.

'Serge?'

There was no response. He looked around the room at the mass of old vinyl records. A half-prepared joint lay across the middle of an album cover that depicted a prism with separated rays of light. Some unusually cool music played in the background and he cast his eye over the tower of antique black boxes.

'Serge? … **Serge!**'

'Urgh, oui, oui?'

'We want to go now, can you take us back to the plane please?'

'One minute, I must pee. Take zis box wiz ze presents. I get my bag.'

'Your bag?'

'Oui, I come also… Urgh, 'ere are ze fangs I 'ave borrowed. I make a mistake and bring zem wiz me.'

'Umm, why don't you keep them, I can always make some more.'

On the journey to the airfield, he couldn't help checking for signs of movement from the mouse.

'Why you stare all ze time?' Serge growled irritably.

'I'm not. Just looking out of the window at the weather, that's all.'

He awoke on Christmas Eve morning with a slight uneasy feeling, knowing that Serge was just a few metres away in the room next door. Going downstairs, he could see that the Christmas preparations were well in hand. Last year's tree still looked extremely healthy and a huge mound of presents had been piled around its base, obscuring the lower branches.

Marco and Stefan seemed more excited than usual as their fashion show was being held that evening. William was sulking because his offer of helping behind the scenes had been rejected in favour of Sazoa. In fact, he was surprised that Sazoa wanted to help at all because she was walking awkwardly and her face was pinched with pain. Her voice had become quite squeaky too and he was glad he hadn't caught whatever it was, because it really did look debilitating.

There was a lot of activity in the ballroom with everyone working hard to get the show ready in time. Gina had put herself forward to co-host the event with Marco, even though this meant working closely with the models. He'd been roped into helping set up the lighting and didn't feel at all safe at the top of the ladder.

'A bit more love, a bit more…stop!' called Marco. 'There, that's perfect. Tighten it up and we'll move on to the blue one.'

'Can't we do the red one next, it's within reach?'

'No, do it my way love. It has to be done in a specific order, otherwise it'll all be wrong. I've spent ages…'

'Oww, oww, ouch!'

'Oh no! Indala, are you all right?' said Marco, clasping his head in anguish. 'Quick, Victor, come down and help her!'

'Oww! Oh, oh, oh, oww! It's broken! I've broken my ankle! I'll never work again!'

'Calm down love, it doesn't look that bad. At least you haven't got any bones poking through.'

'I would not say zat,' said Gina.

'Victor, you'd better go and get Carmen…and bring some ice!'

By the time he'd returned, Indala was sitting in a chair beside the catwalk.

'If you'll all just stand back I'll take a look at the damage,' said Carmen, pushing her way through the gathering crowd.

185

'I'll get the drinks then. I'm afraid we've only got whisky here at the moment. Do you want one Carmen?'

'Go on then, Victor, it is Christmas, isn't it?'

'Ice?'

'Please.'

'Who else wants a top up? Gina?'

'Oui, merci, I will go and find my glass.'

'It just looks like a light sprain,' said Carmen. 'It'll be fine in a few days.'

'It hurts like hell! I won't be able to do the show now.'

'If Indala can't do it, I'm not doing it either,' said Pershia. 'There's this bit where we come down the catwalk together, I can't do that by myself, can I?'

'Oh Pershia darling, you can't let me down. If I don't get to do this show I'll scream!' said Marco dramatically. 'Ooo, perhaps Natasha or Nicole could do it with you instead?'

'No. Neither of them are tall enough to walk beside me.'

'Perhaps we could ask Danii then?'

'Who's Danii?'

'You know, the beautiful leggy blonde who lives here?'

'Can't say I've ever noticed her. As long as it's not that French tart.'

He was glad Gina hadn't heard that remark, otherwise there probably would have been more serious injuries to attend to.

'Ooo, here comes Danii! You're right on cue love,' said Marco brightly. 'We'd like you to take Indala's place in the show tonight, she's only gone and twisted her ankle.'

'I don't think so,' she replied, screwing up her face.

'Go on, you'll be perfect,' said Carmen.

'You know how I hate all that kind of thing.'

'Oh please do it. You'll look a million dollars,' begged Marco, almost in tears.

'He's right, you'll look fantastic, I've seen some of the clothes,' said Hector.

'Oh, okay. God, it's years since I've worn high heels. I'll probably end up twisting my own ankle.'

'Ooo, great!' exclaimed Marco, mincing towards the stage. 'Let's start the rehearsals again. This is going to be fab!'

By seven thirty almost everyone had arrived in the ballroom and taken their seats. He chose to sit between Jasmine and Xenia.

'Ah, Victor. I 'ave asked Serge about zis dog merchant zing.'

'Oh yeah?'

'You are misunderstanding 'im. What 'e 'az said is *don't mention it*, but because of 'iz accent you 'ave 'eard it wrong.'

He kept saying dog merchant over and over in his head until it dawned on him; Serge had actually been trying to be nice. He felt a bit bad, but quickly forgot about it when Gina and Marco came onto the stage to announce the start of the show.

'Good evening ladies and gentlemen! Tonight we 'ave an amazing fashion show for you all. Ze collections 'ave been put togezer by Stefan and Marco, and from what I 'ave seen be'ind ze curtains, zare are some delicious items for everybody's taste.'

'Yes, thank you Gina,' said Marco, 'and thank you all for coming. So, we begin the show tonight with Stefan Dangle and his *Winter Warmers*!'

Stefan set off down the catwalk like a man possessed, stomping in time to the deafening music. Pershia and Hector followed close behind, clad in overcoats, hats and scarves. He didn't find it very inspiring and let out a long yawn as they strode back up the catwalk. Danii immediately made her entrance wearing a short, belted pink mackintosh with white knee length boots. Despite not being the usual thing she would wear, he thought she looked fantastic. No sooner had she disappeared from view, Pershia was out again, stepping purposefully forward in an entirely new outfit. He wondered just how Sazoa was getting them changed so quickly.

'Merci!' said Gina, stepping back onto the stage. 'Now we 'ave a nice surprise. She 'az kindly offered to do a new song for us tonight, so please put your 'ands togezer for ze wonderful… Sheil!'

Unfortunately, Stefan and Marco were dancing for her, so he tried to ignore them and focussed on her short, clingy dress with its plunging neckline. Suddenly, they pranced forwards and began flinging their arms out in front of her face, vying for centre stage. He felt irritated that they were trying to steal the show, especially as they were obscuring his view. Worse still, the sight of their tight PVC sailor suits was making him feel sick.

'Merci! Zank you, Sheil! Now we raise ze temperature a little. We 'ave next season's range of swimwear. I 'ave just seen 'ector, and boy, is 'e 'ot! But first we start wiz ze *beechwear*, naturally modelled by Pershia!'

Pershia strutted down the catwalk in a microscopic bikini. Looking at her fantastic body, he considered what a waste it all was. Danii came out next and got a huge cheer from the audience. Her tiny golden, flouncy bikini was making him drool. It looked as if it was made from micro chain-mail and moved subtly as she walked. He could see Pershia scowling jealously from behind the curtain, so he decided to throw in a few wolf whistles to annoy her even more.

The show ended all too quickly. Some of the flimsy fabrics had caused an effect in his trousers that made it difficult for him to stand and applaud. Waiting for the audience to disperse, he could hear screeching coming from behind the curtain as Gina and Pershia continued to express their dislike of each other.

It was Christmas Day and his first job was to collect everyone from the hotel. He was still feeling rough from the night before and was only halfway down the driveway when he threw up out of the window. It created long streaks down the side of the van, looking like a customised paint job. Staggering into the hotel he found that Ernest and Sanjeev had prepared a full buffet for the evening. He staggered back outside and threw up again.

They arrived at Poffington just in time to receive a Christmas message from the Germans. Everybody crowded around while Mike put Hans on speaker and adjusted the volume.

'Go on Hans, we're all here.'

'Happy Christmas to all! Vee have a little snow ziss morning. Vee have been playing snowballs, so vee have ze weiss men, ze donkey is in ze stables, but vee have no baby, ha, ha, ha! Oh ja, I am forgetting, vee have gut news. Ze eagle has landed!'

'He was trying to tempt this bird with dog food,' he explained.

'Sounds more like one of your tricks, Victor,' joked Carmen.

'Happy Christmas Hans,' William shouted into the microphone. 'We'll visit you sometime in the New Year, bye! ... Phew, had me worried there for a minute, thought they were turning up for Christmas dinner!'

After the meal, people started to filter through to the sitting room where Marco, Stefan and Gina were distributing the presents. He sat in a chair next to his pile, hoping that he had done better than last year.

'Hmm, what's this then Victor?' said William, pulling the watch from its box. 'Seems to be quite weighty, Swiss too. What's it made from?'

'An amalgam of heavy metals and diamond dust.'

'Excellent. *SwissKluck*. Never heard of that brand before. Hmm, quite nice. It'll probably be okay.'

The first thing he unwrapped was his framed certificate from Hector. He was really chuffed and proudly offered it around for everyone to see. Nobody took much notice, as they were too preoccupied with their own presents. Then the dreaded moment arrived, Serge handed him his gift. It sat limply across his lap.

'Oh God, it's a dead animal or something... He's even wrapped each of its legs...urrgghh, it's all bony.'

He tentatively pulled away some of the paper, then let out a sigh of relief when he discovered a set of bagpipes. It was far superior to most of Serge's other gifts. William had received a box containing an assortment of belt buckles and had immediately emptied them over the back of the sofa in disgust. The pets' presents were also extraordinary. Binky got a full-size lumberjack's axe, which nobody thought was a good idea, and it proved quite a struggle to remove it from his grasp. Wolfie was given a framed picture of a hippopotamus, Zeta, a unicycle and Jappa, a French language course consisting of a book and four CD's. To everybody's amazement, Jappa went off on the unicycle and returned with a portable CD player.

'Wait a sec, something's amiss here,' said William, searching through his pile of discarded wrapping paper. 'I don't appear to have my main present from you, Victor. I've only had the stocking filler so far.'

'It's outside. It's from Hector as well.'

'Oh goody! That big, is it?'

'Come on, we'll show you.'

They escorted William to the barn and threw open the doors.

'Go on then, it's under that tarp.'

William approached the object with caution.

'What on earth is it...and why isn't it gift-wrapped? I hope it's not that cesspit.'

'No, it's a flight simulator.'

'Brilliant! Out of my way, I'm having a go right now.'

They watched as the huge box thrashed around on its hydraulic stilts. Judging by the turmoil that was going on outside, he could only imagine what was going on inside.

Chapter 12

'Morning Victor. I've just been on the radio to father. He wants me to pay an urgent visit to Scilly. Apparently there's a collection of exquisite wines somewhere in Troy Town.'

'Toy Town? He's pulling your leg.'

'Troy Town, idiot! T. R. O. Y. It's on the island of St Agnes.'

'Oh, right…when?'

'Today.'

'Today? It's a bit late to be setting off now. Can't it wait until we take Gina and the others home…do a round trip?'

'No it can't! As it happens, it suits me perfectly. There are these two bottles of red I want on St Mary's.'

'Where's St Mary's?'

'It's the main island, idiot! Where we stopped on the way home from holiday. Remember that, don't you?'

'Yeah. Two bottles did you say? Is it worth the effort?'

'Yes, I need them to make a full case. I've only got ten you see. Father doesn't know about these. I discovered their whereabouts in that auction register I pilfered. Anyway, they're situated at Mount Todden, a couple of miles outside Hugh Town. I've got a plan of action already worked out… Land, take a vehicle to collect my stuff first, then take a small fishing boat or something and sail across to St Agnes. It'll probably be too late to do the return journey today, so we'll have to find somewhere to spend the night. Now get yourself ready while I ask the girls to keep an eye on Binky for me.'

'Hey, I've just remembered something. When we were there before, I was reading a newspaper in the Harbour Master's office…'

'Woweee!'

'No look, this is important. There was a headline that said somebody on the island had a pig that was psychic.'

'And what paper was this?'

'One of the local ones, I think it was called *The Scilly Times*.'

'Well there you are then. What a load of rubbish you talk.'

'It's not rubbish. It said that a pig had predicted the end of the world.'

'Pah, what nonsense! You've lost your mind. I've had my concerns about you ever since you chewed my statue.'

'Okay, I'll prove it when we get there.'

Just then Mike came into the kitchen.

'The new *SAR* generator's ready. I'm about to freeze the stratosphere again if you want to watch?'

'No thanks,' said William. 'We're off to Scilly. Wait a sec, are you telling me that you haven't done that yet?'

'No, I've been busy working on other things.'

'So we've been having unprotected fun all this time?'

'Yeah, but we're all right, aren't we?'

'Do you realise that more spaceships could have come? We could have been captured and killed! You are such an idiot. I just hope it turns out to be better than that last piece of shit you made. And be careful when you're fiddling around freezing the sky, I don't want to end up being suspended in close proximity to Victor. Imagine him sitting next to me with a gormless look on his face for eternity, no thank you!'

'It'll be fine. It's pointed at the laser telecom beacon at the airfield like before. This time though, it's poking out of a hole in the lab roof.'

'What?'

'It's a good job...really neat.'

'If it leaks Muffton, Binky will get you in a headlock, then you'll be sorry!'

Jappa was sleeping soundly in his house, so he decided to leave him a note and propped it up outside his door with a small bag of dehydrated fruit. He quickly packed a few provisions, grabbed the camping stove and reluctantly joined William in the *Fido*.

'It's looking a bit unsettled, I think we should put it off for another day,' he said, as they pulled out of the driveway. 'Fuck, I've left my watch by the bed, we'll have to go back anyway.'

'Tough luck! Look Ogroid, I've made a promise. That might not mean much to the likes of you, but it jolly well does to me. We're going, and that's that! It's only fine drizzle, it'll soon clear.'

'If it's only fine drizzle, why have you got the wipers on full speed? You'll wear them out and the windscreen will be all scratched... Oh, they're screeching now! Put them on intermittent before I get out.'

He regretted that William had never learnt to navigate properly and that they relied on following the roads below. Today, because of the low cloud, they were skimming the treetops. It was a terrifying experience and he didn't think he could take much more.

Fortunately, by the time they'd reached Land's End the weather had improved and he relaxed his grip on the seat. He quickly became bored with looking at the murky greyness below and began to reach for a toggle switch just in front of him.

'Don't you dare!'

'What's it for?'

'Don't know, does it matter?'

'What's up with the compass then?' he asked, tapping the glass with his knuckle.

'Nothing.'

'It's not moving...never has come to think of it.'

'Of course it has. Look, if I turn this way, it'll swing.'

'Nah, it didn't move.'

'I can't have turned enough, hold on.'

William put the plane through a series of manoeuvres, this way and that, up and down.

'Drats, it must be jammed. We don't need it anyway... Umm, oh dear. Did you keep a note of which way we should be heading when I was making those turns?'

'You can't be serious?'

'**Help! Mayday! Mayday!** Oh my God, we're lost, what are we going to do? Wait a sec, I think it's going to be okay. There's this trick you can do with a watch...yes, yes, we'll be okay. Right then, umm, it's nearly twelve now, so the sun will be exactly south.'

'It's too cloudy, we can't see the sun.'

'Stop making things difficult Ogroid. Help me look for a bright patch.'

'There! Almost behind us...yes, it's definitely brighter!'

'Good, just need to turn and face it. Hold on...'

'A bit more William, a bit more.'

'Look Ogroid, I don't need you to tell me how to steer a plane, so shut up... Right, we can now assume we're heading south, can't we? Now then, the Scilly Isles should be somewhere west-ish. So, if we do a right turn, we'll be back on course, won't we?'

'No good asking me.'

'Well, I'm right I'm telling you. Now then, at this speed we just need to keep going for fifteen minutes at the most, and the islands will be below us.'

He squinted into the distance, scouring the sea for any sign of land. There wasn't any.

'That's got to be more than fifteen minutes, William.'

'No, no, it's only five. Stop getting so stressed.'

They flew on and on. He'd already finished counting to six hundred several minutes ago and still couldn't see anything.

'We should have seen the islands by now.'

'No, umm, it's still umm...'

Just then, the innards of William's watch flew out and bounced around on the ends of springs.

'Oh no! It's that watch I gave you, isn't it?'

'Might have known it would turn out to be rubbish! Crap, total crap! Well, I want it replaced do you hear? It was a present and...'

'Shut up William, this is serious! It was a trick watch, it was meant to go wrong!'

'What?'

'Yes. It's a high precision trick watch. The time is accurate most of the day, but the microchip is designed to randomly make the hands go backwards or forwards to confuse the wearer, then it all springs apart.'

'Well, that's just great, isn't it? So, while I was setting our heading at noon, you're now telling me it wasn't noon at all?'

'It couldn't have been, could it? Think about it…we left at eleven thirty, so there's no way we could have been over the sea in just half an hour, is there?'

'You are a complete moron Ogroid! We're lost! We're lost!'

'Shit! Okay, try and keep calm, we can work this out. Umm, supposing it was really two when we thought it was twelve, how far off course are we?'

'Umm, two instead of twelve, two instead of twelve… What in God's name possessed you to give me a trick watch? It could have had my eye out! It's a good job I'm wearing goggles.'

'Come on William, think! Given that the time was wrong, which direction did we end up taking by mistake?'

'Oh yes, I see what you're trying to do. Umm, two instead of twelve. Right then…if it was two o'clock, not twelve, we should have pointed the number two at the sun instead, which would have made south further to our left. Fuckety fuck, this is a nightmare.'

'So, where are we then?'

'Somewhere over the sea. What are we going to do?'

'We'll never find the islands now,' he said, studying the map. 'I think we've got two choices. Carry on until we run out of fuel…'

'That's not an option, is it?'

'Or we can turn to face the sun again, then do a sharp left and hope to hit the Cornish coast.'

'Yes, I was just about to suggest that myself. Hold on, here we go…'

After spending the night in Cornwall, they were once again heading for the Scilly Isles. The sky was clear and blue, and they had no trouble locating St Mary's. He fitted a battery to an abandoned car at the airfield and set off in the direction of the harbour.

'Mount Todden's the other way, idiot!'

'I'm calling in at the Harbour Master's office for that newspaper first.'

'Oh really, a detour for a stupid pig story!'

He parked on the quayside and went in, finding the paper exactly where he'd left it.

'See… *JONES' PIG IS PSYCHIC!* Told you so,' he said, climbing into the car. 'Look, centre page… *PIG REVEALS ALL!* Hey, it even looks a bit like you. It's got the same nose.'

'Don't be ridiculous! Come on, we've got to get my wine.'

'I want to call in at Mottle Farm first. According to this map it's on the way.'

'You're wasting time with this damn pig, Ogroid. We're not going and that's that!'

'Oh, okay. You'd better give me directions then.'

He drove slowly across the island, pulling up outside various houses as they searched for the right place. As he reversed down a particularly long muddy track, William ripped the map to shreds and threw it out of the window.

'You're hopeless Victor.'

'It's got to be around here somewhere...look there's another building coming up.'

'We must have driven past it. It'll be miles back in the other direction. It's all your fault, you're not concentrating properly. I wish I'd left you at home now. Ooo stop, stop! I think this is it!'

He parked beside a stone wall in front of the modest looking house. A wooden gate bore the name *Dillberry Lodge*.

'Come on then.'

'No, you go. I want to read the paper.'

'What if the door's locked, how will I get in?'

'Throw a brick through the window or something.'

William sighed sulkily and slammed the door so heavily that the car rocked from side to side. While he waited he read the pig story and then attempted the quick crossword.

'Hmm, let's see... One across, twelve letters... *Mountainous seas awash with goats*...er, nah, thirteen down then... *Astronaut buys loaf in summer*, eleven letters...oh fuck it, I can't be bothered.'

He looked up to see William charging down the garden path like a maniac, stopping at the gate to viciously kick it off its hinges.

'Look at this!' yelled William, wielding an empty bottle.

'Careful! Get it out of my face!'

'That damn pleb! He's only gone and drunk one! That leaves me with eleven. Useless, utterly useless! That kitchen's knee deep in empties. Had some decent stuff too. I've been cheated, cheated. Ooo, if I could get my hands on him I'd wring his neck!'

'Aren't you forgetting something?'

'What's that?'

'The fact that it was *his* wine?'

'He's still a pleb. Nobody in their right mind would drink wine of this quality. Come on then, let's get to St Agnes. Hopefully father's stuff will still be intact.'

They arrived home just before it got dark. William wasted no time contacting Montmaran.

'Yes father, we got there in the end. I found everything you wanted. I've left it in the plane ready for when we bring Gina and co home. Ooo, another good thing, when we stayed overnight in Cornwall I managed to retrieve your old mower, still goes too! Yes...yes, before I go on any more trips I'll recruit a new navigator, the old one was an idiot...yes, speak to you soon then, bye.'

He set off towards the kitchen, eager to share the newspaper story with the others. William was close on his heels so he picked up the pace, sprinting the final ten metres.

'Hey everyone, look at this!'

'Oh leave that for now Victor,' said William, trying to snatch away the paper. 'You've got to help me get that wine into the cellar.'

'It's only one bottle! Why don't you take the lift? This is much more important. It's a story about a pig that predicted the end of the world!'

'Let me see,' said Danii. 'Hey William, this pig looks just like you.'

'That's what I said,' he agreed.

'What rubbish!' scoffed William.

'Let me have a look,' said Carmen, taking the paper. 'Oh yes, if it had glasses, it would be the spitting image. Get me a pen someone.'

'What does it say, Carmen? Read it out,' said Danii.

'Okay... *It was a few weeks ago when I had my first psychic experience with the pig. One night before going to bed, Mary, the name by which the pig prefers to be called, told me that the barn was going to fall down. I went out in the pouring rain in my pyjamas and removed all the cattle, just in case. The next morning I was in for a terrible shock, the barn had indeed fallen down! Since then a number of other inexplicable happenings have occurred and Mary has predicted them all. Yesterday we were just having a chat before getting up, when she suddenly came out with something astonishing. She said that spaceships from another world were going to harvest the entire planet for food!*'

'Zis pig know about ze aliens. Zis pig know somezing,' said Serge.

'Oh really, what nonsense,' said William, shuffling uncomfortably. 'It's just a coincidence, that's all. How many times a year do we get these crackpot headlines?'

'It's still weird though William,' said Carmen, putting the finishing touches to the picture. 'This pig really does look like you...especially with the glasses on.'

It was New Year's Day and he sat propped up on his pillows, thinking back to last year when William had drunk his aftershave. Although he was devastated at the time, with hindsight he could see that it really hadn't mattered. Overall it had been a good twelve months and he was hopeful that 2051 would be even better.

He felt quite hung-over after last night's party and stared over at Jappa, who was sitting quietly by the window wearing headphones, doing his language course.

'Jappa... Jappa... Jappa... Jappa... **Jappa!** Tea, good boy.'

Jappa looked up, raised his finger to his mouth and went *shhh* before reading on. Getting up to make his own tea, he looked out of the window at the grey clouds and thought it would probably rain later. He decided there would be just enough time for a walk to try and clear his head. It was thumping from dehydration and made worse by an irritating tune that wouldn't go away. At ten minutes to midnight William had called Montmaran on the radio and they'd all had to sit and listen to Jean Claude's rendition of *Och Aye the Noo Year* on the bagpipes. It had sounded like a recording and he suspected that it was yet another scam. William had become quite tearful during the performance and had then hummed the tune for the rest of the night.

By midday he'd pulled himself together enough to take that walk and ventured downstairs to collect the dogs. He set off at a gentle pace, zipping up his flying jacket against the cold. Just beyond the lake he stopped to light an especially fat joint and stood admiring the view.

'Phew, that's good stuff!'

He took another couple of puffs and threw a stick for Zeta. He then noticed, way beyond the wooded hill, a column of dense black smoke rising into the air.

'Hello, where's that coming from then? ... Oh no, not the hotel?'

As he jogged back to the house, icy rain began hitting his face. Catching his breath, he staggered into the hallway where William was sitting at the radio.

'Quick, I think the hotel's on fire!'

'What are you talking about?'

'There's smoke, it looks bad!'

'Calm down, it's probably Ernest having a bonfire. Northerners have some strange traditions for the New Year, you know.'

'It must be a pretty big bonfire then. We'd better get over there and see what's going on.'

'Umm okay, but I want to call father first.'

'I'll get Mike.'

He ran through the library and up the spiralling turret stairs to the top landing. Feeling sick and dizzy, he had to support himself against the lab door before he was able to hammer out their secret code.

'What is it Victor?'

'Quick, I think the hotel's on fire!'

'What? Umm, can't it wait? I'm right in the middle of something.'

'The smoke's really bad. I think it's serious!'

'Okay, I'll be down in a minute. Get the fire engine ready.'

He waited for what seemed like an eternity and kept hooting the horn, trying to hurry them up. Mike eventually appeared, but they then had to wait for William, who strolled out wearing full fireman's uniform. He could see that the tunic was at least two sizes too small and the helmet was on back to front. Wasting no more time he sped off with sirens blaring. Getting closer to the hotel, he knew it was no ordinary bonfire. As they skidded up the drive, flames were licking the roof from the upper windows.

'Is everybody out?' he shouted to Ernest, as he jumped out of the cab.

'Aye, nobody being roasted today.'

'I'll get the ladder up,' said William excitedly. 'Luckily there's a hose already attached to that bucket thing, so we won't have to go up with it.'

'I'll nip around the back, see how far it's spread,' said Mike, trotting off.

He quickly scanned the front lawn where everyone had assembled. Natasha and Nicole were calmly sorting through some belongings they'd salvaged, while Pershia and Indala stood cuddled together, watching the flames in a trance. Jasmine and Sheil were consoling Sanjeev, who looked quite upset.

Just then the ladder started to extend and jerkily bounced its way upwards. The elevation was much too steep and William was trying to correct it from the remote control handset. Suddenly the cradle began mashing the roof, all the way along the ridge, creating more outlets for the flames.

'What the fucking hell are you doing William? The roof's all damaged now!'

'It's stuck! The bucket's jammed in that hole. I know, I'll open the valve and get some water on it, flood the place.'

William recklessly began spinning all the valve wheels until a huge spout of water shot out with such force it bowled him across the lawn. For several minutes William flailed his arms and legs unable to get up, but once the tanks had run dry, he struggled to his feet and staggered in slow motion towards the engine.

'What the fuck is wrong with you?'

'Help me Victor! My boots are flooded, I can hardly move. Oh, this is a nightmare!'

'Lean on me and pull them off.'

William wrenched his feet out, tipped the water into a metal pail and handed it to him.

'Climb up the ladder and throw it on. While you're doing that, I'll get everybody to form a chain.'

'Forget it William, it's over.'

He looked on in despair as fire engulfed the hydraulic arm. The rubber hose was melting and fiery droplets rained onto the driveway. Just then the whole roof caved in with a terrifying rumble, forcing flames from the ground floor windows.

'It's hopeless, it's a raging inferno,' shouted Mike, as he came running back. 'I've salvaged some food from the storeroom though.'

'Oh goodness gracious,' said Sanjeev, clasping his hands together. 'All my hard earned cash, up in smoke. I will never again be making such amounts. I am ruined. No job, nowhere to live, I am finished.'

'Don't worry Sanjeev, I'll replace everything you've lost,' he said. 'What happened anyway, did it start in the kitchen?'

'No, not in the kitchen, sir. It is beginning upstairs in the guestrooms.'

'Pershia started it with her hairdryer,' said Jasmine.

'Yeah, spread quicker than any bushfire I've ever seen,' added Sheil.

'But I thought they were smoothies?'

'Sorry Victor, you've lost me there. She left it going on the bed while she went for a pee.'

'Oh right. Umm, a hairdryer, you say?'

'Yeah, strange looking thing it was too.'

'Oh well, there's nothing we can do here,' he said, letting out a sigh. 'Listen everybody, you'd better get over to Poffington.'

The models demanded to be chauffeured and climbed into Ernest's car, refusing to share with anyone else. The actresses took Jasmine and Sheil, while Sanjeev set off on his bicycle.

'What did you go and say that for Victor? We don't want that lot living with us,' grumbled William. 'If they stay the night, we'll never get rid of them.'

'We couldn't just leave them with nowhere to go, could we? It'll only be temporary. We can find another place tomorrow.'

'Hey, perhaps they could stay in the *Ark*?' suggested Mike.

'No,' argued William. 'The *Ark* is to remain a secret. Nobody mention a word about it, do you hear?'

'Fuck, the engine's on fire now! Come on, Jasmine's got several crashed sports cars parked by the garages. I'll see if I can get one going, we'll have to squeeze in together.'

Back at Poffington, William unhappily ushered everyone into the hallway.

'Right, my first priority is to get out of these wet clothes. I'm freezing. I'll probably get pneumonia and die, not that anyone will care.'

'What's going on?' asked Carmen, coming downstairs with Danii.

'I'm soaked to the skin, my uniform's ruined and my fire engine's burnt to a cinder...oh, you tell them Victor...and when I've got changed I'll be wanting a word with you. I might just have an idea to get us out of this mess.'

198

'Fine,' he replied.

'So, what's happened then?' asked Danii.

'Umm, there was a fire at the hotel, a really bad one. Nothing left.'

'Oh no, that's terrible!' said Carmen. 'When we heard the siren, we thought you boys were just playing about. Is anyone hurt?'

'No, but they're all homeless.'

'Well, there's plenty of room here,' said Danii, turning to the group. 'If you'd like to follow me to the attic, we'll get you all organised. Then we can see about getting new clothes and things.'

'Attic?' said Pershia incredulously. 'This must be some kind of joke. We're not sleeping in an attic!'

'We'll take that French tart's room, providing it's fumigated first,' said Indala.

'Well, when I said attic, I really should have said penthouse. It's reserved for VIP guests only.'

'Hey Victor, would you like to see the new chariot?' asked Mike, as everybody trooped upstairs.

'Umm… I was just going to take Jasmine to my room.'

'That's okay Victor, I know the way,' she said.

'Oh, all right, but I'll be there as quick as I can.'

'Take your time, I'll have a long hot bath.'

'Yeah, make yourself at home.'

'Right, first things first,' said Mike. 'Let's get a drink and something to eat. Beans on toast or a sandwich? Hmm, both I think.'

Outside the lab a little later, Mike paused to carefully balance his sandwich on top of the mug before searching his pockets with his free hand.

'You'll be surprised when you see it. All I've got to do is finish a bit of wiring, then we can give it a trial run… My keys! Where are my keys?'

'Maybe you forgot to lock up?'

'That would be unlike me, but…'

Mike reached for the handle and pushed the door with his body, but bounced off when it failed to open. Taking the full force of Mike's coffee, he stepped back out of the way only to skid on something slimy. He looked down to see a large dollop of pickle ooze from the sandwich and cling to the side of his desert boot.

'Fuck, I've only just got these.'

'It's locked!'

'If they're not in your pockets, you must have dropped them when we were tending the fire.'

'No, I remember now. I was just going to lock up, but I dropped the keys…saw my shoelace was undone…picked the keys up…put them in the lower lock…tied my shoelace… Shit, I left them in the door! That means someone's in there. They've locked themselves in!'

'Wait…what's that noise?'

'Oh no, that sounds like the chariot! **Turn that equipment off now! Who's in there? Let me in!**'

'Maybe it's Jappa? He could have come up looking for me.'

'Quick Victor, do something! The *Beam Restrictor Device* isn't connected. It'll envelop everything…the house, the grounds, Woodswell, Dellfield, Oxford…'

'**Jappa! Jappa! If you're in there, open this door now!** … It's no good Mike, he can be very wilful. We'll have to break the door down.'

'We don't stand a chance. It's been reinforced, you've seen the size of the bolts.'

'We'll have to run then.'

'Where to? The whole country could vanish! We've only got a matter of seconds before the beam begins expanding!'

'I know, the lift.'

'No, not possible, the doors are welded up. Come on Victor, think!'

'Umm…umm, okay, wait, er…'

To be concluded…

Don't miss the ending...

STILL STANDING

Join Victor and friends for more
comical escapades in the last of the trilogy.

How do they survive this latest fiasco?
What awaits them inside the spaceships?
Can their existence become any more bizarre?

To be published in 2008

Missed Book One?

STANDSTILL

ISBN: 1-4120-5595-4

ISBN 142511007-X

9 781425 110079

Made in the USA
San Bernardino, CA
14 April 2013